WEBCAM

Someone is stalking webcam models.

He lurks in the untouchable recesses of the dark web.

He's watching you. Right now.

When watching is no longer enough, he comes calling.

He's the last thing you'll ever see before the blood gets in your eyes.

Chicago Homicide Detective Tom Mankowski (THE LIST, HAUNTED HOUSE) is no stranger to homicidal maniacs. But this one is the worst he's ever chased. Someone who uses your own Internet, WiFi, computer, and cell phone to watch you 24/7. Someone who knows your every call, every text, every email. Someone who wants to punish you for being bad.

J.A. Konrath reaches into the depths of depravity and drags the terror novel kicking and cyber-screaming into the 21st century.

WEBCAM

I'm texting you from inside your closet. Wanna play? :)

WEBCAM

WEB CAM

He's watching you. Right now.

J.A. KONRATH

AUTHOR'S NOTE

This book takes place during the same timeframe as my mystery thriller novel RUM RUNNER. It also happens concurrently with the humorous short story WATCHED TOO LONG, co-written with my frequent collaborator Ann Voss Peterson. Some characters, and situations, appear in all three stories, and they overlap and crossover with one another.

You *do not* have to read all three books to find out what happens. Each of these can be read and enjoyed as a standalone. There are no spoilers.

That said, it was an exciting challenge to write three stories that interweave, and I hope readers will enjoy this experiment. If you like WEBCAM, please give RUM RUNNER and WATCHED TOO LONG a try. This trilogy was a whole lot of fun to write.

Also, the pronouns in the novel are all intentionally written that way. You'll understand what I mean later.

As always, thanks for reading.

Joe Konrath

WEB
CAM

CHAPTER 1

TEN YEARS AGO

"What do you need the blowtorch for, Daddy?"

Kendal walked alongside her father, keeping one hand on his wire shopping cart. Her hand would stay there during the entire trip to Home Depot, or else Daddy would get mad.

When he was mad, he wasn't nice.

"I need to use it in the basement."

"Oh."

Kendal wasn't allowed in the basement. It had three locks on the door, and a ghost lived down there.

At least, Kendal thought it was a ghost.

Sometimes, when she walked past the door, she thought she heard noises.

Other times she was *sure* she heard things.

Chains clinking.

Moans.

Whimpers.

"What's in the basement, Daddy?"

Her father stopped the cart. He stared down at her, his dark eyes boring into hers. Kendal wasn't sure if the question made him angry or not. When Daddy was angry, his face always stayed calm.

"The basement is off limits."

"I know."

"You can never go in there."

"I know."

"Never."

"I won't, Daddy. It's just that sometimes... I hear noises."

Daddy's eye twitched. Then he squatted down, so he was Kendal's height.

"Can you keep a secret, Kendal?"

She nodded. Kendal kept lots of secrets.

Daddy looked around, like he was making sure they were alone. Nobody else was in the aisle. He leaned in close and whispered, "There's a monster in the basement."

Kendal felt her tiny stomach get tight, like it was making a fist.

"I thought... I thought monsters weren't real."

"Most aren't. But she is."

"It's a girl monster?"

Daddy nodded. "Her name is Erinyes." He pronounced it *erin-eeeees*. "She's a very bad monster, so I have to keep her locked up."

"Is she bad like Mommy?"

Her father had left her mother, years ago. Kendal hardly remembered her, but Daddy told stories about how mean she was. She was so mean, that Daddy changed their last name so Mommy couldn't ever find them.

"She's very bad, Kendal. She's the worst of all monsters. Erinyes has red eyes, and great, black bat wings, and pointy sharp teeth like a cat. She wears a crown made of biting spiders. And she does terrible, terrible things."

Kendal felt like she had to pee. "What does Erinyes do?"

"Erinyes punishes sinners."

"Sinners?"

"Little girls who have been naughty."

"How?"

Daddy stood and picked up a tool hanging on the rack. It looked like pliers, but with a funny-shaped top.

"She heats up pincers like these in a fire. Until they're red hot. Then she flays them alive."

"What does *flay* mean?" the ten-year-old asked.

"It means to pull your skin off in strips."

"Yuck."

Her father dropped the tongs into his cart, on top of the chains, padlocks, and propane torch.

"It's a terrible thing to see," Daddy said. "And the monster makes you watch."

"How?"

"She cuts off your eyelids so you can't close them."

Kendal closed her eyes, grateful she could, and tried not to think about how awful it would be without eyelids. But the more she tried not to think about it, the more she thought about it.

"I'm scared, Daddy."

He rested his hand on her head, patting it. "Erinyes is very scary. That's why I've locked her up."

Daddy began to walk again, and Kendal forced her eyelids open and tagged along with the cart. "What's her name again? The monster?"

"Erinyes. She is thousands of years old, formed from the blood of the titan, Uranus, when his son castrated him."

"What is *castrated*?"

"Castrated is when a man's genitals are cut off."

"What are geni—"

Her father suddenly spun around and grabbed Kendal hard by the shoulders, giving her a rough shake. "Don't you EVER mention genitals. Do you understand?"

She fought back her tears and nodded as fast and hard as she could. Kendal knew this look in Daddy's eyes; the look when he got so upset he didn't act like Daddy anymore.

"Genitals lead to fornication, which is the biggest sin of all. And if you sin, Erinyes comes for you. Do you want that monster to come for you?"

Kendal shook her head *no*, fast as she could.

"Even though I have her locked up, Erinyes is always watching you. Always. And she pays extra special attention to girls named Kendal. If you hear a strange sound at night, that's her. A foot on the stairs? It's her coming for you. A tapping at the window? It's her staring at you. A scratching at your door? She's there, trying to get in. And if you sin, she punishes you."

"I won't say that word, Daddy."

His eyes softened. "That's my girl."

He released her, and Kendal did her best not to cry as she followed him to the check-out aisle. Even so, she sniffled once, and quickly wiped her nose on her sleeve so her father didn't see.

So Erinyes didn't see.

When they got home, Kendal was immediately sent to her room and told to put on her headphones. Daddy set her iPod to *High School Musical* and told her to stay there and listen to the whole album without stopping.

Kendal obeyed her father. And she didn't move, even though she was really, really scared.

In between songs, Kendal was sure she heard noises.

Coming from the basement.

Kendal knew what it was.

It was the sound of Erinyes, screaming.

CHAPTER 2

PRESENT DAY

Men are assholes.

Kendal Hefferton was sitting on the floor, decked out in slutty lingerie, too much make-up, and pumps with heels so high they were impossible to walk in, staring at the live image of her own cleavage in her laptop webcam and thinking about all the other ways she could be making money.

It had been a slow night. She'd earned a little over eighty dollars, but it was close to three in the morning and she'd been at it since nine. Kendal could have made more waiting tables. Right now she had only one guy in her chat room. A regular who went by the name BigBoy6969. He'd be good for another ten bucks, then she'd probably quit for the night.

`Show me your ass SEXXYGRRL` he typed into the chat box.

Kendal, aka SexxyGrrl, got on all fours and turned around, wiggling her butt at the camera for the customer paying $2 a minute. Next he'd want her to take off her panties. Then her bra. Then touch herself. Then he'd be done, without so much as a goodbye or a thank you.

At least she didn't have to look at her clients, since she had the camera on her but they did not. Watching them jerk it would have been gross. That was the one thing to be thankful for.

Actually, there was another thing to be grateful for. That creep who had been harassing her hadn't shown up tonight. Maybe the sexcam service Kendal worked for finally listened to her complaints and banned his computer's IP address. He'd been cyberstalking her for the last three days, always signing on with a new nickname. Sex chats were often vulgar, and profanity was expected, but this guy was seriously nuts. Just in case anything came of it, she'd saved screen captures of his last visit when he's signed in as *Tilphousia*. Recalling the chat brought a shiver.

TILPHOUSIA: aren't you a cute one?

SEXXYGRRL: thx! ☺ What do you want to do tonite! I'm soooo horny!

TILPHOUSIA: do you like being a cam model?

SEXXYGRRL: I luv it! I get to meet so many sexy guys, like u.

TILPHOUSIA: you're naughty.

SEXXYGRRL: im vry naughty. Do you like my body?

TILPHOUSIA: You need to be punished.

SEXXYGRRL: I like spankings! :)

TILPHOUSIA: I want to fuck you.

SEXXYGRRL: that is sooo hot! Yr turning me on! Tell me how you like it.

TILPHOUSIA: I want to fuck you hard.

SEXXYGRRL: I want that so bad!

TILPHOUSIA: I want to fuck you hard with a butcher knife.

Kendal had to read that twice, but she couldn't make sense of it.

TILPHOUSIA: my knife will fuck you all over.

This guy was seriously disturbed.

TILPHOUSIA: I'm going to cut off your eyelids so you have to watch me do it.

You're a sinning whore and you must have Penance.

I will slice out your guts and

Kendal couldn't kick the creep out of the chat room fast enough.

What the hell was wrong with some people? Who could get off on sick shit like that?

The modeling service she worked for was good about keeping out the creeps.

Happily, BigBoy6969 was a longtime client.

Like what you see, tiger? Kendal typed, wearing the fake smile that came with the job.

Your soooo hot baby!!! Take off your panties.

Kendal eased her panties down, making sure she went slowly. Not to tease him; this was simple economics. The longer he was online, the more money she made. Show him too much too fast and he'd blow his load and sign off. The goal was to make it last for as long as possible.

My god I luv your ass. Its perfect. Im so hard right now.

Kendal was impressed. Not that he was hard—that was to be expected—but at how fast he could type with just one hand.

I like it hard, she typed.

Its throbing. all becuss of you. ten throbbing inches baby.

A genuine smile formed on Kendal's lips. She'd been a webcam model for just under a year, and she'd never had a client less than ten inches long. BigBoy6969 was probably five inches, tops. From his frequent grammar errors and misspellings, she guessed him to be blue collar, maybe a factory worker. Either too fat or ugly to have a girlfriend, or still married to his high school sweetheart who stopped blowing him a decade ago.

Stop talking like that, Kendal typed. **You're turning me on REAL BAD, bigboy. And I'm all alone with no one to fuck me.**

YOUR SO HOT. Take off your bra.

Kendal removed it slowly, her eye on the clock. Three minutes so far. Six bucks. She was still fifty dollars short on rent this month, and it was due in two days. She loved her Chicago apartment, and was able to afford it without needing a roommate, barely.

Kendal wondered if she should take her sexcam work to the next level. Other girls made more money, and got more regulars, by doing more extreme things. Kendal limited what she did to nudity and touching herself. If she used toys, she could make more. Or if she allowed sound and spoke with clients rather than responding by typing. Or if she took her laptop into the bathroom. Apparently some weirdos liked to watch women pee, and were willing to pay extra for that.

But those things seemed too... well... *personal.*

Kendal knew thinking like that was hypocritical, and silly. Workers in this business were called models, but this was closer to stripping or prostitution than posing for magazine pics or walking down a fashion runway. She took off her clothes and touched herself, for money. Why not go a bit farther and make more? What was the big moral issue?

Maybe she should join another chat service. Instead of being paid by the minute, other sites worked on a tip basis using virtual coins. For five coins she'd strip. For ten coins she'd touch herself. There would still be the problem of waiting around for clients—that was the main problem with this business, the waiting around—but at least it would be something different.

You told me you were alone and didn't have a boyfriend.

That's true, Kendal typed. And it was. Since taking up this profession, Kendal began to dislike men more and more. She had enough of them online.

BigBoy6969: So you have a roommate?

No. It was always risky telling clients too much, because some of them could get a little obsessive and stalker-ish. But she usually told the truth when asked non-threatening questions, mostly because it was too hard to keep track of lies.

You live alone and don't have a boyfriend or a roommate.

BigBoy seemed kinda stuck on this. But if he wanted to talk about her living situation instead of whack off, it was his dime.

I'm all alone here, with no man at ALL, she typed.

So who is that standing behind you?

What?

Kendal spun around as a figure in a black ski mask rushed at her. As she opened her mouth to scream, a cold, foul-smelling towel was pressed against her face. The intruder fell atop her, and when Kendal tried to breathe her vision got blurry.

Another breath, and she realized she was losing consciousness.

Her eyes sought out her laptop, at BigBoy6969, hoping he was calling the moderators, telling them what was going on, and that was the last thing she remembered before she passed out.

. . .

Kendal awoke tied to her bed, her arms and legs secured to all four posts with duct tape, a gag in her mouth. The intruder was naked, standing next to the bed, staring down at Kendal. She noticed the butcher knife and screamed.

"Do you know who I am?" the intruder asked.

Kendal shook her head. She couldn't take her eyes off the knife.

"I know who you are. You're Kendal. And you're very, special."

Another frantic head shake. Kendal remembered the webcam. Hoped that the police would be here soon.

"I'm Erinyes. You're a slut and a sinner, Kendal. So I'm here to punish you. Just like I promised."

Kendal screamed in her throat when she saw the tiny, sharp pair of cuticle scissors coming toward her eyes.

"Now let's get rid of those eyelids. It would be a shame for you to miss anything..."

CHAPTER 3

Tom Mankowski's eyelids flipped open at the sound of his cell phone vibrating on the nightstand next to the bed. He squinted at the clock.

4:03 A.M.

Someone in his District had died. And it had to be someone important, or an exceptionally ugly death, or else they would have called someone else. Tom had taken a week off to spend time with his girlfriend, who slept soundly next to him. She was visiting from L.A., and Tom had turned his ringer to vibrate so it wouldn't wake her up, on the off chance someone called.

"Your phone is vibrating," Joan said. She sounded annoyed.

"Sorry."

It vibrated again, rattling the nightstand. In hindsight, ringing might have been quieter.

"Are you going to answer it?"

"I'm on vacation."

"So why didn't you turn the phone off completely?"

Damn. She had him there.

"Did you turn your phone off completely?" he asked. When cornered, attack.

"I did."

"What if some big shot actor calls? Or a studio?"

Joan was a movie producer. Tom had grown to accept the fact that at any moment, no matter where they were, she would answer the phone. Once, while they were in the middle of making love, she took a call from Catherine Zeta-Jones without them actually stopping. Joan's end of the conversation mostly amounted to grunts of agreement or moans of disagreement. Tom pretended to be annoyed, but it was actually pretty hot.

Another tremor rattled the nightstand.

"If someone calls my assistant will handle it. Jesus, Tom, pick up the phone already."

Tom sat up. "I'll take it in the other room so I don't disturb you."

"I'm already disturbed, lover."

Yikes. Joan only called him *lover* when she was really pissed. Tom knew it was an attempt to mask her anger with patience, but it always came out as biting and sarcastic.

Tom picked up his iPhone, saw it was his partner, Roy Lewis.

Maybe it wasn't a homicide. Maybe Tom would get lucky and it was Roy dealing with some terrible personal tragedy. Like cancer, or a car accident.

"Are you dying of carcinoma or trapped in a burning vehicle?" Tom asked after answering.

Hope springs eternal.

"Worse," Roy said. "The Snipper is back."

"Shit." Tom had been fearing that for more than a month. The first murder had been Chicago's goriest in nearly a decade. It was so calculated, so awful, that Tom was sure it would happen again. Someone who went through that much trouble didn't do it one time only.

"Yeah. Your hunch was right, brother. We've got a serial killer."

"Can you handle it?" Tom asked, peeking at Joan. If her eyes were lasers Tom would have been instantly decapitated. Not only did they have plans for the day, but it involved Joan going to the spa this afternoon, giving time for Tom to visit a jewelry store for a very special purchase.

"I know you're off, but you're lead Detective on this one, Tommy. Can you sneak out without Joan waking up?"

"Joan is up," Joan said. "Hello, Roy."

Obviously Tom also had the volume too loud.

"Hey, Joan," Roy said as Tom held the phone away from his ear and put it on speaker. "Sorry about this. It's a big one."

"How's Trish?" Joan asked.

"She's, uh, next to me right now."

"Hi, Joan," Trish said.

"Want to grab some breakfast later? Maybe do some shopping?" Joan asked. "The asshole cops we're dating won't be around."

"How about nine? We can go to Yolk in the South Loop, then walk the Mag Mile. I'll bet your fella would love to buy you some shoes. Roy's gonna buy me some, right Roy?"

"Anything for you, baby." Roy had a sultry baritone and sounded a lot like Isaac Hayes.

"Anything for you, baby." Tom repeated to Joan. He didn't sound like a soul legend. Tom sounded like Michael J. Fox when his mother tried to kiss him in *Back to the Future*.

"See you later," Joan said, then purposely turned around in bed, giving Tom her back. She was still naked from earlier, so Tom didn't mind the snubbing because the view was nice.

"Where's the scene?" Tom asked.

Roy gave Tom the address, and Tom reached out and trailed a finger along Joan's shoulder, down her side, to her hip.

"See you in twenty," Tom said.

He hung up, and snuggled up to Joan, kissing her neck.

"You're ditching me, and you think you're getting a quickie first?" Joan said, snorting.

"Hey, I'm buying you shoes."

"You don't have to buy me anything, Tom."

"Good. Because my cards are maxed, and you earn ten times what I do."

She turned around to look at him, her eyes clear in the dark of his bedroom. "Long distance relationships aren't easy."

"I know." That was the reason Tom's credit cards were near the limit. Travelling to Los Angeles six times a year.

"Neither of us are ever going to quit our jobs."

"I know," he said, kissing her chin.

"This is supposed to be our time. And you're working."

"You do the same thing. Last time I was in La-La Land we were having a romantic dinner at *Bestia* and you invited Johnny Depp to join us."

"That's because you stood up and yelled *Oh my god it's Johnny Depp tell him to join us*!"

"*Edward Scissorhands* is my favorite movie. I always cry at the end."

"You're not taking this seriously. For our relationship to work, we need together time."

"I agree." He kissed her neck.

"Don't start something you can't finish," Joan said.

"I can finish. Can you finish?"

"I don't know." Joan sighed, then her lips met his. "I guess we're going to find out."

. . .

After they'd both finished, Tom dressed and drove and arrived at the crime scene. He held an insulated cup of coffee which advertised a Bruce Willis movie Joan had produced. The victim's neighborhood was upscale, boutiques and cafes and wine shops. The apartments no doubt cost more than Tom paid monthly for the mortgage on his tiny, single-level townhouse in Norwood Park. He parked in an alley behind a patrol car, next to a dumpster that was filled to the brim, and made his way past the police line.

"You had time to make coffee?" Roy asked, eyeing it enviously. Roy looked a lot like Richard Roundtree, but bald. Tom, in contrast, looked a lot like Thomas Jefferson. He even had the longish, reddish ponytail, which was getting to be a pain to brush every day.

"Joan made me coffee after sex," Tom said. "You didn't get coffee after sex?"

"Didn't get coffee or sex. She took my Visa. Trish don't like early morning homicide calls. She revenge shops."

"Ouch."

"No prob. I reported the card lost on the way over."

"Won't that make her mad?"

"I can deal with mad. I can't deal with paying off five hundred dollar boots at 14.9% interest."

Tom paid 22.2% on his card, but didn't say anything. They approached a uniform standing guard in front of the apartment. He looked queasy. Nametag said Wheeler.

"What we got?" Roy asked.

"The apartment belongs to Kendal Hefferton, twenty years old."

"Her name is Kendal?" Tom asked.

The uniform nodded.

"She's the vic?"

"Could be. It's, uh, tough to make a positive ID. She's... it's..." Wheeler took a big breath. "It's pretty bad."

"You first on scene?"

"My partner and I took the call." He raised his eyebrows. "You're Detective Mankowski, aren't you?"

Tom nodded.

"And you're Detective Lewis?"

"Yeah."

"I heard about that thing in South Carolina. That was some heavy shit."

"Neighbors? Wits?" Tom asked. He didn't want to discuss South Carolina, and he knew Roy didn't either.

"Doing a door-to-door now. No witnesses so far. But no marks on the outside door or on this one. It was open when we arrived."

The previous victim's locks hadn't been disturbed, either. As if the killer had been allowed inside.

Or could walk through walls.

"Does the building have security cameras?"

"No. But a few stores on the street do, and so do some TV stations. Live traffic cams. There's a team getting copies."

"M.E. here yet?" Roy asked.

"No. Just C.S.T."

Tom and Roy took disposable polypropylene shoe covers and nitrile rubber gloves from the boxes next to the door. There were also paper face masks and a jar of Vicks. Normally those weren't needed until a corpse had begun to decompose, to cover the smell of rot. Tom raised an eyebrow at Wheeler.

"The vic's insides were... uh... you'll see. It stinks. Bad."

Tom and Roy each took a mask and placed it over their mouths. Three steps into the apartment Tom realized he should have put some menthol gel under his nose. The smell of feces was so strong his eyes watered. Layered beneath it was urine, coppery blood, and acrid bile. The crime scene techies shooting video and ALS digital stills had full hazmat gear on, complete with their own breathing masks.

"I'm grabbing the Vicks," Roy said, scooting back outside.

Tom took a deep, foul breath and held it, then ventured further into the abattoir. He took note of the laptop on the living room floor, open but with a dead screen. A woman's shoe with an exceptionally high heel was next to it. He stuck his head in the open bathroom door; normal, but no shower curtain hung from the curtain rings. Then he walked slowly down the hallway, to where he assumed the murder scene was, based on all the techie activity. Still holding his breath, Tom's eyes began to water from the stench hanging in the air. He came to the bedroom, peered through the doorway, and tried to make sense of what was on the bed.

It was just as bad as the first. The media had dubbed the killer *The Snipper* because he cut off the eyelids of his first victim.. This made for a disturbing corpse; the fully exposed eyeballs, bulging and staring blankly into space, set into a face framed by horror and agony. But in this case, the eyeballs were only a fraction of the atrocities committed upon this poor girl. Her mouth and vagina were mutilated beyond recognition, and she'd been partially eviscerated, loops of intestines knotted around her naked torso.

Smeared on the wall behind her, in blood or feces or both, was a single word.

No shit.

Tom had never seen a homicide with this much fury, and he'd seen some doozies.

Someone touched Tom's shoulder and he spun, coughing out his breath. It was Roy, offering Vicks VapoRub. Tom dug his finger in, smearing some under his nose, but not before he inhaled a stench straight from hell's morgue.

"It's a bow," Roy said.

Tom gagged, spat into his own glove, and wiped it on his shirt rather than contaminate the crime scene. "What?"

"Her guts," Roy said. "The Snipper tied her intestines in a big bow. Like a Christmas present."

CHAPTER 4

Erinyes is searching.

Searching, searching, searching, always searching.

Searching for naughty girls.

So many naughty girls on the Internet. So many who need to be punished.

The Internet is a porn wasteland. A cesspool.

A biblical flood is needed once again, to wipe out all the sinners.

But Erinyes knows that God doesn't care. There won't be another intervention.

Sodom and Gomorrah is so *old* Testament.

Even the New Testament is two thousand years old.

Erinyes is writing the *now* Testament.

God's vengeance, right now.

One dead whore at a time.

Erinyes looks at pornography. So much filth. But it is filth from the past.

Old sins.

So much of the Internet is what people *once did.*

Erinyes cares about what people *are doing.*

Erinyes has to catch the sinners in action.

So Erinyes watches webcams. Webcams are live. Webcams are *now*.

Erinyes searches for the next naughty girl to be punished.

Too many to choose from. But Erinyes is looking for someone specific.

A specific girl.

A special girl.

Erinyes uses a brute-force attack.

Erinyes *IS* a brute-force attack.

Erinyes gets a hit, and logs in as the administrator.

Erinyes is searching.

Searching.

No good.

The specific, special girl isn't there.

Erinyes must try elsewhere.

Sometimes the search takes a long time.

The specific, special girl is tricky. She hides from Erinyes. She doesn't want to suffer Penance.

Erinyes is patient.

Erinyes is *patience.*

Erinyes can wait for as long as it takes to find the right girl.

The *specific, special* girl.

A sound, from the basement.

Moaning. Crying.

Erinyes looks up from the computer. Checks the time.

Breakfast.

Erinyes walks into the kitchen, gets the bag from the cabinet. Gets a bottle of water.

Takes both into the basement.

It's dark. Erinyes' feet creak on the stairs, and that prompts whimpering to emanate from the darkness. Whimpering, and the rattling of chains.

Erinyes sees the bowl on the floor. Pours in dog food. Sets down the plastic water bottle filled with antibiotics, and picks up the empty.

"I punished another one," Erinyes says into the darkness. "Last night."

The darkness doesn't answer.

Erinyes looks at the concrete floor. The dried blood.

Sinner blood.

Old blood.

"Perhaps we once again need new blood," Erinyes says, shivering at the thought.

There is a moan from the darkness.

"I have ordered a new whip. You wore out the old one."

More rattling. More moaning.

Erinyes leaves the basement. Locks the door. Goes to the computer.

Erinyes is searching.

Searching.

Searching.

Searching.

Searching.

Endless searching, for the specific, special girl.

Erinyes checks the time.

Lunch.

Erinyes walks into the kitchen, gets the bag from the cabinet. Gets a bottle of water. Adds antibiotics.

Takes both into the basement.

The darkness swallows Erinyes.

The dog dish is empty. Erinyes fills it with food. Takes the empty bottle. Leaves the fresh one.

"Penance, tonight."

"Please… no more."

"This is for your own good. I'm saving your soul. You should thank me."

Erinyes listens to the crying in the darkness.

Atoning for sins is painful.

Upstairs again.

Searching online.

Searching searching searching.

Erinyes takes a break from the searching, checks the local news.

The police have already found the last one.

Interesting.

Then there's another blunt-force hit.

This one is different than a regular sexcam site. This is a sorority house on a college campus. The girls allow themselves to be watched by those who pay.

Erinyes does not pay.

Erinyes logs in as an administrator.

Six girls. One house.

Erinyes is searching.

There.

The specific, special girl is there.

Now Erinyes is watching.

Watching watching watching.

Then Erinyes is finding out all there is to know about the specific, special girl.

Erinyes knows the deep web.

Erinyes knows darknet.

Erinyes knows port scanners, and worms.

Erinyes can get past firewalls. Past passwords. Past encryption.

Erinyes is no script kiddie. Erinyes can hack almost anything. And if Erinyes can't hack it, Erinyes pays other hackers.

Bitcoin rules darknet.

So Erinyes soon learns about the specific, special girl.

Her credit rating. Who she owes. How much.

Health insurance information. Medical and dental history. Mental health background.

Bank statements. Income taxes.

Scholastic records. Grades. Disciplinary actions.

Court records. Family history.

The specific, special girl has no more secrets. Erinyes knows all.

"Hello, Kendal," Erinyes says to the computer screen. "I'm Erinyes. Penance is coming."

CHAPTER 5

Tom Mankowski returned to his humble, empty home. As he'd expected, Joan wasn't there. Still out shopping with Roy's girlfriend, Trish.

Tom considered calling her. He wanted to hear Joan's voice. After an entire morning spent with a dead body, he needed to speak to someone full of life. Tom dialed, and it went to voicemail.

"Hi, babe. If you haven't had lunch yet, let me know and I'll meet you somewhere. If you have, how about Uno's for dinner? Miss you."

Tom hung up, rubbed his eyes, and wondered if he should hit the gym. Maybe a workout would help clear the ugliness from his head. But if he went that route he might miss Joan's call. Instead, Tom stripped to his boxer shorts, did some push-ups and sit-ups and a quick round of curls with his barbell set.

The sweat came.

But the ugliness didn't leave.

He tried to push away the images of mutilation, and fill his head with facts instead of snapshots.

The girls had much in common, even though their deaths were different.

Both were webcam models.

Both in Chicago.

Both had been murdered in their apartments, bound to their own beds.

Both had been tortured.

Both had their eyelids snipped off.

Both had extensive genital mutilation.

In the first vic's apartment, the killer had written PENANCE on the wall. In the second, FURIE.

And both of the murdered women, perhaps coincidentally, were named Kendal.

Tom thought about the first Snipper murder, Kendal Zhanping, six weeks previously. Her cause of death was exsanguination. She'd died of hypovolemic shock; blood loss, due to traumatic injury to the carotid artery.

The ME guessed the weapon to be a butcher knife. The same one that had been shoved into her vagina had later been repeatedly shoved down her throat. The medical examiner, a no-nonsense guy named Blasky, wrote in his autopsy report that the genital and rectal mutilations "appear as if the victim was repeatedly vaginally and anally raped with the blade."

Tom went from curls to squats, with the weights at shoulder level. Tom hated squats, but as he grunted his way through them he was able to forget about the case and focus on how much his legs hurt.

When he finished, Tom poured a glass of water from the sink, downed it, and poured another. He needed a shower. Not just to wash away the sweat, but to get the smell of death off of him.

Two online sex workers named Kendal.

A coincidence?

Roy would be following up on any links between the victims. He'd made a few calls from the scene. They hadn't worked for the same web modeling site; that would have been too easy. Neither of them had the screen name of *Kendal*, either. He and Roy had done some research into the sexcam business, and the vast amount of performers were anonymous, and took great pains to stay that way. Tom had assumed it was to avoid stalkers. When stripping and flirting on camera, Tom figured you wouldn't want the unknown weirdo watching you to be able to locate you in real life. But it went beyond just weirdos. Tom and Roy had interviewed another model from Kendal Zhanping's agency, and she'd been more concerned about her friends and family finding out than some psycho coming after her.

Made sense. Most people never encountered a serial killer, but everybody had loved ones. Why worry about Norman Bates going after you when a more realistic concern was Dad finding out what you've been doing, or Rita from the day job tattling to everyone at work?

Unfortunately, there *was* a Norman Bates-type psycho killing webcam models.

So how was he finding out where they lived? And did he know their real names?

Was this maniac targeting webcam models named Kendal?

The phone rang, pushing Tom out of his mental stream. He was pleased to see the name JOAN on his iPhone.

"Hey, babe. Did you eat?"

"Not yet, and I'm starving. Trish is a machine. She's like the Shopinator; can't be reasoned with, can't be bargained with, no pity or remorse or fear, won't stop until I'm dead from exhaustion. Oh, and I realized that while I was in LA I left my credit card at the airport when I was checking in. So I had to borrow your card."

Tom didn't understand. He had his Visa on him. "From my wallet?"

"Not that one. The Mastercard you had on your desk. It was just sitting there, you'd already left, I figured it would be okay. Was it okay?"

That was Tom's new card. The one he hadn't used yet, because he needed the entire balance to afford Joan's engagement ring—something he'd planned on buying weeks ago in preparation for her visit.

"Of course it's okay," he said, wincing.

"Also, Roy's card didn't work for some reason, so Trish used yours, too."

The wince became a full blown grimace. Tom's credit had gone to hell in the past few months. He'd been late on the mortgage, twice, due to forgetfulness rather than lack of funds, but it had harmed his credit rating. It was unlikely he'd be approved if he applied for a jewelry store card. If the women had maxed out his new one, there went his proposal.

"No problem," Tom said. "Are you still doing the spa at three?"

"I don't know if I'm up for it."

The best laid plans of mice and men. Tom had been planning to use Joan's time at the spa to get the ring. Not that it mattered if he couldn't afford the ring.

His phone buzzed, and he saw ROY on the other line.

"Is that your other line? Is it Roy?"

"Yeah," Tom said. Joan was eerily prescient sometimes.

"Are you going to get it?"

"I should. But I don't want you angry with me."

"It's your job, Tom. We're not in high school, and I'm not some catty, passive-aggressive teenager who wants to control you."

"Okay. So, to be clear, I should answer the phone?"

"Answer the phone, Tom. And call me if you're going to cancel lunch."

"I'm not going to cancel lunch."

"Sure." Joan hung up.

Tom couldn't be sure, but Joan's tone seemed a bit catty and passive-aggressive. He connected to Roy.

"I got something. You free?"

"I'm on vacation. And you know what I was planning on doing today."

"What?"

"I was going to propose today, Roy. I told you about this."

"When?"

"A month ago. At the Tap Room."

"The Tap Room? We got annihilated at the Tap Room. I don't even remember how I got home."

"I put you in a cab. After I told you I was going to propose to Joan."

"I have zero memory of that. But you gonna marry Joan? Congrats, brother! You free now?"

"I'm meeting Joan for lunch."

"You poppin' the question then?"

"No. I don't have the ring yet."

"So you free now?"

"What do you want, Roy?"

His partner's voice got lower. "We got a witness, Tom. Someone saw The Snipper."

Tom twisted this info around in his noggin. It could be the break they needed. "Was it a good look?"

"Gonna talk to her now. Thought you'd want to be there."

Tom didn't want to be there. But his job meant he *had* to be there.

"Where is the wit?"

"In my office."

"I'll see you in ten."

Tom clicked off, then stared at his phone. Feeling like the worst boyfriend in the world, he texted "Got to cancel lunch. So sorry. I love you."

When he sent it, Tom realized he probably wasn't husband material. Joan deserved better. Maybe proposing was a bad idea.

After South Carolina, Tom had told Joan he was quitting the force. He and Roy had talked about opening a fishing charter business. They'd even gone so far as to shop for boats and investigate loans.

Then Roy had met Trish. Trish had various reasons she didn't want to move away from Chicago, and Roy had various reasons—most of them sexual—he wouldn't leave Trish to head for the coast with Tom. Tom couldn't blame him; he'd had his heart set on a fishing charter in order to be near Joan. So dreams were put on hold, and life went on.

Tom considered his former boss. Lt. Jacqueline Daniels was now retired, having given up police work to raise a daughter. She'd managed to walk away from The Job and stay away from it, for the most part. Tom wondered why he couldn't pull the trigger like that. How bad could working in the private sector be? More money. Fewer hours. A much reduced chance of getting killed. He didn't really like LA, but he loved Joan. There were worse things than giving up your career for the one you loved.

His phone buzzed. He was almost afraid to look at the text, but he did. As expected, it was from Joan.

Text me when you cancel dinner.

Tom made a face, then began to dress. Maybe, if the witness was good, they could catch The Snipper and prevent what Tom was sure would be another murder.

Perhaps the murder of a girl named Kendal.

CHAPTER 6

Kendal Smith switched off the shower camera using the wall switch. The green light on the camera's base blinked, then became red.

She hung a hand towel over the lens, just to be sure, and then turned on the water in the shower and waited for it to warm up. Kendal checked her cell, even though she'd checked it only a moment ago.

12:18.

The Abnormal Psychology test was in thirty-one minutes. It took exactly eleven minutes and thirty-six seconds to walk to the quad—1252 steps—and depending on campus activity between four minutes forty-four seconds and five minutes nineteen seconds to get to class in the Herschell Building. That meant seven minutes to finish showering, another seven to dress and leave the sorority house.

As these thoughts ran through Kendal's head, she'd also been doing a count to thirty-five; that's how long it took for the water to heat up in the shower. Once she reached her count she checked the spout.

The perfect temp.

Then she checked it again.

And again.

Kendal knew how silly it was. And when the cameras were on, she could mostly control herself. But the bathroom was the only true private place in the house, and it was where she indulged in her compulsions. In fact, that was the main reason she turned off the cameras when she showered. Kendal was less concerned about strangers seeing her naked, and more concerned about them seeing her act like a crazy person.

Well, that was *partly* true, at least. The thought of someone watching her as she showered was a pretty awful thought.

I am so screwed up. If OCD wasn't bad enough, I have to be a prude as well.

Thanks for that, father.

Kendal checked the water temp three more times even though she knew it was perfect, then disrobed and climbed into the shower. As Kendal shampooed she willed herself not to count the tiles on the wall.

Her will broke after fifteen seconds, and she began to tick off tiles with her eyes, counting the soap dish as two since it took up two spaces. After shampooing three times, Kendal finished with her shower in exactly three minutes. She toweled and dressed a bit ahead of schedule so she counted to ten before pulling the rag off the camera and turning it back on.

Okay, pretend to be normal. You can do this.

Kendal walked out of the bathroom, conscious of every camera on her. They felt like eyeballs, and gave her the same sensation as when a stranger is staring at you from across the room. She hated them. Hated hated hated them, with all her heart.

She hated them even more because she needed them. The cameras were paying for her college.

Kendal's partial scholarship wouldn't have been enough to cover her tuition without the supplementary income the cameras provided. No one on campus knew about the cameras. And even if they knew, they couldn't watch; the webcams were blocked from everyone in the state of Illinois. But the other forty-nine states, and the rest of the globe, could tune into http://www.hotsororitygirlslive.com and spy on the sisters at Epsilon Epsilon Delta twenty-four hours a day, seven days a week, as long as they had a working credit card.

Some of the sisters performed for the cameras. Of the six that lived in Double-E-D, two were attention grabbers, and two were certifiable exhibitionists. Only Kendal and Linda—Kendal's only real friend and the one who got her into the sorority—were more reserved. They didn't bring their boyfriends back to the house (not that Kendal had a boyfriend) to secretly make-out for the cameras, like the other girls. They didn't strip or masturbate—though Linda did flash her boobs in accordance with her *Free the Nipple* stance. They both (Kendal mostly) kept their client chats non-sexual, even though they'd make more in tips if they cut loose a little.

Kendal wasn't the cutting loose type.

She left the house at exactly 12:29, counting the steps in her head as she walked to the quad. While walking, her mind went over the review sheets for the test today, which covered two sections of the Diagnostic and Statistical Manual of Mental Disorders, Fifth Edition.

Kendal knew more about mental disorders than any nineteen-year-old on campus, and probably more than many of the seniors taking Advanced Abnormal Psych. She'd lived with obsessive compulsive disorder, and with the more extreme mental disorders of close family members, for her entire life.

They'd recently been studying gender dysphoria, and disruptive, impulse-control, and conduct disorders. The latter was a particularly relevant section for Kendal, because it was where the DSM-V categorized antisocial personality.

In other words, it was where they put the psychopaths.

Psychos—particularly Theodore Millon's tyrannical subtype who got off on the pain of others—freaked Kendal out.

With good reason. Kendal had known sadists. She had the scars to prove it. Both mental, and physical.

Oddly, the psychological damage done to Kendal hadn't turned her into a total shrinking violet, and while she erred to paranoia, she was a long way from how she used to be, living in constant fear. She had learned to trust people again. She dated, occasionally. Kendal also sometimes read horror novels; as long as they involved a monster or demon or supernatural element. But she stayed away from torture porn, or serial killer thrillers where the maniac wanted to punish women.

Who thought up sick shit like that and called it entertainment?

At five hundred and two steps Kendal had to swerve to avoid a spider on the sidewalk. Ick. Those things grossed her out, big time. Too many legs. Too many eyes. Curved fangs. Immobilizing victims in webs to suck their blood. She shivered. Awful creatures. And Kendal read, somewhere, that the average person swallows eight spiders a year while they sleep. They're attracted to carbon dioxide, or something, and crawl into your mouth.

As far as the animal world went, Kendal couldn't think of anything worse.

Unfortunately, in the human world, there was worse to be found. Much worse.

But Kendal didn't want to think about that.

At six hundred and eight steps toward the quad, Kendal felt a tingle on the back of her neck.

Someone's watching me.

Kendal knew the feeling well. She lived with the feeling every day, at the sorority house. Eyes were on her, and it made all the tiny little hairs stand out straight on her forearms. Kendal stopped; something she never did when walking to the quad. Then she cautiously looked over her shoulder.

There.

Down the street.

A dark cargo van with tinted windows.

Half a block away, moving much slower than the 25mph speed limit.

Almost as if it was stalking Kendal.

The vehicle stopped a moment after she did, taking up the whole lane. Kendal could hear the engine rumbling, probably a bad muffler or a hole in the exhaust. A car behind it honked, but the van didn't move.

Kendal tried to take a step forward, but had a momentary brain freeze because she'd lost her step count.

What's my count?

I forgot my count!

Kendal had once tried to explain counting to a friend, back in junior high. As the syndrome described, Kendal was obsessed with counting her steps, and the need to do so was irresistible. It was impossible to hold your hand over an open flame, even if you wanted to. Reflexes would make you pull it away. In the same way, it was impossible for Kendal to stop counting. It wasn't a question of willpower. Without counting, Kendal was overwhelmed by fear and dread, convinced she'd done something wrong. This led to shaking, crying, holding her breath, and eventually passing out. She couldn't control it. The fear of not counting was stronger than any other fear.

Including her fear of that black van.

Kendal's mind seemed to bisect, half thinking about some creepy driver intent on doing her harm, and the other half struggling to remember the number she'd left off at.

Her hands trembled. Her bladder clenched. She couldn't breathe, and felt helpless just standing there, waiting for bad things to happen, unable to get away.

Wait! It's 612! I'm at 612.

She blew out a stiff breath. Then Kendal stared at her feet and willed them to move, somewhere between a brisk walk and a jog.

640, 641, 642, 643...

Kendal chanced another look behind her at step 666—a number she loathed due to her strict, religious upbringing—terrified that the van would be right next to her.

But that wasn't the case.

The van was gone.

Leaving Kendal to wonder if she'd imagined the whole thing.

Am I seeing things again? Having a relapse?

Kendal couldn't worry about that now. She couldn't be late for class. Being late gave her panic attacks.

She got to the quad in 1231 steps, but felt no relief. It always took 1252. *Always.*

Already flustered, Kendal risked looking stupid and spent thirty absurd seconds walking in a circle until she hit the number 1252, and only then did she step onto the quad and hurry to the Herschell Building, unaware that the person in the van had parked up the street and was watching through binoculars.

CHAPTER 7

The witness was a tall, sturdy woman in her late teens or early twenties. She had pale skin, high cheekbones that sported too much rouge, a strong jaw, and thick black hair with severely short bangs, like she'd taken a picture of Bettie Page to her hair stylist and they'd gone too far. She sat across from Roy at his desk, her shoulders slumped forward, her posture betraying depression, or exhaustion, or both. But her eyes were bright and alert, and they darted to Tom, locking on him as he approached.

"Detective Mankowski, this is Tanya Bestrafen," Roy said.

Tom offered a hand. Though her expression was meek, the handshake was strong, confident.

"Nice to meet you," she said, in a throaty voice a lot like Tina Turner's.

"Thanks for coming in." Tom took the chair next to Roy.

"You guys are in charge of this case?" Tanya asked.

"We report to our superior, but we're the lead detectives, yes."

Tanya lowered her eyes. "I saw what happened to that girl. On the news. The Snipper murder. Why do they call him The Snipper?"

Tom mentally thanked the media for being so helpful in giving serial killers such delightful names. On the backlog, Tom and Roy were investigating an ongoing series of scalpings that appeared to be gang-related. The local rags had christened the perp The Scalper. Big surprise there.

"He cuts off the victim's eyelids," Tom answered.

Tanya nodded slowly, then said, "So she has to watch what he does to her."

Tom hadn't thought of that. Good insight. Also, creepy as hell. "My partner says you may have seen the murderer?"

"Yeah. After four am."

"Are you normally up at four?" Roy asked.

"Sometimes. I work at home, keep odd hours. I'll go for walks, go grab an energy drink at the nearby 7-11."

Tom glanced down at the witness statement form Roy had started, and saw Tanya lived a few blocks away from Kendal Hefferton.

"Is that what you were doing that night?" Tom asked.

"Yeah."

He picked up a pen and began to take notes. "What did you see?"

"I'd just gotten a Red Bull, and was walking back to my place. He came out of the building, almost ran me over."

"Like he was in a hurry?" Roy asked.

"Like he was in a helluva hurry."

"Did you get a good look at him?" Tom asked.

Tanya nodded. "He was white. Forties. Handsome. Like that Ukrainian guy on that reality show. Maddoks Chmerkolinivskiy."

Tom stopped taking notes after writing a single M. "Who?"

"Mad-doks-im Ch-mer-ko-li-niv-skiy."

Tom had never heard of him. "Uh, how is that spelled?"

"I think Maddoks is with a K and S, not an X, and ends in I and Y." Tanya stuck her hands into her oversized jacket pockets, searching for something. "I forgot my cell. Does yours have Internet?"

Tom nodded. Tanya reached out a hand and Tom gave it to her. She held it to her face, squinting as she pressed the screen with her thumbs. After about fifteen seconds, she put the phone on the desk.

"Maddoksim Chmerkolinivskiy. The nose on the guy I saw was wider, eyebrows thicker, but otherwise they looked like twins."

Tom stared at the Wikipedia page of the actor, who was, as Tanya said, handsome.

"What was he wearing?"

"Long black coat. Jeans. A wool cap."

Roy's turn. "Was he carrying anything?"

Tanya shook her head.

"Plastic bags?" Tom asked. "Shower curtain?"

Another head shake.

"And he was in a hurry, you said?"

"He was practically running. Bumped me. Almost knocked me over. For a second I thought it was Maddoks. You know, from the show. But he also had a gut on him."

"A gut?"

"A pot belly. Maddoksim Chmerkolinivskiy does *not* have a pot belly. He's got the body of an underwear model."

Roy and Tom took turns questioning Tanya for another fifteen minutes, but she didn't add any more details. Roy ended the interrogation with, "If you had to spot him in a line up, could you?"

Tanya nodded. "Absolutely. He got even closer to me than I am to you. So close I could smell his breath."

"What did it smell like?" Tom asked.

"Like meat. Like he'd just eaten a really rare steak. You know. Bloody."

Tom and Roy exchanged a glance. Then they thanked her, and Tanya left.

"What do you think?" Roy asked.

"Send a team to the building. Show all the tenants a pic of Max, or Maddox, or whatever this celebrity's name is, see if he lives there or if he's our guy."

"How about the blood breath?"

"I'll call the M.E. Have him check the body for saliva. If The Snipper is drinking blood, maybe he left some DNA."

Roy nodded. "What did you think of Tanya?"

"She'll make a good witness. Sure of herself."

"Could you tell she was intersex?"

Tom blinked. "Huh?"

"Either intersex or transgender," Roy said. "I'm not sure which. No facial hair, and no equipment—the skinny jeans don't lie. But big hands and feet, thick wrists, slim hips. She's either post op, or intersex."

"I'm not sure what the difference is."

"Transgender," Roy said, "is when a person who presents as one sex identifies with another. Intersex is when someone is born with no distinct gender."

"Like a hermaphrodite," Tom said.

"True hermaphrodites are really rare. But Tanya could have any number of conditions."

"And you know so much about this because...?"

"Trish is intersex."

Tom blinked. "Your girlfriend?"

"She was born with CAIS. Complete Androgen Insensitivity Syndrome."

Tom wasn't sure what to say. "But she looks..."

"Like a woman. I know. She looks completely like a woman. But Trish has a Y chromosome, and no ovaries. She has testes inside her."

"So... she has balls?"

"Don't be ignorant, Tom."

Tom spread his hands. "I'm not trying to be. I just don't understand."

"Externally, she's a woman. Got all the parts a woman does, except she can't grow body hair. Internally, no ovaries. So she doesn't have periods, can't have children."

"Instead, she has testes."

Roy nodded. "Underdeveloped. They don't make sperm."

"And you knew this all along?"

"She told me on the first date."

It was a lot to absorb. "Roy, don't take this the wrong way, but I never expected you to be so... progressive."

"Love is blind," Roy said. "And the sex is incredible. Would you feel any different about Joan if she told you she was intersex?"

Tom didn't have to consider the question. "No. In fact, I'll be honest; no periods would be nice."

"See," Roy said, "you got to be a sexist dick. Here we're having a high level conversation about gender, and you go for the cheap PMS joke."

"It's not a joke. She's like Lon Chaney Jr. during a full moon."

Roy didn't crack a smile. "Why do I tell you these things when you just act like a fool?"

"It's not like I'm saying anything behind Joan's back. She'd admit the same thing. Just because it's a stereotype doesn't mean it isn't true."

"So what stereotypes do you believe about black men?" Roy asked.

"That you're good basketball players, care too much about sneakers, and have big dicks."

"I find that offensive. In my case, all three happen to be correct. But I am offended for my smaller dick brothers who can't hit the fadeaway jumper."

Tom laughed, and Roy stopped pretending to be irritated and laughed along.

"Okay, you want the apartment or the M.E.?"

"I'll take the apartment. Meet you in two hours?"

Tom nodded, they did a fist bump, and Roy walked off. For a moment, Tom thought about Trish. How she probably felt when all of her adolescent friends were getting their periods, and she didn't. He could imagine her going to a doctor, getting the news that genetically she was partly male. Or all male. Tom still didn't understand how that worked. But he did understand what it felt like to be told you were different from others.

Being different didn't feel good. But, to loosely paraphrase Thomas Jefferson, happiness was based on the choices we make, not the conditions we were born with.

He considered all of Jefferson's vast accomplishments, considered his own minimal contribution to humanity, and then got back to work.

CHAPTER 3

1251... 1252.

Kendal stood in front of her house, key in hand. She touched the doorknob three times, then unlocked it, let herself in, and blew out a stiff breath.

Class had been uneventful, but Kendal hadn't absorbed much of it because she'd been unable to stop thinking about the van that had followed her earlier. Walking back from the quad, she'd looked behind her so many times that her neck had begun hurting. Kendal hadn't seen it again.

Which made her wonder if she'd actually seen it in the first place. Which made her wonder if the hallucinations were back.

She checked the mail bin next to the front door, took out two envelopes addressed to her, and walked past the den. Linda and Hildy were stretched out on the sofa, watching one of those movies where the heroine was in love with a hot, angsty teenage vampire who took his shirt off a lot.

"Hey, slut, how was class?" Linda asked, not turning away from the abs.

"I blew the professor, and then had sex with two guys on his desk while everyone watched. Too bad you missed it. What did you guys do?"

"We had a naked pillow fight, then did lines of cocaine off of each other's boobs. Too bad you missed it."

At the beginning of the semester, Kendal and Linda used to make up outrageous lies to tease the subscribers who watched them, pretending that they'd actually missed something epic. They'd gotten so used to the jokes that 'too bad you missed it' was as common to them as 'hello'.

"You got a call," Hildy said. "Message next to the phone."

"Who was it?"

"Some stalker who wanted to cut your head off."

Kendal froze. Hildy was a cheerleading type, and her sense of humor wasn't as subtle as Linda's.

After taking a moment to compose herself, Kendal asked, "Did the stalker have a name?"

"Message is next to the phone."

Kendal walked into the kitchen, found the Post-It note with her name on it beside the old-fashioned push button phone, complete with a twisty cord attached to it.

12:26 P.M. – Dr. Semnai, Carpenter Clinic

Kendal squinted at the words. The Carpenter Clinic was on campus, but Kendal had thought it was closed for remodeling. She dialed the number Hildy had scrawled, and a woman picked up on the fourth ring.

"Clinic."

"This is Kendal Smith," she whispered. "I got a message to call."

"What was the last name?"

Kendal held her hand over the mouthpiece and spelled it. She didn't want anyone watching to know her real name. No Names was the first rule of the house.

"Hold please."

Kendal was treated to the Musak version of an old Nirvana song. She glanced at the nearest kitchen camera, felt her neck go goosepimply, and turned her back to it.

"Miss Smith? We called to schedule a mammogram."

"What, like for breast cancer?" Kendal lowered her voice. "I'm nineteen years old. Aren't mammograms for old women?"

"Your medical history shows you were on several anti-psychotic medications."

"That was a long time ago."

"Medication can continue to harm your body for years after you take it."

"Are you saying my meds cause cancer?"

"They carry an elevated risk."

"Are you sure? Do you know what I was taking?"

"Your medical history was pinged during a routine review. It's important we get this checked out immediately. Have you noticed any lumps? Tenderness? Changes in the look or feel of your breasts?"

She felt herself blush. "No."

"Nipple discharge?"

"What? No. Of course not."

"We'd still like you to come in. I can schedule you tomorrow at a quarter after three. Do you know where we're located?"

Kendal was hit by a wave of vertigo. She put her hand on the counter to steady herself.

"I... this is all happening too fast."

"This isn't anything to play around with, Kendal. The visit is free. It's included in the wellness program as part of your tuition. We really need to take care of this right away."

She chewed her lower lip. The cameras around her seemed to burn like lasers. "Okay. Three fifteen."

"See you then."

The nurse hung up. Kendal stared at the receiver for a moment, then placed it back in the cradle.

Breast cancer? Seriously? WTF?

She walked to her room, ignoring Linda when she asked, "Everything okay, slut?"

No. Definitely not okay.

Kendal closed her door, turned the lock, and sat down at her desk, switching on the monitor. She intended to look up her old medication, and do some searches for breast cancer, but noticed there were eight clients in her chat room.

Shit.

As a cam model for www.HotSororityGirlsLive.com, Kendal got a weekly paycheck for simply living in the house, plus bonuses for extras. Nudity and sex paid the highest, but chatting with subscribers got her double her standard rate, plus tips. Kendal needed the money. Much as she hated interacting with the voyeurs who watched her, it was smart business sense to play nice.

Kendal logged in as SHY1 and began to parse through the questions.

BOFFA DEEZ: Shy, you ok?

Watchdawg: wassup with the cancer, girl?

Prsnal: Need Update!

Unique NY: shy1 what was that call about? u say breast cancer?

ALLEC2: r u scared?

Free-mustache-rides: please tell us what is going on.

Tuscon4evah: this sounds serious shy girl.

Boffa deez: deets, plz!

1rover1: you gonna get you titties squeezed?

Allec2: what meds were you on?

Kendal typed, **thx for caring, guys! I m sorta freaked out right now. I guess I'm gonna see the doc tomorrow.**

She watched as an outpouring of fake sympathy filled her screen. Or maybe it was real sympathy. Kendal had a hard time picturing actual people behind these screen names. They didn't know who she was, or where she lived. She'd never meet any of them in person. For some weird, lonely, voyeuristic reason, they liked watching college girls. It wasn't necessarily prurient. They watched the sisters surfing TV channels, and sleeping, and putting on make-up, and eating. Mundane, everyday, non-sexual stuff. Hildy, who let the subscribers watch her shower, mentioned that some users purposely logged off once she dropped her towel. They told her they were valuing her privacy, even though they stared at her while she clipped her toenails.

Kendal didn't get it. She understood porn. Horny guy sees sexual images and relieves himself. But what benefit was there watching a group of sorority girls do their homework? Where was the entertainment value in that?

For some reason the thought of nameless, faceless dudes watching Kendal read a magazine was even creepier than nameless, faceless dudes whacking off while she exercised. These guys were paying to watch someone else's life. Someone they'd never meet. It was bizarre.

So Kendal dealt with it by not thinking of the subscribers as people. They were more like Tamagotchi to her. She had one of those virtual reality pets when she was a kid. It was a keychain with a digital dog on the screen, and she had to feed and play with it every few hours or it would die. Kendal never warmed up to the pretend animal—it died after a few days. She never warmed up to her subscribers, either. But imagining that they weren't real made them easier to deal with. And the more she interacted, the more money she made.

Her IM screen popped up. Instant messages could be read by her, but not by anyone else in the chat room. This one was from Allec2, a user she didn't recognize.

`Allec2: would you do a private chat?`

Kendal answered that she didn't do any sex stuff. He replied that he just had some specific, private questions. Since Kendal currently had eight paying clients in her room, she declined, saying she was too busy right now.

After twenty or so minutes of broad chitchat about her health and well-being, faux sympathy, and bon mots about how much they cared, Kendal had gotten forty bucks in tips and was down to three subscribers still chatting. Allec2 was one of them, and he tipped her ten dollars, her computer making a *cha-ching!* sound.

Allec2: how about now? Chat?

Private chats paid ten times as much as regular chats. Kendal actually preferred them, as it was hard to keep up several conversations at once. She typed, **ok, as long as you don't get perverted.**

She said goodbye to her other two clients, and went into a private chat room with Allec2.

Shy1: so you finally got me all alone.

Allec2: finally. How are you feeling?

Shy1: still scared.

Allec2: U R really young to need a mammogram.

Shy1: they said I'm at a higher risk.

Allec2: it runs in the family?

Kendal didn't know. It could have. Mom had left when she was young.

Shy1: I was on meds.

Allec2: anti psychotics?

Shy1: yeah. I had some problems when I was younger.

Allec2: sexual abuse?

Kendal shivered. She pulled a blanket around her shoulders and slunk down in her desk chair.

Shy1: I don't want to talk about it.

Allec2: I took clozapine for a while. Made me feel weird.

Shy1: I know, right? I was dizzy all the time.

Allec2: it gave me the shakes. But it helped with the urges.

Shy1: I don't know if it helped me or not. It was years ago. There's a lot I don't remember. My old shrink thinks I blocked some things.

Allec2: the mind tries to protect itself from bad things. We come to believe that abuse is normal.

Shy1: that's what my shrink said.

Kendal never talked about this with anyone. It had been a long time since she'd been to therapy. But Allec2 seemed to get it, on some level.

Shy1: I thought everyone lived like I did. That everyone had a dad like that. That everyone saw things.

Allec2: what kind of things did you see?

Shy1: well, sometimes, when things got really awful, I would go places.

Allec2: in your head?

Shy1: yes! I had an imaginary friend I talked to. But I thought he was real. I could see him. Or I thought I could see him. But he helped me when it got bad.

Allec2: are you sure he wasn't real?

Shy1: he couldn't have been real.

Allec2: so you were just talking to yourself?

Shy1: I guess.

Allec2: could you be chatting with yourself right now? Maybe I'm not even here.

Kendal blinked. This was getting meta.

Shy1: so I'm typing both my responses, and yours?

Allec2: are you looking at the keyboard when you type? Or at the screen?

Shy1: the screen.

Allec2: so your fingers might be typing my response right now, and you don't even realize it.

Kendal kept one eye on her fingers, the other on the screen. Allec2 didn't respond. When she turned her full attention back to the monitor, he replied with:

Maybe you should start taking your meds again.

Shy1: I gotta go.

Allec2: you look a little freaked out right now.

Kendal looked around her room, at all the webcams. Of course Allec2 was watching her. He paid a monthly subscription for the privilege.

Shy1: it's been a tough day. I'm tired.

Allec2: school?

Shy1: yeah.

Allec2: calculus sucks.

Kendal wondered how he knew she took calculus. He'd probably heard her mention it. Or seen her textbook.

Or Allec2 is really me, and I'm talking to myself. Maybe I'm having a schizophrenic break.

Allec2: tell me, Kendal, was your imaginary friend locked up in the basement and screamed like hell when your dad went down there?

Kendal hit the *block* key and pushed away from the computer, her heart halfway up her throat. Then she looked at her hands, fingers splayed out in front of her.

Holy shit, did I just write that?

He called me Kendal.

How did he know my name? He couldn't know my name.

Locked up in the basement?

What the hell was going on?

I'm dizzy.

I want to lie down.

I want to lie down, in privacy.

Kendal switched off the webcams in her room. Her weekly paycheck would take a hit, but she didn't want to be watched right then. When she was finished, she closed her door, climbed onto her bed, curled into a ball, and closed her eyes.

CHAPTER 9

Erinyes's eyes open.

The house is quiet. Still.

But not empty.

Erinyes checks the clock. Almost delivery time. The driver is never late.

Erinyes waits by the door, staring through the peep hole.

Watches the van pull up.

Watches the man drop off the packages.

Watches him take the envelope of cash under the welcome mat.

Watches him leave.

Erinyes unlocks the door and scoops up the brown boxes. They all have fake return addresses, paid for with stolen credit card numbers. Darknet purchases, sent to a PO Box in a false name, via a mail forwarding service, and dropped off by private courier.

No way to trace them. Too many layers of protection.

Erinyes spreads the boxes out on the dining room table. Picks up a utility knife.

It's Christmas time.

Santa brought Erinyes some goodies.

Spironolactone.

More vantablack make-up.

Cyproterone acetate.

Eratigena agrestis eggs.

Gamma-Hydroxybutyric acid.

A master key set for Sargent locks.

Clindamycin.

A new cat o'nine tails.

Erinyes inspects the whip. The previous one had broken after repeated use. This one seems to be higher quality. The nine lashes are supple cowhide. The handle is wrapped steel, giving the weapon greater weight. Each tail ends in a sharp metal barb. So sharp Erinyes draws blood on a fingertip after touching it.

This isn't a cheap S/M toy to flog your spouse while playing Fifty Shades of Grey in the bedroom. This is the real thing, meant to administer severe corporal punishment.

Penance. Penance long overdue.

Erinyes unlocks the basement door and walks downstairs.

"The Eratigena have arrived," Erinyes says to the darkness. "Soon you'll have your crown."

Whimpers, and a tinkling of chains being dragged across the cement floor.

"UPS also delivered a new whip."

A moan.

"You shall atone for your sins with spilled blood. The punishment will cleanse your soul."

"Please… don't." The voice is meek. Feeble.

"Don't you want your sins forgiven?"

No reply. Erinyes hits the cell phone record button.

"Do you think you have suffered enough for your crimes?"

"Mercy. Please."

"Erinyes does not know mercy. Only punishment."

Erinyes raises the whip.

"Don't hurt me anymore."

"It is your sins that have hurt you. I am here to give Penance."

Erinyes begins.

The Penance is very loud. And very bloody.

CHAPTER 10

"I cut open dead bodies for a living, and this one made my stomach turn."

Tom was using Facetime on his cell phone with Dr. Phil Blasky, who was in session at Cook County Morgue. Blasky hovered over the corpse of Kendal Hefferton, his voice booming through the refrigerated room, bouncing off concrete and stainless steel.

"Look at this," Blasky switched to the rear camera. Tom didn't like it when Blasky did that, and he winced at the sight of the victim.

"These wounds here in the vagina and anus all have increased histamine levels, indicating the injuries were pre-mortem."

"She was alive," Tom interpreted.

"Alive and struggling. Lots of defensive cuts."

"Did the killer leave any trace?"

"Not a goddamn thing. I've been over every square inch of her with an alternate light source, swabbed every part of her I could think of, and the perp didn't shed so much as an eyelash."

That wasn't good. While DNA rarely led to suspects, it often led to convictions. Tom had been hoping the killer left something behind.

"The tape used to bind her?" Tom asked.

"Standard duct tape"

"Prints?"

"Oval spots where he touched the adhesive, but no prints. He wore gloves."

"Any evidence of rape?"

"Other than with the butcher knife? None I could find. No skin under her nails. If she fought back, she didn't scratch him."

"We think he might have tried to drink her blood."

"Then he did it clean. No saliva I could find."

Tom thought of something awful, and winced when he spoke. "Could he have maybe used a straw?"

"You mean poked into a vein and drank her like a juice box?"

"Yeah."

"There's something wrong with you that you think of stuff like that. But if the killer did it, I can't find the entry point."

Tom sighed. "So what can you tell me?"

"Her molars are loose, but no bruises on her face or cheeks." Blasky stuck a gloved hand in the victim's mouth and wiggled a tooth. "It's a guess, but I think she was gagged and bit down hard on it."

"Ball gag?"

"More like a bit."

"Like for horses?"

"That's what I'd bet on. Wedged into the back of the mouth, buckled around the head. Common bondage item. So I've heard."

"Tox screen?"

"Waiting on results. Lab takes forever, you know that. But I have a theory how he tied her up."

"Could it be consensual? A cam model decides to make extra money as a call girl, the client is into bondage."

Blasky switched the camera back to himself, and he made a face. "Would you let some guy you didn't trust tie you up?"

"There was no evidence of B&E. She might have let him in."

"Or she might have been knocked out." He turned the phone around. "See the small mark above her nose, and one under her chin?

"Yeah."

"I'm a sucker for antique medical equipment. Did you know I have over a hundred pre-1950 reflex hammers? It's crazy the shit you can find on eBay. Those burns, to me, look like they'd line up with a chloroform mask."

Tom thought back to old black and white movies, an assailant sneaking up on a woman with a chloroformed rag to knock her out.

"Can you still buy chloroform?"

"You can buy anything. A hundred reflex hammers, remember? Chloroform masks were made of wire or mesh. They fit over the mouth and nose, and held a rag in place. You find the mask, I can match it to her injuries. Just as good as DNA evidence."

Blasky then began to talk about his 1923 tonsil guillotine, and Tom was spared the details because he had another call.

"Gotta take this, Phil. Call if you find anything." Tom switched over. "Hi, babe," he said to Joan. "What's up?"

"I'm checking to see if we're still on for dinner."

"Of course we're on for dinner. Nothing could keep me from dinner with you. Are you still with Trish?"

"Yes. We ate at Uno's."

That's what Tom had planned on for dinner, but he supposed he could figure out an alternative. "How was it?"

"They didn't have goat cheese."

"Of course they didn't have goat cheese. This is Chicago, not Rodeo Drive."

"Don't get snotty with me. You're the one who stood me up."

"I wasn't getting snotty, hon, I—"

"Are you still at work?"

"Yes. Not for long, though. Want to maybe check out the Art Institute? There's an O'Keefe exhibit."

Tom's other line beeped. He ignored it.

"Are you going to answer that?" Joan asked.

Tom checked the number. It was the crime lab.

"I can call them back."

"I hear your tone. It's important."

"You're the one who is important, babe."

The beeping continued. Tom wondered why the hell his voicemail didn't pick up.

"The Art Institute sounds nice," Joan finally said.

"Want to meet there in an hour?"

"Sure. That way, when you don't show up, at least I'll have something to do."

"I'm going to show up, Joan. I've been thinking about you all day."

"Uh-huh."

She didn't sound convinced. Tom's phone finally stopped beeping.

"I have."

"Okay, fair enough. But why does it have to be you're at work, thinking of me, or you're with me, thinking of work?"

"We promised we'd never make our jobs a thing between us," Tom said. "That's why you still live in LA and I still live in Chicago. They're part of who we are, and we decided not to ask each other to change."

"What if we did?"

"Huh?"

"What if I asked you to give up your job for me, Tom? Would you do it?"

"Are you asking?"

"Do you want me to ask? Or do you want to ask me?"

"We said we wouldn't ask. I know your work is important."

"But movie deals aren't as important as catching killers, right?"

"I didn't say that," Tom said.

"You don't need to. I get a call in the morning, I have to talk a director off a ledge so he doesn't derail a two hundred mil blockbuster. You get a call, someone died. So obviously, you think your job is more important."

Tom's other line beeped again. Same number.

"You should answer it," Joan said. "Someone else might be dead."

"Can we continue this discussion at the museum?"

"A coward is much more exposed to quarrels than a man of spirit."

"What is that? Is that a Jefferson quote? Did you just quote Jefferson to me?"

"Text me when you cancel," Joan said, then hung up.

Tom wanted to be irritated, but he didn't want to miss the call again, so he shelved his frustration and picked up.

"Mankowski."

"Detective, are you in your office? I can come up."

"Who is this?"

"Firoz."

"Excuse me?"

"Detective Firoz Nafisi?"

"Excuse me?"

"I'm the CPD computer guy. I did forensics on Kendal Hefferton's laptop. You're lead on the case?"

"Me and Roy Lewis."

"Can I come up?"

"Yeah. Sure."

"Be right there."

Tom opened up the folder containing his crime scene report of the first victim. He let himself drift back to it. The sight of her, tied to the bed, mutilated almost beyond recognition. The smell. The bloody writing on the wall. Tom was no stranger to violence. He'd seen it. He'd been the recipient of it. But this was a whole new level of psychotic. There was careful planning here. The perp had gained access to the apartment, brought along his torture tools, tape, gag, chloroform and mask. But there was so much raw rage, so much savagery, in the murder, that it looked like the work of someone severely unhinged.

"Detective?"

Tom was startled by someone speaking so near to him. He looked up.

"I'm Firoz."

The man who extended a hand looked familiar, and Tom hid his surprise.

He looked a lot like Maddoksim Chmerkolinivskiy, which meant he looked like the suspect Tanya Bestrafen had described leaving the second victim's apartment.

CHAPTER 11

The man bleeds.

The man hurts.

The man pulls at the chains.

The man knows there is no escape.

The man thinks about monsters.

The man knows they are real.

The man cries.

The man cries for himself.

The man cries for the world.

The man knows there is no forgiveness.

For anyone.

CHAPTER 12

Kendal picked up her cell phone.

"Hello?"

At first, there was silence. Then:

"Do you think you have suffered enough for your crimes?"

The voice sounded weird. Far away. "Hello?"

"Mercy. Please."

"Who is this?" Kendal asked.

"Erinyes does not know mercy. Only punishment."

"Don't hurt me anymore."

"It is your sins that have hurt you. I am here to give Penance."

Then there was a cracking sound, and a scream that made all the fine hairs on Kendal's arms stand on end.

The horrible sounds continued. Smacking and screaming, and Kendal realized she was listening to someone being beaten.

She hung up, holding the phone at arm's length.

Caller Unknown.

What the hell had just happened?

Kendal hurried out of her bedroom, into the kitchen, brushing past Linda, grabbing a glass drying in the sink, and pouring herself some water from the tap. She sucked it down in a few gulps.

"Thirsty much?" Linda asked, laughing.

Kendal didn't answer, pouring herself another glassful.

"Hey, girl, you okay?"

Kendal finished the water and sucked in a breath. "I just got a really weird phone call."

"Like obscene weird? Some guy yanking his crank and moaning? You lucky slut! I never get calls like that."

"I mean like someone being beaten."

"That's even kinkier."

"Really beaten. Screaming for their lives beaten."

Linda raised an eyebrow. "Was it some kind of joke?"

Kendal leaned against the counter, her shoulders slumping. "If it was, it wasn't funny."

"Who was it from?"

"It said caller unknown."

"You can *67 or *69 him to call him back, even if it's unknown."

"I don't want to call him back."

"Give me your cell."

Kendal hesitated, then handed Linda her phone. Linda's thumbs were a blur on the screen.

"When did you get the call?"

"Just a minute or two ago."

"There's no record of it."

"What?"

"The last call you got was yesterday."

"But someone just—"

"Could you have deleted it?"

Kendal's face pinched. "I don't know."

"If you deleted it, we can't call it back."

Linda handed the phone over. Kendal stared at it, wondering if it really happened.

Had she been asleep?

Dreaming?

Hallucinating?

Hallucinations were one of the big symptoms of schizophrenia. Another one was paranoia. Thinking people were watching you.

Kendal took an easy look around at all of the cameras in the kitchen. People actually *were* watching her.

But were they out to get her?

She thought about the van following her on the way to school. Had that been real? Had the chat with Allec2? The phone call she just got?

Or were past afflictions coming back to haunt her?

"Shy?" Linda asked, using her screen name. "You look like you're seriously freaking out."

"I think I just need to take a walk. Can you come with me?"

"History essay. I need to cut and paste some Wikipedia pages and change enough so it passes the sniff test. My prof searches phrases on Google."

Kendal gripped her arm. "Just to the corner, get some ice cream or something. My treat."

"You know I'm dieting, bitch."

"Fine. We'll go for celery. Please?"

"I heard celery has negative calories. It actually burns more calories to chew it than you digest."

"So let's go. I'll buy you ten pounds of celery, and you'll be a size 2 by the time we get back."

Linda made a face like she was severely constipated. "Ooh, it's tempting, but I really have to do this paper. I've played around enough today."

Linda left the kitchen. Kendal stared at her phone again.

Had I erased the call?

Or, maybe, had Linda erased the call?

Is it still paranoia if everyone is actually out to get you?

Kendal closed her eyes. She thought about her father. All the things he'd done to her. All the things he'd threatened to do.

But he was gone. Long gone. Kendal needed the webcam money, but if there had been a single chance in a billion that her father could somehow find her, she would have run away with the clothes on her back and not stopped until the soles of her shoes had worn down to nothing.

Kendal opened her eyes, forcing herself not to stare at any of the cameras, but feeling them on her body like hands pawing at her. She had to get out of there. Immediately.

She counted her steps—eighteen—to the front door, touched the knob three times before turning it, and then began the six hundred and eight step trip to the corner store.

Twenty-nine steps into her journey she shivered. It was cold, and she hadn't taken a coat. She crossed her arms, hugging herself, and picked up the pace.

Turning the corner at one hundred and fifty-five steps, Kendal saw the van. The same one that might have followed her earlier. Dark, tinted windows, creeping along under the speed limit.

Coming toward her.

Kendal froze. Should she run? Call the police? Pinch herself to make sure it wasn't a psychotic delusion?

The van pulled up alongside her and stopped, idling there.

Run! Kendal told herself.

But she'd forgotten her count.

As before, Kendal couldn't draw a breath. Her legs began to tremble, but her feet might as well have grown roots.

The corner was 155. She knew that. How many steps had she gone past that point? Ten? Fifteen?

The side panel door of the van inched open.

Kendal cast a frantic look around, seeking help. Up ahead, coming her way, was a police car.

I need to scream. If I scream, the police will stop.

But her lungs were as frozen as her feet. She watched, her eyes blurry with tears, as the cop car rolled past.

The van door opened. It was dark inside, but Kendal thought she saw a figure crouched inside. Someone wearing black. But it was strange, almost like a shadow rather than a person.

Where did I leave off?!?

Kendal began to mentally count up from 155, hoping a number would seem familiar. She was getting dizzy from the lack of air, and the shadow inside the van seemed to shift and twist, as if coiling up to pounce.

One seventy-two, one seventy-three...

That was it! One seventy-three!

She sucked in a breath and began to sprint back toward her sorority house, running as fast as she could count. When she made it home, panting and shaking all over, she was trying to hold her key steady enough to get it in the lock when her cell phone vibrated with a text message.

Kendal didn't want to look.

She looked anyway.

You can run. But I know where you live.

Kendal turned slowly around, and saw the black van parked only a few meters away.

Then the world went swirly, her legs went rubber, and she passed out.

CHAPTER 13

"Detective Nafisi?" Tom asked, eyeballing the man standing next to his desk.

The man extended his hand, and shook Tom's with surprising force. "Call me Firoz."

"Tom."

"I wanted to do this in person, Tom, for two reasons. First, I wanted to meet you. I heard about South Carolina, what you and Roy Lewis went through. Must have been intense."

Tom nodded. "What's the second reason?"

"I found something on Kendal Hefferton's laptop, and I need to confirm it in person." Firoz looked at the empty chair across from Tom. "May I?"

"Please."

Firoz dragged it over next to Tom, then turned it around and straddled it like it was a horse, propping his arms up on the back. "I heard you were tortured," Firoz said.

Tom didn't mind a man who was direct, but something about Firoz was off-putting. Tom felt like he was being scrutinized.

"What did you find?" he asked, ignoring the comment.

Firoz stared at Tom for a moment, then said, "The victim was having problems with one of her online clients. He was cyberstalking her."

"Is it traceable?"

Again Firoz paused before answering. "To a degree. But the better the cyberstalker, the harder he is to trace. Do you know a lot about computers?"

"As much as anyone, I guess."

"When devices communicate with each other over a computer network, each has a unique Internet Protocol address. This can be traceable, unless someone takes steps to make sure it isn't. If it's something like an email, the IP is recorded. But in a chatroom, like the victim used for her webcam modeling, tracing after the fact is practically impossible. Once the stalker disconnects, there is no way to find him. But Kendal was smart. She kept screen shots of the harassment. The last time, he used the name *Tilphousia.* His threats match up to the way she was killed."

"How do you spell Tilphousia?" Tom asked, pen in hand.

Firoz spelled it out.

"Do you have those screenshots?"

"I emailed them to you before I came up. Check to see if you got them."

Tom turned to his computer screen, accessed his department email, and saw he'd gotten a new one from superhackercop17. Tom clicked on it, then clicked on the attachments, creating a slideshow of screen captures. Half the screen was a picture of Kendal Hefferton, a snapshot of her live feed. She was in lingerie, looking disgusted. Tom could understand why. The other half of the screen was chat text. Tom read through some of Tilphousia's threats and felt himself become disgusted as well.

"Yeah, he's quite a psycho, isn't he?" Firoz asked.

Tom nodded.

"Keep looking. The next to last jpeg is of an email Kendal received. It's a different name, but the tone is the same."

Tom found it and began to read.

Little girls who do naughty things must be punished. Accept your fate and accept your Penance. Vengeance comes from the blood of Uranus, whore.

"Can you trace the email?" Tom asked.

"I already did. Click on the last picture."

Tom did. He stared at the screen, blinking a few times, confused.

"Don't you recognize it?" Firoz asked, his eyes narrowing.

"I don't understand," Tom admitted.

"What's so hard to understand?" Firoz asked. "That email, the one I found on Kendal's laptop. Do you know where it came from?"

"Of course not. Why would I?"

"Because it was sent from your account."

CHAPTER 14

Erinyes watches.

It is easy to watch when there are so many cameras.

Cameras in businesses.

Cameras on streets.

Cameras in homes. Security cameras. Nanny cams.

Cameras on computers. On tablets. On cellphones.

Taking a selfie? Erinyes can see it.

Video chatting? Erinyes can watch it.

Surfing the web? Erinyes can turn on your webcam and stare at you, and you won't even know it.

Does your ebook reader have a camera?

Look at it. Examine the edges. Is that a camera on the front, up on top?

Are you being watched right now?

What is that on the bottom? A microphone?

Is someone listening to you breathe? Hearing you clear your throat? Recording your every movement, every sound?

How secure is your network?

How unbreakable is your password?

Do you think your firewall is unbeatable?

Do you think your antivirus software can protect you?

Do you really think you're safe?

There is no such thing as safe. If you are connected to the Internet, if you're part of a network, if you're online or on the phone, surfing, talking, chatting, texting, you can be seen.

Are you frightened?

You look frightened.

CHAPTER 15

Tom stared hard at Firoz. "You think I sent this email?"

"You tell me. Veteran cop, went through a horrible experience, became dangerously unhinged, began stalking webcam models."

Tom was about to protest, but Firoz smiled for the first time. "No, it isn't you. No offense, man, but you don't have the brains for it."

"You went from practically accusing me of murder, to saying I'm an idiot."

"Look at your desk, Detective. What are those?" Firoz pointed.

"My notes."

"Written on paper? In pen? What are you, a Neanderthal? Don't you know there are apps for that? Have you heard of typing? Voice to text? A stylus for digital notes?"

"A pen never runs out of batteries," Tom said.

"Move over." Firoz nudged Tom aside, his hands a blur on his keyboard. A few screens flashed by, almost too fast for Tom to see. "You were spoofed."

"Spoofed?"

"Someone forged your sender address, made it look like you were sending the email. When was the last time you ran your anti-virus program?"

"Uh..."

Firoz clicked the mouse a few times. "The answer you're looking for is *never*. So either you have a Trojan or a worm, or someone used a fake mailer. I'm going to need to do an analysis."

"That's why you wanted to meet," Tom said. "To check out my computer."

"Or to arrest you if you tried to get away," Firoz grinned.

"How long is this going to take?" Tom asked. He wanted to get a closer look at the screen captures from the victim's computer that Firoz had emailed him.

"An hour. Maybe more. Depends if you have an infection, and how bad it is." Firoz dug a pen drive out of his pocket and plugged it into one of Tom's USB ports. "I brought some basic tools with me. If we're lucky, and this guy hacked your computer, maybe I can find him."

"Can you print up those screen shots for me?"

"Print?" Firoz said the word like it was an expletive. "Why you want to kill trees, man? Don't you like trees?"

"I wanted to—"

"Don't you have email on your cell phone? Wait, you don't still have a flip phone, do you? Tell me you've got one of those old Motorola RAZRs with the clamshell case." Firoz began to giggle.

"I have an iPhone," Tom said. "The latest version. 4."

"A 4s?"

"Uh, no. Just 4, no s. So I'm just a model behind."

"The latest version is 6s. You're five models behind."

Tom stood up. "I'll be at my partner's desk if you need me."

Tom took his handwritten notes and the case files, went to Roy's workstation, and sat down. Then he stared at his partner's screen saver, Chun Li from the Street Fighter videogames. Chun Li offered no inspiration on what to do next. But detective work wasn't about inspiration. It was about pounding pavement and doing research. Since Roy was out pounding pavement, looking for video footage of the perp, Tom fired up Google and looked up *Tilphousia*, the screen name of the guy who'd harassed, and possibly killed, Kendal Hefferton.

Tilphousia, Megaera, and Alecto are three infernal goddesses in Greek mythology, known as Erinyes or Furies.

Tom could still see the word FURIE written on the wall of the last crime scene. He read on.

They had the wings of crows, and bloodshot eyes, and wore crowns of live spiders, and they punished the wicked for their crimes with pain and torture.

Tom clicked on a hyper-realistic drawing of a scowling, witch-like woman with spiders in her hair, flaying the skin off a screaming man's back with a studded whip.

He searched for more information, and learned all about the furies' history and depiction in art and literature. They were frightening, sadistic creatures, whose sole purpose was to inflict suffering. Tom read a scholarly paper about the absorption of Greek gods into early Christianity, and how the furies were refitted as demons, dragging sinners into hell for atonement.

Tom had no doubt this was his killer. A psycho who thought he was an avenging deity, taking out his warped agenda on webcam models. Just like his mythical counterpart, he first stalked and hounded his victims, tormenting them before swooping in to torture and kill.

Tom went back to the first report, the murder of Kendal Zhanping over five weeks ago. He and Roy had done extensive interviews with the webcam agency she'd worked for, along with a competitor. Their security was top notch. Models could live anywhere in the world, and they had full control over their client list. For example, a webcam performer who lived in Chicago could prohibit anyone from Chicago, or Illinois, or the Midwest, from accessing her page. Their own locations were hidden from clients, and the agencies gave the models tips on how to make their performance areas untraceable. Unlike sex workers, or exotic dancers, or even adult actors who go to conventions and greet fans, webcam models were particularly hard to find. And it made sense. You didn't want stalkers finding you. But you also didn't want your postman recognizing you from your Hitachi vibrator show.

Webcam models didn't use their real name. The websites all used secure, encrypted connections. The models could block individual users, or entire regions. Yet The Snipper found two victims, and they were both named Kendal. Not their cam names. Their *real* names.

If it had been the same website, Tom would have suspected someone on the inside. But the two agencies weren't related in any way.

"Hey, Firoz," Tom called over the desk.

"What?"

"How hard is it to hack an encrypted website?"

"Depends. Different sites have different levels of security. What kind of site?"

"A porn site. Webcam models."

"You're too cheap to pay?"

"I want to know how The Snipper is finding out who these models are, and where they live."

Firoz pushed away from Tom's computer and laced his fingers behind his head. "Lots of ways. There are tools and programs. He could hack the source code to find passwords. If the site has HTTPS he could use a brute-force attack."

"Sounds violent."

"It means you use a program to keep trying random passwords until one works. This can technically be used on any system. Depending on password strength it can take minutes, or millennia. For example, it took me thirty seconds to crack your Facebook password. For the record, your last name plus the year you were born is used by millions of people. So are ascending numbers, like 1-2-3-4, or the word *password*. I hope your bank password isn't so easy. Some morons use their social security number. Anyone who steals your wallet has your Social. People are idiots."

Tom made a mental note to change his bank password. "So if you were looking for webcam models named Kendal, how would you do it?"

"I'd find the top webcam model sites, and I'd be searching for administrator passwords. That would give me webmaster access, so I could search employee records."

"What if I needed you to start looking?"

"Then you'd need a warrant. And you aren't going to get one. NSA aside, you can't just hack the whole country hoping to find evidence of a crime. That's not how the law, or the Constitution, works."

Tom knew that. But he wanted to plant a seed in Firoz's head, in case the man wanted to do a little hacking outside normal work hours. "That might be the only way we catch him. To find out who his next target is. It will be a webcam model in Illinois named Kendal. How many can there be?"

CHAPTER 16

Kendal opened her eyes, unsure of where she was. Linda stared down at her.

"Hey, slut. You scared the heck out of us."

Kendal realized she was lying on the couch, in the living room. "What happened?"

"We heard something pound on the front door. It was your head. You were passed out on the porch."

She reached for the sore spot on her scalp, found a lump. "How long ago?"

"Just happened. We were about to call 911."

Kendal saw Hildy in the kitchen, the land line receiver in her hand.

"No!" Kendal said, louder than she'd wanted to. "I'm okay. I don't need a doctor."

Kendal knew where that path would lead. If she told anyone at the ER about the things she'd been hearing and seeing, they'd admit her for observation. That meant missing several days of school. Or weeks, if they decided her mental health issues were severe enough. Kendal could deal with it on her own.

"I'm fine." She nodded at Hildy. "Really. I just tripped."

Hildy said, "Whatevs," and hung up.

The memory returned to Kendal. The dark van. The text. She patted her pockets. "Where's my phone?"

Linda winced, then held up Kendal's Samsung Galaxy, the screen cracked in a spiderweb pattern. Kendal reached for it. The cell didn't even turn on.

"Shit," Kendal said.

"I've got like six old cell phones. You can have one of mine. Just stick your SIM card in, it'll work fine. But you should play this up." Linda leaned forward and whispered, "Do a chat, show everyone. They'll feel sorry for you and tip you crazy cash."

Kendal didn't want to do a chat. She wanted to get away from all the cameras. She could feel them all, like weights pressing down on her. Drills, boring into her bones. But the idea of leaving the house frightened her. Maybe the van was just a hallucination, or maybe it wasn't. Kendal wasn't ready to prove it one way or the other. She just needed some alone time, to think. Someplace dark and quiet.

The basement?

The sorority house had an unfinished basement, cement floors and walls, exposed beams and columns. It was dusty, and probably full of spiders.

No, thanks.

The bedroom, then. Cameras off, even though Kendal needed the money now more than ever.

Kendal said, "Good idea," to Linda, then stood up. There was a pinch of dizziness that quickly passed, and then she was counting the steps to her bedroom. She touched the knob three times, went inside, and locked the door behind her.

After making sure all the cameras were off, Kendal logged onto her laptop computer. She stared at the built-in webcam at the top of the screen, frowned, and stuck a Post-It note over it. Then she went on Google and searched for "schizophrenic hallucinations." She found the usual sites; Wikipedia, the National Institutes of Health, WebMD, but it was all the same stuff she'd known for years. Take your meds. Get counseling. Keep a journal. Confront the voices in your head.

But what if it wasn't voices? What if it was a van? Or a text message?

The chat balloon appeared. A subscriber wanted to reach Kendal. She clicked on IGNORE.

The balloon appeared again.

I know you're seeing things.

Kendal froze.

I can help you.

Kendal wasn't sure what to do. If this was a hallucination, the doctors recommended confronting it, ordering it to go away.

But if it was some pervert, stalking her, Kendal needed proof.

How? Take a picture of the screen? Her phone had just broken.

Wasn't there a way to do some sort of screen capture?

Kendal Googled it.

You can't ignore me, Kendal. I'm your destiny.

Who r u? Kendal typed.

Some call me Megaera.

What do you want?

What all people want. I want the righteous to prosper. And the wicked punished.

Kendal quickly read how to print a picture of your computer screen. All she had to do was press one key, PRTSCN. But where was that key?

Whores need punishment. I can give you Penance for your sins.

How do I know you're real? Kendal typed.

You'll know I'm real when I stick the knife in.

Kendal spotted the PRTSCN button, above the INSERT key. She pressed it.

Nothing happened.

She went back to the Google page, and realized she needed Photoshop or something like it; some art or picture program to paste the screen capture she took. She clicked on the Start icon and began to search Windows for art apps.

What are you doing?

She clicked on the Accessories folder. There! A program called *Paint.*

Stop it, Kendal. I'm warning you.

Kendal opened Paint, clicked on Paste. A screen shot of the chat filled the page, and offered her a choice of format options to save it as. Kendal chose jpg and—

Her computer switched off, leaving Kendal to stare at a blank screen.

CHAPTER 17

Joan stared at the blank screen, then switched on Tom's laptop. As it whirred to life she sipped the swill that passed for coffee in his house. His Mr. Coffee was ancient, with more scales than a komodo dragon. It wasn't a water issue, because she used bottled. It wasn't a coffee issue, because she bought the coffee. It was strictly a machine problem. Every time Joan visited, she fought the impulse to buy a new one. But this was Tom's place, and men didn't like their cave messed with. Usually, she could subsist on Starbucks, but Joan was hungry, and if she went to the coffee shop she wouldn't be able to resist getting a scone, and that would spoil her appetite and ruin her upcoming dinner with Tom, which she hoped would still happen despite all signs pointing to him cancelling. So it was drink sludge, or go without caffeine, and Joan needed caffeine like scuba divers needed oxygen.

Tom had given her permission to use his computer, but it still sort of felt like she was spying on him. They'd been dating, exclusively, for years. Because it was long-distance, there was still an intimacy gap that would have ended had they been living together. So Joan was in *his* small house, drinking *his* shitty coffee, sitting at *his* lumpy sofa, with *his* laptop, which was eight years out of date and had a WiFi connection slightly slower than the Pony Express.

On the plus side, the place smelled like Tom, which she loved. And she certainly loved him.

But she didn't love living apart from him, and didn't love Chicago, and didn't love his job, which was worse than a mistress because mistresses usually came second, and Tom put his work first.

Joan knew she also put work first, but she made ten times the amount of money he did, so she allowed herself the double standard.

After dealing with a few emails that would have been a pain responding to on her phone, Joan noticed a folder on Tom's desktop called SNIPPER.

Without thinking, she clicked on it and the pictures began to flash in a slideshow.

Big mistake.

Joan had produced several horror movies. She'd even done a sequel in a franchise about a serial killer who built his own unique weapons, which the liberal press gleefully dismissed as *torture porn*. And Joan, herself, had dealt with violence in the past, at the hands of some people who were the worst of the worst that history had to offer.

But she'd never seen anything, in movies or real life, that even came close to the atrocities in those pictures. They were beyond obscene. Those poor women had been butchered like... well... meat. Horrified, Joan couldn't look away, even as one photo after another was branded onto her brain. By the time she'd managed to close the folder, Joan had seen things she'd never be able to unsee, enough for a lifetime's worth of nightmares.

How could Tom stomach that?

Why did he continue to expose himself to such evil?

Joan didn't ever think about marriage, and especially not children. But if Tom was the guy she was going to spend the rest of her life with, how could she allow that kind of darkness in her family? Joan had a hard enough time separating work life with private life, and a bad day for her was a superstar throwing a hissy fit on set. Tom was dealing with some seriously dark shit. She'd seen him moody. How long before the moodiness became the norm? At a Christmas party, Joan had met Tom's former boss, a woman named Jack Daniels. Joan's impression was that Jack had burned herself out. Jack was a tough broad, but the job still beat her down.

Was that the road Tom was headed down? Where catching psychos outweighed being happy? Where dealing with human misery put a permanent stain on your soul?

That's when a spider chose to crawl up over her hand

It was less than a centimeter long, brown, and its hairy legs tickled as it strolled across her thumb.

Joan yelped, then did the *I'm a girl who hates icky things* dance, flapping her hands, then her arms, then her hair, graduating into a full body shudder.

She immediately hated herself for her wimpy reaction. Joan had faced some scary things in her life. Scary in a life-threatening kind of way. To overreact to a bug made her feel weak and embarrassed.

Still, she could never get over being bitten by a spider when she was in third grade, and a kid at school telling her it had laid eggs under her skin and baby spiders were going to burst out. As the bite swelled up, Joan became hysterical and her mother had to pick her up.

Joan once had a chance to produce a horror movie about killer spiders, and turned it down without any serious consideration. The picture had gone on to become a minor hit. She never saw it, and had thrown away the screener DVD.

She checked her hand; the spider was gone, of course, because she'd flung it across the room. Then she did a quick inspection of her body, and the surrounding area. If Tom had a spider infestation, she would refuse to stay there for another night. This was Illinois, home to the infamous brown recluse. The bite of the brown recluse was so venomous, it caused more annual fatalities than the black widow. And almost as bad as death was permanent disfigurement. Unlike her third grade tormentor's fairy tale, brown recluse bites were real and serious. She'd researched Midwestern spiders—and snakes—before her first extended stay with Tom. Joan had seen pictures on the Internet of swollen-to-bursting spider bite wounds with blackish necrotic tissue that had to be surgically removed.

Could that have been a brown recluse? Joan hadn't looked long enough to notice any distinctive violin shape on its back. There was also another biter known as, believe it or not, the *aggressive house spider*. Just thinking the name gave her the willies. If Tom had—

Her cell rang, startling Joan so badly she yelped again. She took a calming breath before she looked who it was.

Tom.

And Joan could guess why he was calling.

Irritation chased away the fear, and she picked up.

"Hey, babe. Something big just came up. I'm going to be a little late."

"Of course you are," she said. "See you whenever you get home."

"I can still make a late dinner."

"I already ate," Joan lied.

"You did?"

"Did you know you have spiders in your house? One almost bit me."

"I... uh... I didn't know that. Should I call someone? An exterminator?"

"You know I don't like spiders, Tom."

"Are you okay?"

"I'm fine. Go catch your bad guy."

Joan hung up, then went to find her jacket. She'd go grab a Starbucks, and a scone. Maybe several scones.

Erinyes watches her through the laptop webcam.

CHAPTER 18

The sting of Joan's words still fresh, Tom climbed into his car to meet with his partner. Roy had called five minutes earlier, to update Tom on his progress sweeping the neighborhood, looking for surveillance footage. He hadn't found any evidence of the mystery man Tanya had mentioned. But he had caught a convenience store video of Tanya walking past the storefront, clutching a large bundle wrapped in plastic.

"Looked like a shower curtain," Roy had told him.

Tom had noticed the shower curtain had been missing from Kendal Hefferton's apartment. A plastic shower curtain was an easy way to wrap up bloody evidence from a crime scene and take it with you without dripping everywhere.

Then Roy had called a contact at ABC News, which ran dozens of traffic and weather cameras around the city, and had picked up Tanya two blocks away, a few minutes later.

No plastic bundle. She'd dumped it.

So Roy and Tom were on Dumpster duty. According to a quick check of Google Maps, there were six possible routes between her two video appearances, and six alleys where she could have dumped the bag.

On the way to the scene, Tom called the number Tanya Bestrafen had given them.

It was disconnected.

Tom radioed Dispatch to locate Tanya's apartment and DMV info. Tanya's address, and name, were fakes.

They'd been played.

While at a stoplight, Tom Googled *Bestrafen.*

It meant *punishment* in German.

Tom clenched his teeth so hard his jaw ached. The person calling herself Tanya Bestrafen might have been The Snipper, and they let her just waltz right out of the station without even checking her bona fides.

He found Roy in an alley on Halsted, staring at a Dumpster, looking as miserable as Tom felt. Tom parked at the mouth.

"Stinks," Roy said.

"Sure does. We screwed up."

"We do stink as cops. But I'm talking about that garbage bin. Smells like someone puked on a dead chimpanzee. I say we call up some uniforms, let them paw through it. Builds character."

The smell hit Tom, making his nose hairs curl and his eyes water. He swallowed back the gorge in his throat. "Not a bad idea."

At least, it wasn't a bad idea until the garbage truck began to drive up the alley.

"Shit, Roy, garbage pickup is today."

"So?" Tom watched his partner's face as he put it together. "Aw, shit. They could take the evidence."

"If they haven't already."

If Tanya was the killer, lying to the police wasn't enough to pin the murders on her. They needed physical evidence. They needed whatever was wrapped in the shower curtain.

Tom held up his badge and approached the truck. The garbage man looked like the kind of guy who grew up to be a garbage man, and the expression he wore was both world-weary and suspicious.

"What?"

Chicagoans weren't much for small talk.

"We're looking for evidence that a murderer threw away. It might have been on your route."

"So?"

"So how big is your route?"

"So big that I'm running late, and the boss don't pay no overtime."

Tom could have turned prick, making threats, being the cop that made people hate cops. Instead he went another route.

"No shit. Us civil servants don't get any respect. My boss is an asshole, too. And he's got me hunting through alleys when my girlfriend is in out of town."

"Your point?"

"Ten minutes, tops. My partner checks out the back of your truck, I check out the Dumpster, you guys go have some coffee on me."

Tom fished out ten bucks.

"This is Chicago, officer. Where are we gonna get two coffees for ten bucks?"

Tom had four more bucks in his pocket. "That's all I got."

"I don't got to do this, you know. You ain't got no warrant or court order."

"I know. I appreciate it."

"Make it quick," the man said, hitting the hydraulic switches to lift the shovel and open the hopper.

"Got extra gloves?" Tom asked.

"Not for no fourteen bucks." Then he climbed out of the cab and headed toward his partner. The two of them had a loud chuckle, then headed up the street. They bypassed the Starbucks and went into a bar.

"They left," Roy said.

"You should be a detective."

"Didn't you pay them to sort through the trash?"

"I paid them to go have coffee."

Roy made a Mr. Yuck face. "So we gotta do it?"

"Chain of evidence. If they touch Tanya's bundle, that's one more way for the defense attorney to discredit it."

"Did they have extra gloves?"

"I've got latex gloves in the car."

"Latex gloves won't protect me from junkie hepatitis needles."

"So don't stab yourself with junkie hepatitis needles."

Tom climbed up the side of the truck and peeked into the hopper, quickly figuring out the task ahead was impossible. The garbage was several meters deep, and already compacted. To properly sort through it, Tom would have to get permission to seize the truck, dump it someplace, and comb through it with a team of at least ten cops. And that was just for this load. There had to be dozens more garbage cans and Dumpsters in the area. They'd all have to be searched.

This meant a call to the Captain, to authorize funds, space, and manpower. It was doable; The Snipper was high-profile, and the mayor would spare no expense to catch him. But this was an all-night affair, and Joan would resent him for it.

But this was supposed to be Tom's vacation. Maybe he could appeal to Roy's good side and get his partner to take over without him. It was worth a—

"Oh hell no!"

Tom shot a look at Roy, who was backing away from the Dumpster, holding his wrist as blood trickled down from his sliced hand.

"This is NOT happening."

"Was it a needle?" Tom asked.

"It was a goddamn rat. Tommy, a goddamn rat just bit my finger."

Tom rubbed his jaw. It was going to be a long goddamn night.

CHAPTER 19

"Call the police," Linda said, sitting on Kendal's bed.

"And what do I say? I don't have any evidence."

Kendal had more or less told Linda about all the weird things that had been happening, leaving out the growing possibility that it was all in Kendal's head. If this was actually a psychotic break, Kendal would deal with it on her own. She'd die before she went back to a mental institution.

Linda chewed on her lower lip, pouting for cameras that Kendal had turned off. She was a natural ham, and had trouble dialing it down. "Then we need to get some evidence. So it's been calls, texts, and chat?"

Kendal nodded. "And the van that's been following me."

"Okay. Let's look for the van."

Linda took Kendal's hand, led her out of the bedroom and to the front door. Kendal was aware of the cameras on her, watching. Was the stalker watching her now? Or was he still outside, in the van? Or was she just going insane?

If I really am going nuts, do I want to know?

Kendal hesitated, holding back.

"You scared it's there?" Linda asked.

Kendal was actually more frightened that it wouldn't be there, but she kept that to herself. "Can you check for me? Please?"

"You're really that freaked out?"

Kendal nodded. Linda shrugged, strode over to the door, and stuck her head out. She remained that way for ten seconds.

"Hey, girl," Kendal said, avoiding Linda's name because of the cameras.

Linda didn't reply. She didn't move at all. Kendal's mind cycled through ridiculous horror movie scenarios. Was Linda so terrified she couldn't move? Was someone holding a knife to her throat? Would she fall backwards, like an axed tree, with an arrow sticking out of her forehead?

"Hey!"

Linda finally poked her head back inside, her expression serious.

"Is it there?" Kendal asked.

"Is it a black van?"

"Yeah."

"And is the driver wearing a clown mask?"

Kendal blinked. "What?"

"And holding a giant ax?"

Kendal felt her whole body tense up and her bladder shrink two sizes. "What are you saying?"

Linda flung open the door, revealing an empty street. "There's no one out here, girl. If there was a van, it's gone."

"But you said—"

"I was putting you on. Don't they have jokes on your planet?"

"That wasn't funny."

Linda did a dramatic eye roll. "Everything is funny. If you can't laugh at life, it's not worth living." She shut the door. "So what next? You said this pervert is threatening you in chat? Have you reported him to the mods?"

"Huh?"

"The moderators. Have you reported him? They keep records of chats, and record IPs, to keep out the freaks. We went over all of this when you joined the house, skank."

"I... uh..."

Linda took Kendal by the hand. "Come on."

They marched back to Kendal's room, and she was too occupied counting her steps that she couldn't fully process what Linda had said. They kept records of chats? If so, this could be the evidence

Kendal needed. Either that someone was stalking her, or that she was riding the relapse train to Crazytown.

Linda logged onto Kendal's computer—how did she know the password?—and opened the chat app.

"How did—?"

"I used the Administrator ID. It's a backdoor into the program."

"So how did—?"

"Duh, I'm into computers. You know that's my major. Did my first DDoS when I was sixteen. Crashed a big oil network. Bombarded them with pictures of sea otters in a spill. Okay, here's the record of your last two hours of chat. Who's the stalker?"

"He used the screen name Megalon, or something like that. And before that, Alex2, or Alec2."

Linda scrolled through the past messages. The threats Kendal remembered weren't there.

"I don't see anything, babe. You sure you were in your account? Did you log in as another sister?"

"No. It was my account."

Oh, jesus, I'm crazy. Am I going to have to go back to the hospital? Can they force me to? I'm not a minor anymore. Wouldn't I have to check into a nuthouse voluntarily? What if I don't? Maybe I can get better without going back to the institution. Without medication. But how can I—

"Hold on, let me run a scan. I've got a packet sniffer on the network. Maybe someone has been poking around. Any third rate hacker with a bit of computing power can go blunt force searching for passwords. And there are programs that aren't random character generators. They start with the obvious first, names and common numerical sequences. You'd be surprised how many people use dates as a password. A fast system can check every date in human history in a microsecond. If you used your anniversary, you're fu—hey, what's this? Looks like we have a visitor. Let's search his IP."

Kendal watched, not knowing what Linda was doing but riveted just the same.

"Located in Guam. My ass. He's using TOR."

"Huh?"

"An onion router. It relays a user's location, bouncing it around the world, so they can be anonymous while online."

"Is this my stalker?"

"I have no idea. Could be. Could be our webcam host, who just likes anonymity. Could be some teenager who doesn't want to pay the monthly subscription fee. Or just someone curious."

"Can you block him?"

"I don't know how he's getting inside the network. And he might be legit. Even if I could block this IP, he could just log in using a different one. Our site has decent encryption, but there is no such thing as fully secure. Anything that links to the Internet can be compromised. Modern computer security isn't about keeping people out. It's about detecting them quickly once they get in."

"So what should I do if he comes back?"

"Alert the mods. And take a screen capture."

"It's creepy."

Linda logged off and pushed away from the keyboard. "Welcome to the twenty-first century. No privacy. No secrets. We all live in a fishbowl, and everyone can watch. Be happy; at least you're getting paid for it. All those unaware suckers on their webcams, their phones, their tablets are being spied on and don't make a dime, or have a clue."

CHAPTER 20

As the night progresses, Erinyes listens.

The app on Detective Tom Mankowski's cell phone is linked to his camera and microphone, but the phone is in the cop's pocket so there is nothing to see but black. Still, Erinyes can hear.

Street sounds.

A truck.

People talking.

Tom's partner, Roy Lewis, saying something about a shovel.

They're digging through a Dumpster. Looking for the shower curtain.

Good luck. It's the wrong Dumpster.

Idiots.

Still, they caught on pretty fast. Faster than anticipated. Erinyes had planned for the possibility that this might happen, but was impressed just the same.

Sniff away, doggies. Follow the trail, see where it leads.

Erinyes leaves the computer, heading for her bedroom. Walking down the hallway, she stops and looks in the full-length mirror. Erinyes studies herself, running a finger over her slender jaw, trailing it down her neck.

Identity. Some are born with it. Some search for it.

For some, it changes. Plastic. Fluid. Heads or tails, depending on the flip.

"I see you," she tells the monster in the mirror.

Erinyes has spent a long time dealing with nightmares. But the secret to beating them was something the shrinks never told you.

Pain can be passed along. The quickest cure for suffering is to make someone else suffer.

Then she goes to her bedroom closet to check her bug-out bag.

CHAPTER 21

Though it was going to seriously cut into her weekly check, Kendal kept her bedroom cameras off. Though some clients paid to watch sorority girls sleep, and it was easy money, Kendal didn't like it. She could handle being watched during waking moments, when she was alert. Being spied on while unconscious was a little too creepy. She valued her sleep too much.

Kendal crawled into bed, reached for her Kindle, touched it three times, then turned it on.

She was on location 2375 of a scary book called *Hellmonger*. Kendal had no idea why she read scary books. Life was scary enough. Her past was the stuff of nightmares. Why read about make-believe horrors, when there were so many real horrors in the world?

And yet, she lapped this stuff up. Maybe it was akin to self-medicating. A form of stress relief. Or maybe she was just warped. But as long as it was make-believe, Kendal liked being scared.

Kendal found the bookmark where she'd left off, and began to read.

> *The bedroom clock was closing in on 3 A.M. The witching hour. When witches, demons, and ghosts were at their most powerful.*
>
> *Jayden stared at his closet.*
>
> *There was a monster inside.*
>
> *He was sure of it.*

Even though he was twelve years old, and shouldn't believe in monsters anymore. Things can exist even if you don't believe them.

But Jayden did *believe. He and Charlie shouldn't have been playing with that tarot deck. That old gypsy had warned them not to fool around with it. They'd awoken something.*

Something evil.

Something that was now in Jayden's closet.

Jayden gripped his cell phone, along with the Ten of Swords card. He slowly pushed back his blanket and swung a bare foot onto the cold, wood floor. The card brought the monster. The card should be able to vanquish the monster. As the floor took his weight, the board creaked.

Did the monster hear it?

Jayden held his breath. He stared at the closet door. He imagined the monster on the other side, also staring at the door. Waiting to pounce.

I AM WATCHING YOU

Kendal startled. That pop-up caught her. For a moment, she thought the message was for her. But it must have been part of the ebook she was reading. Jayden had his cell phone in the story. The monster in the closet must have sent him a text.

She read on.

Jayden felt his bladder clench. He'd never been so scared. His hands trembled, and he forgot how to swallow, his throat feeling like a giant knot.

He took another step toward the closet, and the floor creaked.

Step, creak.

Step, creak.

Step, creak.

Creak.

There was a creak, but Jayden hadn't made another step.

The monster had made the sound.

He tore his eyes away from the closet, wondering if he should run. Get out of his room, go tell his parents. They'd think he was silly. A baby. But at least he'd be safe.

You cannot get away

Again, Kendal flinched. That really looked like a pop-up screen. But it didn't look like it was part of an ebook.

It looked like someone had sent her a text message.

Did Kindles even have text messaging?

Freaking out a little, she exited the book, and went to Google, typing in "Can Kindles be hacked?" and began to scroll through the results.

Before she found the answer, she had an even bigger question. Did Kindles have cameras? Could someone be watching her through the camera? Watching her as she read?

Kendal knew a guy who was so paranoid, he put black tape over the cameras on his cell phone. But maybe that guy was onto something.

What if someone had hacked my Kindle and was watching me right now?

Kendal giggled nervously. That was ridiculous. This wasn't really happening. This was just the ebook she was reading. The author was being meta, trying to make her believe she was the one being watched.

Jayden was the one getting the pop-up texts. He had to be the one.

Kendal kept reading, flipping ahead for the scene where Jayden answered the message.

> *Jayden reached for the closet doorknob, and stopped before touching it. He needed to tell Charlie first. If anything happened, Charlie had to know it was because of their demon stupid incantation.*
>
> *Jayden brought up his cell phone, preparing to dial. But his battery was dead. He wondered if he should plug it in, try to*

I see you

Kendal's heart threatened to jump out of her mouth. She stared at the message, still unable to tell if it was part of Jayden's story, or happening to her in real life. Jayden's phone was off, but the demon he'd summoned could probably still send him messages supernaturally. That was probably the—

You are going to die

KENDAL!!!

The Kindle flashed, and a picture of Kendal's frightened face appeared on the screen. She threw it across the room, hugged her knees to her chest, and began to sob.

Why is this happening to me?

What did I do?

Am I a bad person? Did I do something to deserve this?

Haven't I suffered enough?

Through the panic, a tiny idea fought for attention.

Proof. This is proof. I can take this to the police.

She scrambled out of bed, scurrying to the Kindle, turning it over and seeing the large crack running down the glass. The screen was black. Repeat pressing of the power button didn't do anything.

Kendal was sure of what she'd seen. Her own face, eyes wide with terror. That hadn't been a hallucination.

But had her stalker done it? Or had Kendal taken a selfie and freaked herself out?

She turned on all the lights and returned to bed, tears stinging her cheeks.

The cameras in her room were off, but she could still feel them watching.

Kendal went to the bedroom closet, reaching inside of her backpack, taking out the duct tape. One by one, she taped off every camera in her room. Then she went behind her desk and unplugged her computer.

Maybe they'd kick her out of the house. And without money, she'd surely be kicked out of school.

But at that moment, Kendal didn't care. She hadn't been this scared in years. Since her father…

Stop it. I don't want to think about that.

I don't want to think about anything.

I just want to sleep.

But Kendal was too afraid to close her eyes.

CHAPTER 22

"You smell like garbage," Joan told Tom when he walked into the house at 2 A.M. She was sitting on the sofa, laptop on, her face and tone so completely devoid of expression that Tom knew she must be fuming.

"Sorry. I'll shower."

He trudged into the bathroom, turned on the water, and began to strip. Two hours into Dumpster diving and Tom had blessedly lost his olfactory sense. But he knew his clothes probably needed to be burned, and he'd no doubt stunk up his car, and his house. He hopped into the shower while it was still lukewarm, reaching for the soap dish, coming away with a sliver of soap that was as thin as a library card, working hard to get a lather and failing, stepping out of the shower and checking under the sink for a fresh bar, remembering that he was out of soap and had been meaning to pick some up before Joan came over, got back into the shower and dumped shampoo over his body, and tried to scrub away the last five hours.

He wasn't able to.

The search for the shower curtain had been a bust. He and Roy had gone through the entire Dumpster, and the garbage truck, and then had called in back-up to check the surrounding Dumpsters in the area. When Tom left, there were still men and women waist-deep in refuse, and Roy was trying to locate the truck that had already picked up the remainder of the trash.

Some vacation.

After wrapping himself in the robe Joan bought him the time they'd stayed at the Hilton in Beverly Hills, Tom brushed his teeth, used some mouthwash, and slapped on some of the aftershave Joan bought him, even though he didn't like aftershave. He knew she was pissed. Hell, he was pissed at himself. The time they spent together was good. Real good. But Tom knew the time apart was strangling the relationship. Skype and texts and phone sex couldn't ever compare to being in the same place at the same time. Love wasn't meant to be experienced long-distance. So the rule was, whenever they were together, they made up for lost time.

But Tom had broken that rule. He'd hurt Joan. He knew it. And this was the woman he wanted to marry.

He had a half-assed plan to make up for it, at least in the short term. Joan loved foot rubs. Maybe that would warrant a little forgiveness.

Tom checked the living room, didn't see her there, and went into the bedroom.

Joan was wrapped in the comforter, snoring softly.

He sat at the foot of the bed, thinking. It wasn't polite to wake her up. But who didn't like being woken up to having their feet rubbed?

He snaked a hand under the blanket, found her leg, and began to gently knead it. Joan's breathing changed.

"I'm sorry," he said.

"Did you catch him?"

"No."

"Was it worth going in?"

Tom recognized the question was a trap. If he answered yes, the job was more important to him than Joan. If the answer was no, then he had no reason to go in.

"I missed you," he said. "I don't like myself very much right now."

"At least you smell better." She extended her leg and made an *mmm-mmmm* sound.

"I want to make it up to you," Tom said. "You know how you've been wanting to go to *Bonne Nourriture*? I got reservations for tomorrow night."

"You hate French food."

"But I love you. And you love French food. You put up with my work, I can put up with some foie gras."

"I don't like foie gras. They force feed the duck to make the liver fatty. It's cruel."

"So… you don't want to go?" Tom tried to sound nonchalant. He'd asked a favor of a pretty unpleasant guy to get reservations, and now owed the man.

"Of course I want to go. They were rated the best Coq au vin in the country."

"Do I want to ask what that is?"

Joan sat up, placing her hands on Tom's shoulders. "It means *cock with wine*."

"Well," Tom said, "we don't have to wait until tomorrow for that. I have a pinot grigio in the fridge."

Joan's fingers laced through his hair. "Well, that's half the recipe. What about the other half?"

Tom's cell phone buzzed in his robe pocket.

Joan took her hands away from him. "Are you going to answer that?"

"No. I'm here with you."

"What if it's the case?"

"I'm on vacation. Roy will figure it out."

"What if it's Roy, in some kind of trouble?"

Tom pressed his lips together. His phone buzzed again.

"Tom, why is your phone even on if you have no intention of answering it?"

"I thought I'd turned it off."

"You thought you turned it off, and still put it in your robe?"

"Just tell me what you want me to do, Joan."

"I want you to be the kind of man who turns off his phone before he climbs into bed with me."

Tom took the phone out of his pocket and pressed the button. "Done. It's off."

"Who was it?"

"I didn't look."

"Of course you looked."

Tom couldn't ever win an argument with Joan. She was always half a step ahead of him. Smart lady, one of the many things he loved about her.

"It was Roy."

"Does he normally call at 2 A.M.?"

"No."

"So this could be an emergency?"

"Yeah."

"So you want to make love to me while thinking about Roy?"

"Yeah. No! Joan, look, I'm trying here. I've had a real shitty day."

"My day was shitty, too. I spent it waiting for my boyfriend to remember that I flew in from LA to visit him."

Tom reached for her face to stroke her cheek, and she flinched away.

"Joan, how about we just ignore the phone and pick up where we left off?"

"Can we do that, Tom? Is that even possible? We're both going to be thinking about the call. You're going to be wondering what the emergency was, I'm going to be thinking that another poor girl is going to die because I want to be selfish and keep my man for myself. And the fact that you didn't shut off your phone—whether it was intentional or not—shows where your priorities really are."

The ring startled them both. Tom's landline, on the nightstand next to the bed.

"Are you going to get that?" Joan asked.

"I'd rather not."

Joan picked it up, not breaking eye contact with Tom. "Hello?"

Tom heard Roy mumble something apologetic.

"It's okay, Roy, I was already up. He's right here."

She held the phone out to Tom. He didn't move. When her eyes narrowed to slits he took it.

"Yeah, Roy."

"We found the shower curtain, Tom. Had a knife in it, blood still on it. Enough to link DNA."

"That's great, Roy. But this could have waited until morning."

"Crime Scene Team lifted latents. Ran them at the scene. Tom, we got a match."

Tom's heart rate kicked up, but he kept his face and voice neutral. "Okay."

"Tom, did you hear me? We got him. Perp is on file. Registered sex offender named Hector Valentine. Thirty-eight years old, lives in Logan Square off of Fullerton. I called Judge Harbough, warrant is meeting us at the perp's house."

"It's a man? What about Tanya? Isn't she the suspect?"

"Could be his girlfriend. Or daughter. She's an accomplice, we know that much. Hell, maybe he dressed up as her to throw us off."

Tom held eye contact with Joan. "Well, congrats, Roy. Call me tomorrow, let me know how it went."

"Tom, you drunk? We need to roll on this, partner."

"I'm on vacation. You can handle this without me."

"Is it Joanie? She angry with you? Tom, we're going to catch a serial killer. This is a big deal. Tell her to chill."

"I'll tell her," Tom said, intending to never tell her. "But I'm not going, Roy."

"You need to go," Roy said.

"You need to go," Joan said.

"See, Tom? She told you to go."

Tom frowned. "Apparently you both can hear each other."

"Your phone is ridiculously loud," Joan said.

"She's right, Tom. It's real loud. Sorry to take your man away, Joanie, but this is big. He should be there."

"He's all yours, Roy. We weren't doing anything anyway." Joan narrowed her eyes. "I was just about to go to sleep."

Ouch.

Tom listened as Roy gave him the address. Joan laid down and turned her back to him.

"We're going in with two teams, Tom, Crime Scene and Special Response. Meet you there?"

Tom hesitated.

"Tell him you'll meet him," Joan said to the wall.

Tom sighed. "See you in ten, Roy."

He hit the hang up button and stared at the woman he loved.

"Go on," she said. "Go arrest the bad guy."

"Joan... I'm..."

"This is who you are, Tom. I know that. I fell in love with that. Now go be you."

Tom considered trying to kiss her goodbye, realized he wouldn't take it well if she rejected him, and instead began to dress, trying to seem like he wasn't in a hurry even though he was.

Sixteen minutes and some bad traffic later he pulled up in front of the residence of Hector Valentine. The SRT—Chicago's version of SWAT—was already there in force, as were Roy and the techies. Tom was apparently the last to arrive.

He walked up to Roy, who was talking with a Special Response Sergeant with the nametag *Breach*, which was so appropriate for a cop who broke into homes that Tom wondered if it was a nickname. Breach wore standard gung-ho tactical gear; a vest, helmet with faceplate, combat boots, a utility belt with so many dangling things it would make Batman envious. Tom listened in as Breach laid out the entry plan.

"Got four guys in the alley out back, one on each window, and four doing the entry. We also have snipers on the roofs there, and there."

"Valentine inside?" Tom asked.

"Thermal reading on the upper floor. Hasn't moved in five minutes. Suspect appears to be asleep. We're going in three."

"Good luck, Sergeant."

Breach nodded, adjusted his helmet camera, then commandoed over to the rest of his team.

"Dispatch read me his rap sheet on the ride over," Tom said to Roy.

"Yeah, typical scumbag. Raped a sixteen year old girl. Served seven out of ten."

"He works as a fry cook at a burger joint."

"Your point?"

"Guy dropped out of high school, Roy. Does this sound like a cyberstalker with hacking skills?"

"A print is a print, Tom. And we got three of them, all different digits, on the curtain, and the butcher knife."

"I dunno. Something feels off."

"Your optimism is the reason I love you so much."

They watched the techie's video monitor from behind Roy's car as Sgt. Breach breached the front door. It was a clean entry, and within seconds they were upstairs and bearing down on a terrified, unarmed Valentine. Less than a minute later, they were dragging the cuffed perp out into the street.

"Think he'll talk?" Roy asked.

It didn't really matter. The chain of evidence had the man, cold. Tom guessed the CRT would find even more evidence in the house, something that would likely lead to Tanya. Angry as Joan might have been, Tom felt a surge of pride. This was why he stayed a cop. To take really bad people off the streets. It was important work, and he was good at it. Maybe it interfered with his personal life sometimes but—

"Ah, hell," Roy said.

"What?"

"Check out his hands, Tom."

Tom's eyes trailed down the perp's back, to his cuffed wrists and hands.

"Ah, hell," Tom repeated. "Those prints, were they lefty? Index, thumb, and middle finger?"

"Yeah. Shit."

Shit and then some. Hector Valentine only had two fingers on his left hand, and they weren't the ones Tom just mentioned. Tom knew a little something about fingerprint evidence, and he was pretty sure the owner of the fingerprints needed to be in possession of said fingers in order to convict. Unless they found Valentine's severed digits in a box in his house, this wasn't their perp.

Tom followed Roy over to the man. Up close, he did look like a picture of that Ukrainian actor Tanya had mentioned, Maddoks with the impossible to pronounce last name.

"When did you lose your fingers, Hector?"

Tom noted the stumps had healed, and healed well. This was an old injury.

"Back in June. What are you arresting me for? I didn't do nothing. I've been clean. I couldn't do anything, even if I wanted to."

Valentine stared at his feet. He seemed more defeated than indignant—not what Tom would expect from someone dragged out of his bed by the cops in the middle of the night. If he really was clean, he should be angry, not glum.

"How did it happen?"

"What, my fingers?"

Tom and Roy nodded.

"The darkness took them. To punish me."

"What does that mean, Hector?"

"I was asleep, in my room. The darkness came up to me while I was sleeping. It sliced my fingers off and vanished."

"Do you do drugs, Hector?"

He finally met Tom's eyes. "It wasn't drugs! Drugs don't chop your fingers off in the middle of the night!"

Roy, using his *I have infinite patience voice*, said, "Tell us exactly what happened."

"I want my lawyer."

Tom placed his hand on the perp's shoulder. "Hector, we found your fingerprints at a murder scene. But if you can tell us about your missing fingers, then it could prove you didn't commit the murder."

Tom watched Valentine's face spark with hope. "It was the darkness! I swear!"

"Okay, how did the darkness take your fingers?"

"It was late. I was in bed, watching TV. And the closet door opened."

"Someone was in the closet?"

"The darkness was in the closet. It came to me. I raised up my hands to keep it away, and the darkness cut them off."

The guy seemed sincere enough. "How?"

"First they were there, then they were gone."

"Where did they go?"

"I told you. The darkness took them. To punish me."

"How do you know it was to punish you?" Tom asked.

"Because the darkness told me so."

"What did it say, exactly?"

"It said, 'You're a bad man, and must be punished.'"

This wasn't getting anywhere productive, but Tom gave it one more try. "Hector, this darkness, can you describe it?"

"Black. The blackest thing I've ever seen. No shape. I couldn't see the edges. And it wasn't thick. It was like it was flat. Like a shadow."

"Anything else?"

"Yeah. The darkness had eyes." The hope on Valentine's face fractured, and fear shone through. "The darkness had brown eyes."

Five minutes later they were in Hector's bedroom, wearing the standard booties and gloves. Hector Valentine was a pig as far as his sexual deviancy went, but he was also a pig when it came to cleanliness. His house was a sty, and smelled just as bad as the Dumpster Tom had climbed out of earlier. Old food wrappers, dirty clothes, and body odor cut through the aftershave Tom wore and made him wince.

"Last forty-eight hours, I'm about ready to cut off my nose," Roy said.

"It'll spite your face."

"I'll deal with the spite."

"Look on the bright side. Guy obviously doesn't have a maid. So maybe we can find some trace of the darkness, even though it has been five months."

"You believe that bullshit he was spouting?"

Tom looked at his partner. "Do you?"

"He sounded sincere. For a rapist."

They walked around a discarded pizza box and Tom noticed the closet. Standard cheap hollow-core door, aluminum knob. He opened it slowly, as if some supernatural darkness was going to spring out and start lopping off digits.

"Is that a hole?" Roy asked, pointing.

There was a black spot on the inside of the door, at eye-level. Tom squinted at it.

"I don't know what that is."

He touched it with his finger. It wasn't a hole. It was solid. And though he could feel the door behind it, he couldn't see the door. It was as if his finger was touching something that was both solid, and a void. Some of the black rubbed off on his purple nitrile glove, which was one of the weirdest things Tom had ever experienced. Where the black was smudged on his finger, his finger seemed to disappear. Like it had been erased.

"Don't tell me someone invented vanishing cream for real," Roy said.

Tom peered closer. The black made his finger appear two dimensional. There was no depth to it. Blacker than black.

"The darkness," Tom said.

"You mean some dude was hiding in the closet, wearing that black stuff all over his body?"

Tom nodded. He noticed more of the black substance on the inside doorknob, and on the closet carpeting, Then he left the closet and surveyed the room. In the corner, on a desk, was a flatscreen monitor. Tom went to it, and noticed the webcam attached to the top. It was pointed at the closet.

The left and right hemispheres of Tom's brain ping-ponged some ideas around.

Tanya said she saw someone who looked like that actor, Maddoks.

Hector looked like Maddoks.

Tanya was seen walking down Kendal's street with a package.

That package was found in a Dumpster. It had fingerprints belonging to Hector.

Hector lost those fingers months ago. Someone in black make up took them.

Tanya must have taken them, and left those prints on the knife and shower curtain.

Tanya was trying to frame Hector.

Did Tanya know Hector?

Hector was a registered sex offender. Anyone could look up where sex offenders lived. There was a database online. If The Snipper—and Tom was working under the assumption that Tanya was The Snipper—could hack Tom's computer, then she could hack Hector's. The Snipper found webcam models online and watched them before killing them, and probably watched Hector as well. And, like the webcam models, there would be no way to connect Hector with The Snipper.

Dead end.

So why come to the police station and file a phony report? Why go through all the trouble of leaving false fingerprints? Why not stay out of the investigation completely?

Tom was missing something. He knew some serial killers basked in the attention of the authorities and the media, but The Snipper didn't seem like a glory hound. The Snipper had some kind of agenda.

Tom thought about the furies. Greek goddesses of vengeance. Punishing the wicked.

Hector was wicked. Why wasn't he murdered, like the webcam girls? How did he escape with his life, only missing a few fingers?

Tom remembered something Hector had said, on the street. He turned to Roy. "Got your radio?"

"Yup."

"See if they've carted off Hector yet. I have one more question for him. And get some ALS and luminol up here."

Roy spoke with Breach, and Hector was still in the police van, parked in front. Roy asked them to stay put for a moment, and they waited for a CRT member to come up for a spray and light.

"He said he was in bed?" Tom asked Roy. "When he lost his fingers?"

"Yeah. This whole area here," Roy told the techie.

The crime scene guy began to spritz luminol on Valentine's bed and the floor around it. Then he used an alternate light source to search for blood. If any was there, it would fluoresce.

There was no telltale glow. Tom and Roy exchanged a glance.

They went back downstairs. The night seemed to have gotten colder, nipping at Tom's cheeks and neck. He turned up the collar on his wool pea coat and shoved his hands into his pockets, and they walked to the police van.

Hector brightened at seeing Tom again. "You're letting me go?"

"You told us that you couldn't do anything, even if you wanted to. What did you mean by that?"

Hector went sheepish. "I mean I been staying out of trouble."

"Roy, what is this gentlemen's rap sheet like?"

"He's been a rapist since he turned eighteen. Probably earlier, but his juvee records are sealed."

"So why did you stop, Hector? Because you feared going back to jail? Because you lost a few fingers?"

Hector stayed silent and went back to his signature move; studying his shoes.

"When you lost those fingers, did you go to the hospital? You know, to get stitched up?"

More silence.

"There would be a record if you did. Happen to have a doctor bill lying around, Hector?"

"I want my lawyer," he mumbled.

"You're free to call your lawyer, Hector. But I'm trying to help you here. You told me you lost your fingers while you were in bed, but there was no blood in your room. Did your maid service come by afterward, mop it all up? Or are you leaving something out?"

Silence.

Tom pressed. "Did you cut your own fingers off, Hector? Cut them off to cover up a murder?"

Valentine moved so fast that Tom's hand automatically went for his gun. Hector Valentine stood up, his face twisted in rage, tears streaming down his cheeks.

"You think I did this to myself, you stupid pig?!" he yelled, hands cuffed behind him, thrusting his pelvis out like he was in a Nicki Minaj video.

Tom looked down, and saw that the place between a man's legs that normally sported a bulge had no bulge at all.

"Darkness came to my bed, knocked me out. I woke up I was missing three fingers, and my junk. You hear what I'm saying? Darkness took my dick and balls. Cut that shit off and sewed me up. All I got is a goddamn tube down there. Now why don't you get on your knees and suck it, you asshole."

Tom elected to pass on the offer. He and Roy got into Tom's car to get out of the cold. Tom noticed that he was subconsciously cradling his privates, as was Roy.

"I've seen some shit, but that's messed up," Roy finally said.

"Rapist gets castrated. There's a warped kind of justice there."

"Ain't no justice in cutting up webcam models. Rapist is a rapist. Model ain't hurting no one."

"Flaunting her body. Making men want her."

"Asking for it? You victim-blaming, Tom?"

"I'm trying to figure out why The Snipper neutered Valentine and left him alive, but tortured two women to death. It seems disproportionate. Like it isn't the same person."

Roy looked at Tom. "What if it isn't?"

"You mean…?"

Roy nodded. "Two perps. What if The Snipper has an accomplice?"

CHAPTER 23

Kendal couldn't sleep.

She was exhausted, but when she closed her eyes she started to freak out. That led her to counting every blink, restarting each time she reached a hundred.

Counting blinks made her think of her father. It was something Kendal once did to distract herself, when he came to her room at night. Lie perfectly still. Count to a hundred. Don't scream, or it will get worse. It will all be over soon.

She didn't want to think of that. But she couldn't stop blinking, and one thought led to the other.

It was the lights. Kendal was afraid to turn them off, but couldn't fall asleep with them on. She'd turned off all the cameras, unplugged her computer, put her Kindle and cell Linda had given her in the bedside drawer, but still didn't feel safe in the dark.

So she blinked. And counted. And tossed. And turned. And blinked. And counted.

Sometime around two am she felt like clawing her own eyes out. She stared at her bedside lamp, needing it and hating it at the same time, finished her hundredth count to one hundred, then crept out of her bed and counted the steps to Linda's room. Predictably, her sorority sister was awake, video chatting with clients.

"Come on in, slut."

Kendal froze. She felt the cameras on her. Like X-rays, tearing away her robe and underwear. She wanted to start blinking again, but people were watching. They'd think she was a freak. She might get kicked out of the house. Kendal wouldn't be able to afford college without the webcam income.

Not giving in to her counting was like trying not to scratch a gigantic itch. Her brain and body wanted so badly to do it, even though Kendal knew it was neurotic and wrong. She could resist for short periods, but the neuroses always won. But Kendal didn't want it to win in Linda's room, with the cameras on.

"Can you come here a sec?" Kendal asked. She was opening her eyes as far as she could, and probably looked insane, but she was able to control the blinking.

"Sure." Linda rolled out of bed and met her in the doorway. "Sup?"

"I can't sleep," Kendal whispered. "Can I use your vape?"

Linda's face glowed with delight. "You never want to get high. You sure?"

"Yeah. Something that will relax me."

"I just got some wicked indica juice that's sticky as hell. Lemme get it."

Linda bounced over to her bedside drawer, waved at her appreciative fans, and told them she'd be back in a minute. Then she took Kendal by the hand and led her back to her bedroom. They sat on Kendal's bed, and Linda held up an electronic cigarette. The base was black metal, attached to a clear plastic cartridge that had fluid inside.

"This shit is crazy sticky."

"I'll be careful not to spill it."

Linda smiled. "Dummy, sticky means it makes you stick to the spot. A few hits and you can't move."

"Will it put me to sleep?"

"This would knock out Snoop Dog."

Linda lifted the e-cig to her lips, pressed the round button on the side, and inhaled. She held it a moment, then blew out sweet smoke. The smell of marijuana washed over Kendal. Marijuana, mixed with something else. Strawberry or watermelon.

"I get this from a boy in Biology. Has glaucoma or some other eye bullshit. Lucky bastard got a medical ID. Can you believe the luck?"

Kendal wasn't sure having glaucoma qualified as lucky, but she gratefully took the offered e-cig. She'd smoked before, and always found it to be harsh and unpleasant. But when she inhaled the vapor, Kendal was surprised that it didn't hurt her lungs. She blew it out without the usual accompanying cough.

"That's smooth," she said, hoping she didn't sound stupid.

"Have you ever vaped before?"

Kendal shook her head.

"It's just water and sugar, along with THC. Smooth as a virgin's tit."

They passed it back and forth two more times, and Kendal was surprised she'd forgotten to count her blinks.

Then things got really slow.

Linda was talking about the boy in Biology class, and she seemed to be talking forever, on and on, but when Kendal looked at the clock not even a minute had passed.

"You feel it?"

Kendal nodded, her head heavy. She might have been smiling, but couldn't really feel her face.

Linda launched into another endless babblefest, and Kendal stared at her hand, wondering how millions of years of evolution culminated in cashmere matte nail polish. For some reason that seemed like an extremely profound thought. She started to share it with Linda, but forgot what she was going to say.

An hour passed, which in sober-time was really just two minutes, and then Linda was saying something about going back to her room and suddenly she was gone and Kendal was alone.

But it was okay being alone.

In fact, it was great.

Kendal was great.

She knew she was stoned, but she also felt like she hadn't been able to see things so clearly. The cameras around her room were off, and Kendal vaguely remembered being afraid of them for some reason, but that seemed silly now. Everything that had happened to her in the past few days seemed silly. Silly, and somehow far away.

"Maybe I'm stalking myself," someone said. Someone who sounded a lot like her.

Kendal locked the door to her room out of habit, and thought about turning the cameras back on. Then she thought about ice cream. Then she thought about a movie she saw when she was younger, about some people who went to the center of the earth and were in some kind of boat on a river of lava, which seemed like a really fun thing to try.

The lights in her room were bright. Too bright. Kendal shut them off, and then laughed because she didn't touch the switch three times like she always did. In fact, the whole concept of counting seemed ridiculous. Even more ridiculous was the idea that marijuana was still against the law when it was without a doubt the greatest thing *ever*.

She laid back on her bed, in the dark, listening to herself breathe but not counting her own breaths, and fell asleep feeling like all was peaceful in the world and everything was going to turn out okay.

• • •

Kendal dreamt of spiders.

A big spider with eight red eyes and long hairy legs was perched on her foot, stroking her sole. Kendal was afraid to move, because it had two large, curved fangs, sharp and shiny like hooks, poised above her big toe and if she moved she knew it would bite her.

So Kendal stayed completely still. She didn't move. She didn't breathe. She didn't want to do anything that would provoke the spider. It crawled up her leg to her knee, stopped there, and began to whisper to her.

"The eetsy… beetsy… spiiiiiiiider… went… up… the… waaaaaaater spout."

Kendal startled herself out of sleep, jerking up to a sitting position, slapping at her bare knee. It took her a moment to get her bearings.

I'm in bed. I was asleep. It was a dream.

She squinted, looking around the room. Moonlight slivered in through the crack in the window drapes, enough for her to see she was alone. The only thing in her bedroom was her, and the darkness.

Kendal plopped back down into bed. Her brain was still fuzzy from the weed. She looked at the clock. A little past four-thirty. She blinked, three times, then let sleep claim her again.

The spider came back.

This time it was on her neck. Stroking her cheek with its leg.

Singing to her in a soft, low voice.

"Down... came... the... raaaaaaaaaain... aaaaaaaaand... washed... the spiiiiiiiiiider out."

Kendal flinched, pushing away the tickling spider with her hand—

—and felt it.

Again Kendal bolted awake. The spider might have been a dream, but when she reached out she was sure she'd touched something. Something soft, with a stiffness to it.

She also sensed something else. Something far worse than any spider nightmare.

There's someone in the room with me.

Kendal peered into the dark, not sure what she was looking for. There was nothing to see. The room was empty.

But it didn't feel empty. It felt like there was someone nearby. Moving through the same space. Breathing the same air.

Standing next to her and staring.

"Hello?" she whispered.

The darkness didn't answer.

Kendal held her breath, listening.

She didn't hear a sound. The room, the whole house, was still.

It was a dream. Or the weed. I'm being paranoid. There's nothing—

Then the floor creaked.

Right next to the bed.

Kendal reached for the bedside switch, flicking it on.

The light didn't work.

She turned it a few more times, and in her panic knocked it off the nightstand. It hit the floor with a thump. Kendal reached over, seeking the lamp, finding it and again seeking the switch and twisting it.

No light.

Kendal slapped her palm on the nightstand, finding the drawer, taking out her cell and powering it on. It took a few seconds, but the phone flickered to life. Kendal pressed the flashlight app and jerked the tiny cone of light around the room.

As far as she could see, her room was empty.

She turned to the lamp, set it back on the nightstand, and noticed that the cord was unplugged.

Did I do that?

Maybe when I was high?

Kendal couldn't remember. She plugged the lamp back into the wall and when it came on the intensity blinded her for a moment. She shielded her eyes with her hand and again searched her room.

Empty.

She no longer felt like someone was standing next to her. In fact, Kendal wasn't sure if she'd imagined it. Maybe it had been no more real than touching the nightmare spider on her neck. She was dreaming. Or tired. Or still stoned.

Or having a psychotic break.

When Kendal was younger, rational thought helped her keep the hallucinations under control. If she thought she saw something that wasn't plausible, she knew to dismiss it.

A spider on her neck, singing to her?

Implausible.

Someone in her room?

Also implausible. The sorority house had good security locks and deadbolts on all the doors. Kendal had also locked the door to her room. She turned to check it, to make sure it was still closed.

The door was open.

Just a crack.

Kendal had one of those lame privacy locks that could be opened with a fingernail. But she had locked it.

So she either misremembered locking it earlier—

Or someone had gotten in.

Another spike of adrenaline, and Kendal clutched her cell to her chest. She took another nervous look around the room, wondering if there were any places for a person to hide.

No room behind the computer. The desk was against the wall.

Laundry hamper? Not big enough.

The bed?

When Kendal was small, she had a friend named Julia who was afraid of monsters under the bed. Kendal knew that was silly. Monsters didn't hide under your bed. They called themselves "Daddy" and came in through your door.

But, still, the thought that there was someone directly beneath her was freaky enough to cause a shiver. Someone lying there. Waiting for her to sleep.

Tickling her, and singing soft and low.

Kendal peered over the edge of the bed, lifting up her sheet—

—and seeing the box spring was directly on the floor.

She blew out a stiff breath, feeling silly. For a moment there, she really was afraid that someone might be under her bed. Next she'd think—like in that ebook she was reading—that someone was hiding in the closet.

The closet.

Kendal stared at her bedroom closet.

The door was open a few inches.

She thought about what was in the closet. Clothes. Her suitcase. A plastic tub of shoes.

There was more than enough room in there for a person to hide.

Kendal pulled her eyes away from the closet long enough to glance at her bedroom door.

I could run for it.

Get the hell out of here.

Wake up the other girls.

They'll think I'm crazy, but Linda is my only friend here anyway.

And what if someone actually is in my closet? It's better to be wrong and look foolish than be brave and be dead.

But Kendal knew it wasn't just about looking foolish. It was about looking crazy.

Kendal would rather die than go back to the institution. That had been hell. Almost as bad as what she'd gone through at home. One of those ignorant shrinks even had the audacity to say she'd made up all of those stories. That they were in her head. That there was no proof at all that her father had—

The closet door moved.

It had been just a tiny move. Less than an inch. But Kendal was sure it had opened just a little bit more.

She stared at it, refusing to blink, refusing to breathe, waiting for it to move again while hoping it didn't.

After a full minute Kendal blew out the breath she'd been holding, her heart beating so fast and loud she could hear it.

The door hadn't moved.

I'm going crazy.

Or going crazier.

So what now?

Kendal wasn't going to get help. She'd become an expert at keeping people out of her neuroses, and wasn't going to start because she'd vaped some grass and had a bad dream.

But there was no way she could go back to sleep until she checked the closet.

Kendal stood up. She took a small step, wincing as the wood floorboards creaked under her weight. As if it would alert the person in the closet that she was coming.

"This is crazy," Kendal said, the sound of her own voice reassuring her. "I wasn't being tickled by a spider. And there is no one in my closet."

Kendal forced herself to walk normally. She reached out her hand for the closet doorknob.

There's no one in there.

I'm being crazy.

Kendal wasn't sure which concept was scarier, and found she'd broken out in a light sweat. But she touched the knob—

—began to pull the door open—

—and then her phone vibrated in her hand, causing her to yelp.

Kendal stared down at her cell. Saw a text message on the screen.

You're right.

The text was from *Unknown*. Kendal had no idea who it was from, or what it was referring to. But staring at the words made her knees shake. She moved her thumb over the text to delete it, and her phone buzzed again and another text appeared.

It wasn't a spider. It was a feather.

Check the bed.

Kendal turned, slowly. The last bit of weed fog cleared out of her head, and hyper-awareness took over. She felt like she was in some terrible horror movie, the zoom lens focusing in on her face as she struggled through excruciating slow motion, focusing on her widening eyes as the realization of her situation kicked in.

There, at the foot of the bed, half covered by her blanket—

A long, gray feather.

It wasn't just a dream.

Someone had been in my room.

Someone had been tickling me with a feather while I slept.

Her phone vibrated again, and it scared Kendal so badly she dropped it. The cell bounced on the wood floor, landing face up, and Kendal read the next text.

You're also wrong.

Kendal stared down at the phone. Her mouth had gone dry. Her bladder felt like it had shrunk four sizes. Then her phone buzzed once more.

I AM in the closet.

In front of her, the closet door creaked.

Kendal jerked away from it, planting her foot on the phone, slipping backward as the scream escaped her lips—a scream so loud it could shatter glass—and then she was falling and her head slammed against the floor and the whole world exploded into a giant starburst and her vision went wiggly.

Kendal tried to blink away the dizziness as black encroached on the edges of her vision, and then a shadow was pressing on her chest and grabbing her hair, pounding her head against the wood again and again and again...

As Kendal's world blurred out, she swore she heard the shadow whisper,

"See you soon."

Then consciousness faded and returned, like she'd just awoken from a dream, and the shadow seemed to transform into Linda, who was kneeling next to Kendal and holding her hand.

"You okay? You fell."

Kendal sat up, so fast it made her dizzy. Her head hurt. Her ears rang. She reached up and felt a tender spot at the base of her skull. Two other sorority sisters stood in her doorway, staring.

"Someone was in my room," Kendal said. Her voice sounded small.

"What?"

Kendal jerked her head around, looking at the bed.

The feather was gone.

She searched the floor for her cell phone, scrambling to it and scooping it up.

The texts were gone.

Linda leaned in, a smile curling her lips. "Are you still high?"

High?

Or insane?

She thought about that awful therapist when she was in the institution. The one who accused her of making it all up.

Could she have been right?

Could I have imagined all the abuse?

Is it happening again?

Kendal started to say something, but it stuck in her throat and became a strangled cry. As she sobbed, Linda stroked her hair.

"It's okay, babe. You're just scared."

That was the understatement of the decade. Kendal's reality seemed to be fracturing. It made her feel like she was eight years old again. Terrified. Helpless. A victim.

And there was no worse feeling in the world than that.

"Get into bed, honey," Linda said, helping her up.

"I'm too scared to sleep."

"I'll stay with you. It'll be like a slumber party? Remember those when you were a kid?"

"I never had one."

"Never? You had some kind of deprived childhood, then."

"Something like that."

Kendal got into bed, and Linda climbed in next to her.

"Now what?" Kendal asked.

"Well, when I had slumber parties we'd do all sorts of stuff. Talk about boys we had crushes on. Play games. I'm a rockstar at Chinese Checkers and Mall Madness. Sneak some of our parents' whiskey. Read magazines. That was how I saw my first peter, a friend brought a Playgirl. I thought it looked stupid." Linda laughed. "I still think it looks stupid. I mean, how do guys walk around with that hanging between their legs?"

"I don't know," Kendal said, honestly.

"Sometimes we'd do each other's make-up. Or talk gossip about the lacrosse team. Or dance to some boy band. I was soooo in love with Nick Jonas."

"I don't know who that is."

"You don't know the Jonas Brothers? They were on Hannah Montana, back before Mylie started doing the freaky thing with her tongue and taking her clothes off all the time. She's cool, though. She owns it, y'know? Her body, her rules, everyone else can go to hell. I wish I had that much confidence."

Me, too, Kendal thought.

"What else did you do?"

"Well, whenever the first girl fell asleep, we'd put her hand in a bowl of warm water."

"Why?"

"To try to make her pee herself."

"Why?"

"It's funny, I guess. No one ever peed. They always woke up because we were laughing too hard. And don't worry—I won't do that to you. I mean, we're not ten years old. And I'm sleeping in the same bed. That would be self-defeating."

"Linda?" Kendal was aware she'd used her real name, but it was okay because the cameras were off.

"Yeah, slut?"

"Thanks."

"No problem. Sweet dreams, okay?"

But Kendal didn't have sweet dreams. As soon as she fell asleep, she dreamt of monsters.

CHAPTER 24

Erinyes sits in the van outside the sorority house and watches.

Tonight was not the night. Kendal isn't ready yet.

But she will be. Very soon.

The app Erinyes put on Kendal's cell phone is hidden. It's the same app Erinyes uploaded to the cop's phone. The app is free in the Apple Store. A rudimentary tennis game, similar to Pong. But that's just the shell. What the app really did was allow a remote user access to the phone's root directory. So Erinyes can access the phone's cameras, among other things.

This Kendal is weaker than the other Kendals that came before. Erinyes hasn't seen this Kendal take off her clothes, yet, but it's only a matter of time. She's a slut, just like the others. A bad girl. Any woman who takes off her clothes for men on camera needs to be punished.

You shouldn't tempt men. It's a sin.

A wicked sin.

But Penance was coming.

Erinyes switches to Tom's phone. The camera is dark, but there is snoring.

Penance is coming for him, too.

Erinyes starts the van, pulls onto the street, and begins to cruise the dark, Chicago streets.

He's excited.

He's been in several Kendals' homes. But they hadn't had roommates.

This Kendal has five roommates. All sluts.

It makes Erinyes think. And he gets so lost in thought that he almost doesn't notice the woman on the curb.

Skinny. Old. The mini skirt on her hangs on her flat hips like a square lampshade. Her boot heels are so high she looks like a parody of a hooker. But she's no parody. She's the real deal.

He pulls over, rolls down his window.

"How much?"

She leans inside, looking at the interior of his van. The back is dark so she can't see what's in there.

"Twenty for a suck."

He nods and unlocks her door. She climbs in.

Up close, Erinyes realizes she's younger than he'd originally guessed. Maybe even a teenager.

"Where should I park?"

"Here is fine. It's dead this time of night. No one will bother us."

That's exactly what I wanted to hear.

Erinyes rolls up the tinted windows and she takes a condom out of her purse.

"Money?" she says.

He fishes two tens out of his pocket, hands them over. She tucks them away and leans over, unzipping his fly.

When she starts to laugh he places the stun gun against the side of her neck and hits her with the juice. The whore does the two million volt boogie for ten full seconds, then collapses on his lap.

He duct tapes her wrists. Her mouth. Uses a four inch metal spring clamp to attach her pony tail to the passenger side headrest. Then he's on the road again.

When she tries to kick, he zaps her.

"Hurts, doesn't it? If you try to move again, I'll put this on your eyes. It'll fry your eyeballs and make them burst."

Erinyes has no idea if that's true or not. But she doesn't try to move again.

"Do you know what the furies are?" he asks as he drives.

The whore doesn't answer. She's crying, and her runny eyeliner makes her look like Alice Cooper.

"The furies are monsters. They have great, batlike wings and talons on their hands and feet. Their eyes are red; red as blood. They wear crowns of spiders. There are three of them. Alecto, Tilphousia, and Megaera, and they were created by God to punish sinners. Sinners like you."

The whore whimpers behind her tape gag.

"Lust is the worst sin of all. It leads women to cheat on their husbands. It leads men to rape. You sell your body like the mother of harlots. The whore of Babylon. You bring misery to the world. Your soul needs to be cleansed. But first I need to know something. And I want you to tell me the truth, or I'll do that eye-melting thing."

Erinyes turns and stares at the woman. "The truth, now. Is your name Kendal?"

She shakes her head.

Too bad. Kendals were the worst sinners of all. If she'd been a Kendal, she would have required special attention.

Erinyes drives to his house. He takes the alley to his unattached two-car garage, uses the electronic opener, and backs the vehicle inside. With the van off and the garage door closed, Erinyes holds the stun gun against the whore's arm until she passes out, then exits.

The space is cool and smells like car exhaust and spoiled milk. A quarter of the garage is taken up by twelve fifty-five gallon metal drums. The barrels are black, carbon steel, epoxy-lined, with half inch valves at the bottom. He forgets which are full and which aren't, and raps a few until he hears the telltale hollow sound.

The whore wakes up when he lifts her lower body into the barrel. She fights him, but her hands are bound and Erinyes is bigger and stronger. After another zap from the stun gun, she slumps over.

He spends a few minutes zapping her unconscious body.

Her eyes do not melt. Though they do puff up and turn a milky color.

Erinyes pushes her completely into the barrel, then seals a lid on top with a boat ring. It's an airtight seal, and experience has shown him that when the body begins to decay, it releases a lot of gas. The inside pressure can build to the point that the barrel expands. No barrel has ever leaked, but if it did it would be bad; the decaying human body has a distinct, powerful odor, which is a big red flag for the police. To offset this expansion, Erinyes uses an electric vacuum pump to remove some of the air in the barrel.

Forty seconds into the vacuum process, the whore wakes up. There is some pounding, some shaking, a muffled cry for help.

All movement stops within a minute.

Erinyes closes the valve, then rolls the barrel into the far corner, next to the ten other full ones.

Ten souls, given Penance.

Ten souls, saved from damnation.

Hard work. But worthwhile.

He goes into his house.

Prepares and delivers an intramuscular injection of Delatestryl.

Sits at his computer and opens TOR.

Checks his forum.

Rubs some Fortestra gel on his thigh.

Hears crying. Coming from the basement.

Erinyes opens a can of dog food, cuts open two clindamycin capsules, pours them into a full bottle of water, and takes everything downstairs.

The smell is getting bad again. Time for a new toilet bucket.

Erinyes pours the dog food in the bowl and says, "I saved another soul today."

After a moment, a meek male voice whispers, "Please kill me."

"You haven't atoned for your sins yet. Don't you want salvation?"

"I'm sorry. For everything."

Erinyes stares at the pitiable creature in chains.

"So am I," he says, and goes back upstairs.

CHAPTER 25

The phone woke Tom up.

But it wasn't his phone.

He glanced at the clock. A bit past 7 A.M. Then he turned and stared at Joan, who was squinting at her cell.

"Work?" Tom asked.

He hoped it was work. Maybe that would help Joan forgive all the work he'd put in over the last few days, which strictly violated their *no work while visiting* agreement.

"It's Trish," Joan said.

"Roy's girlfriend?"

Joan nodded, then picked up. "What's up?"

Tom couldn't make out Trish's words, but she sounded upset. He sat up in bed, staring pointedly at her. If something had happened to Roy, Joan would tell him. But Joan didn't look his way at all. She kept making backchannel sounds; uh-huh, hmmm, uh, yeah, and so on, which indicated she was listening intently, but it didn't tell Tom a thing.

He finally gave her a poke and mouthed, "Is Roy okay?" And she narrowed her eyes at him and rudely turned her back.

Prior to Joan, Tom had been in several relationships. He blamed himself for those romances failing. On the job, he thought he was pretty good at reading people. Witnesses. Suspects. Cops. But Tom wasn't as keen with personal relationships. One of his past girlfriends intentionally cheated on him to see if he would notice. Tom had been oblivious until he got their wedding invite in the mail.

With Joan, Tom tried to be attentive. He made an effort to notice the subtle stuff, like the underlying meaning to things she said, and how she looked at him, and how often she smiled. So when she snubbed him, it hurt.

He poked her again, making a sad face. She gave him a sideways glance, an eye roll, and went back to mmm-hmmming. Joan eventually ended the call with, "I'll meet you there."

"Well?" Tom asked.

"Trish thinks Roy is cheating on her. Is he?"

"What? How should I know?"

"You're partners and best friends."

"Yeah. But we're guys. We rarely share personal stuff, and when we do we mostly ignore it."

"So could he be cheating?"

"I don't know. I thought he was happy."

Joan got that little crease in her forehead, an indicator he'd said the wrong thing. "Since when does happiness have to do with cheating? So if you weren't happy with me, you'd cheat?"

"I don't cheat. I'm committed to you." Tom reached out and stroked Joan's thigh. "Did you know Trish was intersex?"

"Of course. And what does that have to do with anything?"

"Nothing. I didn't know about it. Just found out."

"What should it matter?"

"It doesn't."

She frowned. "What if I told you I was intersex?"

"I love you for you, Joan. And if there are some extra chromosomes in there, that wouldn't matter."

Joan stared at him, then put her arms around his neck and kissed Tom behind the ear. "That's the sweetest thing anyone has ever said to me."

"Is Trish okay?"

"She's a wreck. She was paying bills and saw one of Roy's credit card statements. An eight hundred dollar room bill at the Sheraton. Dated last month."

"Did she ask him about it?"

"He's at work. She's afraid to ask. Figures maybe he did it because of the baby thing."

"Baby thing?"

"They're talking about having a baby, and she can't get pregnant. Didn't Roy tell you?"

"Did they get married and I missed it?"

"You don't have to get married to have a baby with someone, Tom. This isn't 1950. Marriage is an archaic, patriarchal tradition rooted in religious dogma and societal enforced gender roles. Give it another two hundred years, marriage will vanish from our culture."

"Really? I thought women cared about marriage."

"Married women care about marriage. Single women are having too much fun to care." She kissed his neck again. "I'm meeting Trish for breakfast. I figured it was okay, because it's an emergency."

"Of course."

"Plus, you're working."

"I'm not. I'm taking the day off."

"Seriously?"

"You're here for four more days, and I'm making every one of them count."

"No shit?"

"No shit. I swear."

This time Joan kissed his mouth. The moment they touched tongues, she pulled away.

"Morning breath."

"I don't mind," Tom said.

"I do. It's like kissing a dead salmon."

"You've kissed a lot of dead salmon?"

"My ex-boyfriends are none of your business." Joan winked, swung her legs out of bed, and padded over to the bathroom. Tom admired the view for a moment—was there anything sexier than a woman wearing one of your old tee shirts?—and then went in after her.

His sink was tiny, so he stood behind her as they both brushed their teeth. Joan leaned with one hand on the sink, and Tom pressed against her back and put his hand next to hers.

It felt… right.

Then he leaned forward to spit, missed, and got it all over her hand.

Joan giggled, and she wasn't the giggling type. She turned around, slipping into his arms, mint Colgate dribbling down her chin.

"Do you know why we work?" she asked.

"We need the money?"

"No. Us. Why we work as a couple."

"Because I got really, really lucky?"

She grinned, eyes glinting. "We both got really, really lucky. And we both know it. And that's why we work."

Joan kissed him, and they both tasted like toothpaste anyway so it didn't matter Tom hadn't finished brushing, and then her shirt was off and his boxers were too and Tom was on his back on the cold tile floor while Joan bounced on top of him and he realized that he needed to do whatever he could to make sure he spent the rest of his life with this woman. Even if her views on marriage were different than Tom's, he had to ask her.

Now probably wasn't the right time, though.

CHAPTER 26

Erinyes cannot see them, because the camera on Tom's phone is on his nightstand, facing the ceiling.

But she can hear.

Tom and Joan are rutting. Like swine. Moans and grunts and flesh slapping flesh.

Sinners.

Erinyes doesn't want to listen anymore, but she's weak. She touches herself between her legs. Runs her hand over the bumps and ridges.

The tears come, and as she cries she also screams; a harsh, guttural noise that sounds more monstrous than human.

CHAPTER 27

After Joan left for breakfast with Trish, Tom forced his way through some pushups, then dug his twenty-five pound dumbbell out of the closet and curled it, left arm then right arm, until he couldn't anymore. Then he showered, thinking about life, and Joan, and life with Joan.

He didn't think about The Snipper. Or his job. Or anything to do with policework.

But he did have several unpleasant thoughts about his credit score.

After toweling off, he picked up his cell and spent ten humiliating minutes on hold listening to recordings of how his bank card was working for him, then two more humiliating minutes being told that his credit couldn't be extended. All he had was four hundred dollars left. Also, his bill was due in four days; it wasn't late yet, but that was a friendly reminder.

Okay. Plan B.

Tom went back into his closet, and found the white cardboard box under a bag containing old sweaters and a pair of hiking boots. He hefted the box onto his bed and took off the rectangular top.

Last he remembered, there were roughly a hundred comic books in the box. Before moving out of his parent's house after college, Tom had taken care to bag and card each issue, on the off chance that one day they might be worth something.

Today he was going to find out.

He pulled out a few random issues, judged them to be in decent shape, and then used his phone to Google comic shops in Chicago. There were many, but the biggest seemed to be a place that also sold sports memorabilia and used jewelry, called Golden Treasures, on Addison.

Tom called, confirmed there was an appraiser there, and then dressed and carried the box out to the car. Twenty minutes later he was walking through the door, approaching a mousy-looking man a decade his senior, who wore a Wayward Pines tee shirt and smelled like he was allergic to showers. Tom propped the box up on the counter and said, "I called a little while ago."

"Let's see what you got."

The clerk began pulling out issues, arranging them in some order known only to him, and mumbling stuff to himself.

"Copper age. More copper age. Turtles. ASM #238. New Mutants. Alpha Flight. Secret Wars. Dark Knight Returns in 8.5. Maybe 9. Hey, an Uncanny #120!"

"Is that good?" Tom asked.

"First appearance of Northstar," said someone behind Tom. A thirty-something, skinny jeans, hipster beard.

"From Alpha Flight." Tom remembered the character. Canadian, could fly, emitted energy blasts. Superheroes were probably the reason Tom had grown up to become a cop. Though Joan said it was because Tom was genetically wired for life, liberty, and the pursuit of happiness. It was an inside joke.

"Northstar is the first openly gay superhero in the Marvel Universe," said the hipster.

"Really? I must have missed that."

"CCA wouldn't allow it," said the clerk.

"The Comics Code Authority." Tom nodded. Though he'd outgrown comic collecting, he could still speak some nerd. Or was it geek? He got the two confused.

"Came out in Alpha Flight #106. Married Kyle Jinadu in Astonishing X-Men #41."

"Number fifty-one," said the clerk.

"Is it worth anything?" Tom asked.

"I'll give you forty bucks for it right now," said the hipster.

The clerk nodded, "Take it, I could only offer thirty. He's also got a lot of New Mutants."

"Karma?" the hipster asked, coming over to sort through Tom's comics.

"Yeah," the clerk looked at Tom. "Gary collects LGBT titles."

"Karma was gay?" Tom said.

The clerk and the hipster exchanged a look that said *duh.*

"Any transgender superheroes?" Tom asked.

"Mystique could change gender," said Gary. "And she was bisexual."

"Sasquatch. Remember the Wanda Langkowski years?"

Tom did recall that one of the strongest Alpha Flight members was trapped in the body of a woman for a few issues. It caused a bit of confusion for the character. "How about intersex?" he asked.

"Shining Knight in the New 52," the clerk said. "And Alysia Yeoh."

"She's trans." Said the hipster.

"Okay. How about Sera from Asgard's Assassin?"

"Also trans."

"She was assigned male at birth."

"Are you sure?"

As they went back and forth, Tom walked up to a jewelry display case. Among the antique brooches and necklaces was an eye-catching ring. Light yellow stone, a solitaire cut, in a silver setting. He'd been stopping in the occasional jewelry store for the past few months, keeping a look out for something that looked like Joan's style. Tom took out his cell and snapped a picture, wondering if maybe he could take it to a jeweler and have them do something similar in gold with a diamond.

Tom then wandered around a bit, found some back issues of Fangoria, and thumbed through some old Dr. Cyclops reviews until the clerk called to him.

"Gary wants your Alpha Flight run."

"I'll give you four-fifty," Gary said.

"A fair market value. You've got some average issues, but some good ones. The Dark Night #1 can go for $700. You've got the first ten TMNTs, but the condition is only very fine. Be worth a lot more if you didn't read them."

"What would be the point then?" Tom said.

"Just sayin'. Don't kill the messenger. Your best is your New Mutants #98. First appearance of Deadpool. One just sold for two k."

"So what would you give me for everything?"

He squinted, then chewed his lower lip. "I'd go... four thousand for everything."

"Plus my four-fifty," Gary added.

Less than forty-five hundred bucks? It was a lot lower than Tom expected.

"I thought they were worth more," Tom said.

"You could get more, if you sell them on eBay one at a time. That's what I'll do with most of them. You the original owner?"

Tom nodded.

"You paid a buck for most of these. Four thousand percent mark-up is pretty good for a thirty year investment."

True, but Tom was less concerned about how much his goods had appreciated and more about getting Joan a ring. He was a grown ass man. He caught bad guys for a living. But financially he was no better off than he was a decade ago. It was damn depressing.

"What can you tell me about the ring in the case?" Tom said.

"Which one? The yellow diamond?"

"It's a diamond?"

"Almost a full carat. Set in white gold. It's a Cartier."

"French? Really?" Tom asked. His disappointment at the lowball offer vanished. A diamond? And French? Joan would love that it was from France. Another inside joke.

"Yeah. Over a hundred years old."

"What are you asking for it?"

"I couldn't go less than seven grand."

"How about in trade? The comics for the ring?"

The clerk's face twisted in thought. "Nope. Couldn't do it. Got too much in it. I'd have to get another $1500."

Tom considered his bank account, which was a perpetual balancing act just shy of overdraft. He'd just paid rent, had been spending money on Joan's visit, and didn't think he had more than five hundred bucks left until next payday.

"How about a grand?" Tom asked. "I want to propose to my girlfriend."

Gary spread out his hands, "C'mon, Jerome. Guy is selling his comics to get married. Cut him a break."

Jerome the clerk rubbed the stubble on his face, then nodded. "Okay. Who am I to stand in the way of love, right? The comics, plus a grand."

Tom took four hundred and fifty bucks from the hipster—who carried around cash like that?—and then handed his credit card to Jerome, hoping it would go through.

A minute passed. An uncomfortable, sweaty, breath-holding minute where every second lasted ten.

"This damn machine," Jerome said. "It disconnects all the time. You okay if I do a handwritten transaction?"

Tom was very okay with that.

Five minutes later he was sitting in his car with the ring in his hand, staring at it, grinning like he'd just gotten the deal of a lifetime. He just knew Joan would like it. It was her style, and it felt right.

But would she say yes?

Tom didn't have a clue.

His cell buzzed, and Tom expected to see Joan's name come up. When it did, he decided he'd meet with her right then, and ask her to marry him the moment he saw her.

But it was Roy.

"I'm on vacation," Tom said. "I've told you this. Repeatedly."

"But you answered anyway. What does that say about you, brother?"

"I'm hanging up now."

"Wait! We got a hit!"

"You can handle it."

"Can you listen just a second? I been up all night, working the sex offender angle. Our boy, Hector, he broke down. Told me about this online help group for pedos. *Fight The Feeling*, they call it. It's a message board for child molesters who want to resist the urge. So I got a fake account, logged on, started poking around, see if anyone got themselves castrated lately."

Tom didn't say anything.

"You still there, partner?"

"I'm listening," Tom said.

"Because you want to know what I found out. That's the cop in you. That part don't go on vacation."

"You're just daring me to hang up on you."

"Hold up, hold up. I got in a chat room. Seven dudes, Tommy! The Snipper cut the shit off of seven dudes, in just that forum. Our perp is castrating kiddie rapers. Doing the world a goddamn public service."

"Can we talk to any of these people in person?"

"Way ahead of you. Forum is anonymous, for obvious reasons. Don't have any real names. So I checked out the domain registry, got the address of the guy who runs it. Check it; he lives in Bucktown."

Tom was only a few blocks away from Bucktown.

"You'll need a court order, get him to give up user addys."

"I know. But it doesn't hurt to ask. If The Snipper is targeting guys on that forum, they're all in danger of losing their junk. That's even more persuasive than a warrant, don't you think?"

It was much more persuasive. But that didn't change anything. "You can handle this without me, Roy."

"I know. But seeing as how our ladies are at breakfast anyway."

"You know about that?" Tom asked.

"Yeah. Trish texted me. Said she and Joanie were grabbing a bite."

"She say anything else? Why they were going?"

"No. Why?"

Tom almost asked Roy about the hotel bill, but awkwardness stopped him. That was a big bomb to drop over the phone.

In person would be better. Even though it was a conversation Tom didn't want to have. He and Roy were good at a lot of things. Intimacy wasn't one of them. But Tom didn't want to see his partner blindsided. Friends looked out for each other. Even when mistakes have been made.

Especially when mistakes have been made.

"Where are you at?" Tom asked.

"Precinct."

"I'll pick you up in ten."

"See you then, partner."

Tom put the ring in his front pocket, then started the car. As he drove, he imagined proposal scenarios. Get down on one knee? Do it in public? Talk about all the things he loved about her first, or just come right out and ask? Tom saw a movie where the guy put the ring in a champagne glass, but he couldn't remember what happened next. Did she choke to death? Or swallow it and then they had to wait a day or two to get it back?

Probably shouldn't go that route.

Roy was waiting outside the precinct house, sipping a coffee. He hadn't brought one for Tom. When he climbed in he gave Tom the address.

"So, Trish called Joan this morning, upset," Tom said.

Roy didn't answer. He was fiddling with his phone.

"She saw a credit card statement," Tom continued. "Some big hotel bill."

Roy grunted something.

"She thinks you're cheating on her."

"I ran the domain guy for priors. His name is Dennis Dale Cissick. Got nothing on him but a name."

"I also sold all my comics and bought Joan an engagement ring."

"Google brings up zip on Dennis. He don't even have a Facebook page. What twenty-something don't have a Facebook page? Isn't it some sorta law?"

"Are you listening to me?"

"What? No. I'm talking about this dude we're going to see. Now that last name rang a bell. Cissick. You remember that name?"

It did sound familiar, but Tom couldn't place it. "Remind me."

"Ten years ago. Some kid found a woman's severed finger on the sidewalk. Got lucky with the ID. She worked at a bank, so her prints were in the system. Lilyana Cissick. Married, and a mom. Never found her. Husband Walter had filed a missing person report earlier that week."

Tom nodded. "I remember now. All over the news. No one knew if it should be treated as an abduction or a homicide."

"Body was never found. So I checked the husband. His Driver's License expired a few years ago, he didn't renew. But his address…"

"Is the one we're going to."

"Correctomundo."

Tom played around with it in his head. He couldn't work out how a missing woman from a decade ago was related to a maniac butchering webcam models and castrating pedophiles.

"I'm thinking Cissick and son maybe figured Mom was raped and killed, put up the *Fight the Feeling* site to punish other rapists."

"What about the women?"

"No idea. But there may be two perps, right? Maybe one targets men, the other women."

"Maybe. Or maybe it's a weird coincidence, and the message board has nothing to do with The Snipper, who has nothing to do with these assholes getting castrated."

"Lots of coincidences. I don't like coincidences in a homicide investigation."

"Me, neither."

"You say something about Trish and comics?"

Tom pulled onto Artesian Avenue and parked next to a fire hydrant. "It can wait. We're here."

They got out, dead leaves from the large oaks lining the street blowing past their feet. The home was small, gray, two stories, stairs leading up to the front door, typical old school Chicago house. It was flanked on either side by similar structures, and a walkway led to an alley in back. Tom took his shield out of his pocket, flipped it open so it hung from his jeans, and automatically gave his jacket a pat to make sure his Glock was there.

The wooden steps were in need of a paint job twenty years ago, and Tom used the rail because he wasn't entirely confident they'd hold his weight. At the top there was a handwritten note attached to the storm door.

Don't knock. Just leave package.

"You bring a package?" Roy asked.

Tom shook his head. Roy knocked.

Then he knocked again, harder.

Tom tried the doorbell, but there was no sound.

"Does Dennis have a car?" Tom asked.

"Cargo van. Ford Transit."

"Let's check the garage, see if he's out."

As they walked around the house, Tom felt it. What he called his *cop-sense.* A little warning tingle that something wasn't right.

"You hear that?" Roy said.

Tom listened. "No."

"Someone screaming?"

"I don't hear anything."

But then Tom did hear something. Something very faint, but shrill. They picked up their pace, following the length of the house around the back, into the yard. There were concrete steps descending to the basement door, blocked by boxes filled with old newspapers. Roy knelt next to the building, put his ear next to the brick.

"Anyone there!" he yelled.

This time Tom knew for sure it was a scream.

"Do you need help?" Roy yelled.

There was a stuttering sound, sharp and staccato, that went on for several seconds.

Sobbing?

Or some kind of crazed laughter?

Roy used his radio and called it in, and Tom walked up the back porch stairs. The door looked heavy, formidable. The windows had old, rusty, iron bars covering them in an ugly fleur-de-lis pattern.

Probable cause gave them permission to enter the home, but this wasn't going to be easy.

"How long for back up?" Tom asked his partner.

"Three minutes. See a way in?"

"No easy way." Tom banged on the back door, announced himself as a police officer. There was another mournful wail from the basement.

"Tom! Side of the house!"

Tom followed his partner's voice to the walkway. Roy was staring up at a side window, about three meters off the ground.

"You gonna fly up there?"

"Get on my shoulders. You can reach."

"How about you get on my shoulders?"

"I weigh more. Muscle. Come on."

Roy laced his fingers together and Tom stepped onto his hands, placed his palms on the side of the house, and climbed up to his shoulders. The window didn't have bars across it, but it was a security model with wire mesh inside the glass. Tom squinted inside, but couldn't make out anything in the dark room.

"It's safety glass," Tom said. "I don't think I can break it."

"Check to see if it's open."

There was no handle on the outside, so Tom took the Emerson folder from his front jeans pocket, and wedged the tanto blade under the window. He gave it a tentative pry, not wanting to bend his knife, and the window went up a few centimeters.

Tom folded his knife, clipped it back inside his pocket, eased his fingers underneath, and lifted. The movement wasn't smooth, but the window opened. The air inside was warm, and had a faint, unpleasant odor; a cross between a well-used public restroom, and a high school gym.

"It's open. Boost me up."

Roy grunted, getting his hands under Tom's feet, and for a few seconds they did an awkward acrobat act until Roy pushed Tom up far enough for him to climb inside.

"Let me in the front door," Roy told him.

Tom paused, hanging halfway over the window frame, letting his eyes adjust to the dark. After fifteen or so seconds he could make out a bed and dresser. Tom shifted his weight, pulling himself inside, handwalking until his feet were through and he was kneeling on the floor.

The smell was stronger, and had a harsh, chemical undernote. He sensed the room was empty, but recently used. Tom recalled how his house felt when he got back from visiting Joan; after a week away the air inside was always stale and empty when he returned, like the space knew he'd abandoned it. This room didn't feel that way. Someone had been in here recently.

In his shoulder holster, next to his Glock, was a Fenix penlight. Tom tugged it free and panned two hundred lumens around the bedroom. The wood floor first, to make sure there was no pet fur; Tom didn't want to be surprised by a Rottweiler or a leaping Tabby. Finding it clean of both dust and hair, he turned the beam upward.

Pink walls. Purple sheets. Stuffed animals on the carefully made bed. Posters on the wall of the Powerpuff Girls and Dora the Explorer. Dolls on the nightstand, a lone Barbie and five or six Kens in various stages of undress, some with their pants off and sporting their asexual, featureless groin bumps. A toy pony that looked too big for Barbie and crew. A jump rope with glitter handles, hanging on a drawer handle.

This was a young girl's bedroom. But something was off about it.

Tom did another quick scan of the room, trying to spot what was missing. No TV. No computer. No stereo. An old clock radio that appeared to be unplugged. Besides the bed, there were two dressers and a bookshelf full of paperbacks. Tom didn't recognize any of the authors, but they looked like teen romances of the *Sweet Valley High* variety.

Tom looked at the outlets for a cell phone charger, or a tablet.

Nothing.

That was odd. The room looked like time stopped in the year 2002.

He took a step and almost tripped over a pair of blue Converse All-Stars with neon green laces.

The shoes were larger than Tom's.

The occupant of this room was a big girl.

"This is the police," he said, loudly. "I heard a scream from inside, and I'm upstairs. Is anyone home?"

He listened for a reply.

None came.

The silence was so complete, Tom could hear his own pulse. His heart was beating faster than he would have liked. The key to dealing with stressful situations was being able to maintain calm. Fear caused mistakes.

He took a moment to slow his breathing, then headed for the open door and stepped into a hallway, the floorboards creaking under his feet. There were no lights on and the house was dark. Tom reached for a light switch, flipped it on.

Nothing happened.

Being in someone else's house never ceased to be a creepy experience. Trespassing didn't feel nice. Tom always felt sneaky, and a little ashamed, when he was in a stranger's home uninvited. Even though he was legally allowed to be there, it made him nervous and he didn't like it.

Blame his childhood. Tom was raised on a diet of 1980s VHS slasher movies like *Don't Open the Window* and *Don't Go in the House* and *Are You in the House Alone*; titles that seemed oddly appropriate at that moment. In those scary dark house movies you always knew that some crazed maniac would leap out of the shadows with a meat cleaver. It didn't help Tom's imagination that, in this particular case, they were actually chasing some crazed maniac. He recalled the last victim, her eyelids sliced off, intestines tied in a bow, and he considered drawing his firearm. But there was protocol against doing that, and Tom didn't feel threatened. Just on edge.

He passed a door, peeking his light inside. Bathroom. Sink. Shower. Toilet. Towels. Seemed ordinary enough.

Further down the hall was another bedroom. Tom peeked inside. This one belonged to a boy. Batman sheets. Star Wars and

GI Joe figures on the dresser. A poster above the bed with Batman punching Two-Face. Harry Potter and Tolkien on the bookshelf. No TV. No computer. No stereo. But there was an older model iPod with headphones on the floor next to the bed.

Just like the girl's bedroom, this one looked like time stopped ten years ago. But it was dust free. And the bed was unmade, the covers pushed down.

Recently slept in?

Next to the bed, on the nightstand, was half a glass of water.

Tom felt an adrenaline surge, and all the tiny little hairs on his forearms went erect. Roy had done a background check on this homeowner, but there hadn't been any mention of kids. It was Saturday, so no school.

Where were they?

It was creepy.

Something else was creepy, too. Except for the toys and posters and color scheme, this room was exactly like the girl's room. Beds and dressers and bookcases all the same type, in the same spots.

Maybe the children were strange, fraternal twins who imitated each other.

More old horror movies from Tom's youth flashed into his head. Movies with weird kids. *Children of the Corn. The Brood. The Shining.* What weekly allowance Tom didn't spend on comics, he spent renting fright flicks at Blockbuster Video. As an adult, Tom had seen enough real-life horror to make all of those old films seem trivial. But for some reason, as he walked through this house, he felt like there should be eerie violins playing in the background, raising in pitch until the shocking monster revealed itself.

Tom realized he was freaking himself out a little. He needed to let Roy in to help search the place.

He walked past the bedroom and froze.

Ahead, in the hallway, was a dark, huddled shape.

Someone was squatting next to the stairs.

One of the children?

"I'm Detective Tom Mankowski, Chicago Police Department," Tom said, using his authority voice, pointing his light at the figure while automatically reaching for his gun with his free hand.

There was no response.

It took Tom a second to realize why. He'd just announced himself to a pile of dirty laundry.

He blew out a breath, walked past the dirty clothes—a combination of male and female items—and slowly descended the staircase, watching his step.

The funky smell grew stronger. The stairs ended at a living room, and Tom saw a large desk with three computer monitors set up on it. Flat screens, up-to-date. All were off. But underneath the desk, in a large snarl of cords, there were blinking router and modem lights. The computer tower's cooling fan hummed softly.

Besides the desk, there was a well-worn sofa, an older model TV from the era before flatscreen, and a blanket hanging up on the wall. Tom guessed it was covering the window. He walked in the direction of the front door, and was reaching for the handle when an abrupt knock startled him.

"You in there, Tom?"

Tom let out a small, nervous laugh—stress relief—and tried to open the door to let his partner in.

The door didn't budge.

"Deadbolt on this side needs a key," Tom said, flashing his light at it. "Key's not here."

"You find anyone?"

"Not yet. You didn't tell me there were kids here."

"I didn't know. You found kids?"

"Their bedrooms. Boy and a girl. Teens or younger."

"Cissick is twenty-one. Couldn't have children that old."

"Maybe a brother and sister?" Tom asked. "Did Walter have more kids?"

"Not that I know. Dennis was an only child."

Tom's imagination took him for another unpleasant ride. Deformed siblings, hidden from the public, raised behind closed doors. Inbred and homicidal. Probably cannibals. The stuff of B-movies, but reality as well. Tom had known real life instances like that. He knew a couple named Deb and Mal who had gone through it.

"I'll go around back," Roy said. "Meet me there. And don't shoot any kids. Maybe they're the ones made the noise."

It was possible. Kids home alone, playing in the basement. Roy had called to them, and they yelled back as a joke. And now a cop had broken into the house and they were freaked out and hiding. Though Tom still could cite probable cause as his reason for entering, if an angry homeowner called Tom's boss—or worse, some reporter—it could cause a lot of trouble.

But that cry for help hadn't sounded like kids goofing around. It had sounded genuine.

Tom walked back through the living room, into the kitchen. The smell had gotten worse. Like someone was keeping a large animal in the house and not cleaning up after it. Tom went through the kitchen, into a utility room with a washer and dryer, and to the back door.

Another deadbolt without a key.

Now the only way to let Roy in was to break down a door or window. And if it was only children…

POW POW POW!

"Tommy, you there?"

Tom flinched. It was just Roy, pounding on the door.

"Door is locked here, too," Tom said.

"Shit. Team will be here in a minute. But if those are kids in there, and we break down the door…"

"I had the same thought."

"You check the basement yet? That's where the sounds came from."

"I'm doing that now."

"Well, move your ass. It's about to turn into a circus out here. You want Fox news to show up?"

"I had the same thought," Tom said again.

"Stop thinking, start searching."

Tom played the flashlight around the utility room area, saw a heavy door with a steel security bar going across it. That eliminated the *children playing around* theory; there was no way they could lock themselves into the basement and then drop the bar back down.

He went to the door, lifting up the metal barricade, setting it next to the jamb, wondering who would lock a basement in such a way, and why.

Tom reached for the knob slowly, like it would give him an electric shock when he touched it. More videos from his misspent youth clouded his thoughts. *Beyond the Door. The People Under the Stairs. Don't Look in the Basement.*

Just dumb movies. Tom was overreacting. He grabbed the knob, and just as he was ready to turn it—

POW POW POW!

—his partner banged on the door again, making Tom jump a few inches.

"Team is here."

"Hold up. I found the basement."

"What you waiting on?"

"It's spooky."

"Spooky? You serious?"

"There was a big metal bar over the door."

Roy didn't answer.

"Roy? You still there?"

"How about you get out of there, let the team go in."

A few years ago, Roy wouldn't have said that. Their ongoing bromance insisted they pick on each other's weaknesses, and in the past Roy would have mercilessly teased Tom for being a coward. But after what they'd gone through in South Carolina, and the PTSD that followed, neither man played the action hero anymore. If things got scary, they both knew to wait for back-up.

Except back-up was already here. And even if this was getting scary, what did Tom have to fear from something locked in the basement?

"I'll just do a quick check," Tom said. Though the words felt weak coming out of his mouth.

"You sure?"

"Yeah."

"Put your cell on speaker phone, so I can hear what's going on. Say the word and the cavalry will rush in."

"Got it." Tom slipped his cell phone out of his jacket, speed dialed Roy, and hit the speaker button.

"You hear me?" Tom asked.

"Loud and clear, partner. Be careful."

"Roger that."

Tom held his iPhone in the same hand as his penlight, and with his other he turned the knob and pulled. The door swung open with an obligatory, creepy creak.

The smell that wafted up was awful; garbage and sewage and rot surrounding him like a foul breeze. Tom put a sleeve over his mouth and coughed.

"You okay?" Roy, through the phone.

"Bad smell. Going down now."

"Maybe announce yourself first?"

"Good idea." He cleared his throat and yelled, "This is Detective Tom Mankowski, Chicago Police. Is anyone down there?"

Silence.

Followed by silence.

The seconds ticked by, and Tom could feel every single one of them. He searched for a light switch on the wall, didn't find one, and shined his light on the staircase.

Here goes nothing.

"I'm going down," Tom told Roy.

The stairs were wooden, old. They curved to the left, so Tom couldn't see the bottom. He went down a step, letting it take his weight, then paused to listen.

There was a tinkling sound, coming from below. Like a chain being dragged along the concrete floor.

"Hello?"

More silence.

"I'm here to help," Tom said. Though he felt as if he was the one who needed help.

Then came a response. Of sorts. A soft, high-pitched, protracted yipping sound rose up from the darkness below.

Tom shivered, his arms mottling with gooseflesh. The appropriately-sounding technical term was *horripilation*; hair standing on end from fear. Tom knew the word because it had been a question on a game show he'd just seen.

"What the hell was that?" Roy said.

"Hello?" Tom called again.

The ghostly voice got louder. It resembled a sound effect straight out of a haunted house; off-kilter and manic and insane. It might have been a sob. It might have been a giggle. Either way, it was scary enough to make Tom tug out his Glock. He held it with one hand, his flashlight and cell phone with the other, his arms outstretched like he was warding off vampires with a wooden cross and a wreath of garlic.

While Tom did not believe in the supernatural, he had total faith in the depravity of human nature. Whatever was in the basement may not have been paranormal, but it was still damn far from normal.

He went down another step, every muscle tense, finger on the trigger, his breathing matching his increased heart rate. Tom forced himself to take deeper breaths; it wasn't a good time to pass out from hyperventilation. But this was the first truly scary thing to happen to him in a while, and the fear was asserting its dominance over him.

"I'm here to help," Tom said to the darkness.

Another step. He could see the concrete floor.

"I'm a cop. I'm armed."

The acrid smell seemed to double with every stair he descended. Piss. Shit. Blood. Body odor. The stench became so thick Tom was tempted to fan his hand in front of his face, like he might waft away smoke. But he kept both arms fully extended. Gun. Light. Phone. All of them potential life-savers.

While fear of the unknown was common to most of humanity, Tom's fear was more primal. He was afraid of pain and death. The fight-or-flight response activated in his reptile brain had historical precedent in his life. Tom remembered all-too-well what it was like to be hurt. To almost be killed. Even worse was helplessly waiting to be hurt and killed. Being restrained, to be vivisected like a lab rat. No mercy. No hope. Tom knew that feeling, intimately, and it was the same feeling that crushed him now.

But this time, Tom wasn't bound. He was free to get the hell out of there. Which is what every cell in his body ached to do.

I'm safe. I have a gun. I have back-up outside. I can get away if I need to.

He tried to take another step.

His feet didn't listen.

From the darkness came another giggle.

"I'm frozen," Tom told Roy. His ears reddened in shame.

"Are you hurt?"

"No."

"In danger?"

"No."

"I feel you, brother. Been there. We can come in. Just say the word."

Tom thought of the engagement ring in his pocket. He thought about Joan. About the many happy years ahead. Was his job worth risking all of that? He was willingly marching into a bad situation to prove...

What exactly am I trying to prove?

"We're coming in," Roy told him.

"Gimme a second."

"Tom—"

"A second, Roy."

Whenever a police officer shot someone, professional counselling was mandatory. If you didn't get a pass from the district shrink, you didn't get to return to the streets. Tom had been through the process before, and he understood its purpose. The point wasn't to make the cop feel better. The point was to make sure the cop could still shoot someone if the situation warranted it. A version of getting back on the horse that threw you.

Tom knew, if he called for help, he'd never be able to get back on the horse. He either had to face the fear now, or hang up the badge.

A soft giggle wafted up the stairs.

Hanging up the badge seemed like a pretty good idea.

He was about to tell Roy to send in the cavalry when the voice in the basement spoke to him.

"Is... heeeee.... dead?"

The voice was hoarse, a high tenor. Tom couldn't tell if it was male or female.

"Holy shit that is some eerie shit," Roy said.

Tom told his partner to be quiet. "Is who dead?" he asked the person in the basement.

"Erin... eeeees..."

"Who are you?"

"Erin... eeeeeeeeeeeees."

"I'm here to help you," Tom said. Letting the urgency of the moment fill his courage reserves, Tom made it to the bottom of the stairs. Then he played the light around.

Concrete floor and walls. Posts with I-beams supporting the bare first floor joists. Various pipes snaking through the exposed ceiling. And in the corner—

A horribly stained blanket. Spread out in front of a large, wooden box.

The box had a hole cut in the front. Like a dog house.

Attached to the side of it was a heavy chain. It led into the box's opening.

"We're going to need an ambulance," Tom said. He noted the bowls on the floor, water and dry kibble. "There's someone down here chained up like an animal."

Tom tried to shine his light inside the box, but whoever was inside hid in the shadows.

"Are you hurt?" he asked, taking a step closer.

"I... hurt..."

"Can you move?"

"I... hurt... so.... much...."

Tom adjusted the angle of his approach, and caught the sight of a bare leg, mottled with filth and dried blood. It quickly retracted out of the light.

The person in the box began to giggle again.

Tom hesitated. His natural desire to help and protect wrestled with primal, deeply-ingrained terror.

There is a human being inside that box, Tom told himself. *One who needs medical attention.*

So why do I think it's going to spring out and attack me?

Yet another artifact from many an old horror film; the creature locked up in the basement, too dangerous to unleash upon an unsuspecting world.

I'm never watching another freaking horror film ever again.

"Help is coming," Tom said, less to reassure the person in the box, and more to reassure himself. "We're going to get you out of here."

"Erin—eeeeees... won't... like... that."

"Erinyes isn't here."

Tom stepped to the left, trying to get a better angle to see inside the box. His beam still failed to illuminate the corner where the person was hiding.

"Erin—eeeees sees everything."

"That's impossible," Tom said, though he did a quick sweep of the basement to make sure no one else was there.

"Erin—eeeeees sees all. Knows all. Punishes sinners."

Tom moved closer. All the clichés about fear were holding true. His mouth was dry. His legs were rubbery. His heart was hammering. He'd never gone sky diving, but he imagined this is what it felt like right before you jumped out of the plane.

"Do you sin... Tom?"

Tom flinched at hearing his own name. How did this person know it? Then he remembered announcing himself at the top of the stairs. Tom swallowed, then adjusted the grip on his Glock because his hands were sweating.

I'm overreacting. I have a gun. This poor bastard is chained up in a doghouse. I have nothing to be afraid of.

"We're trying to get in," Roy said, his voice on the phone surprising Tom and making him flinch. "This door is a mutha."

"Roger that."

Tom took another step toward the box.

"We all sin. We all need Penance."

"Come out of there," Tom said. "I'm not going to hurt you."

"I deserve to be hurt."

"No one deserves this."

"I do, Tom."

"No, you don't." Tom stepped over the dog bowls and crouched down. He was only a meter away from the box.

"I'm... wicked. I'm a sinner."

"Sins can be forgiven. God forgives sins."

"God does." There was another wicked giggle. "Erin—eeees... does not."

Tom finally got the correct angle to shine his light on the person in the box.

He wished he hadn't.

It was a naked man, but he was so emaciated the only way to tell he was male was by his patchy beard, which was bare in spots like he had mange. The chain attached to a collar around his ankle. Beneath all of the grime and dried blood, the man's skin was covered with a crisscrossing network of wounds and scars. He sat with his back to the rear wall of the box, his legs pressed to his chest, rocking back and forth. It was horrible to look at, and impossible to look away from.

"You're okay now," Tom said. It was one of the biggest lies he'd ever told. Even with fifty years of intense mental therapy and physical rehabilitation, this man would never be okay.

"What year is it?" the man asked in his scratchy, high voice.

Tom told him.

The man giggled again. The laugh morphed into a keening wail—

—and then he pounced.

Tom squeezed the Glock's trigger out of fright, but managed to pull the shot so he didn't hit the guy.

That proved to be a mistake.

The man rushed at Tom, pushing him off-balance with surprising strength. Tom fell backward, his gun skittering off in one direction, his cell phone flying off in another, as the man straddled him and locked his hands around Tom's neck.

Tom felt jagged, dirty fingernails dig into his skin. He'd managed to retain his hold on the Fenix, and aimed the flashlight into the man's eyes. The close up look at his face was horrifying; half of his nose had been cut off, and so had most of his ears, making him resemble a living skull. His mouth was a red, infected cavern of missing and rotten teeth. He snarled, his breath causing Tom to gag, and he tried to push the guy off but the thin man wouldn't budge.

But he did bite.

The few teeth he had left locked onto Tom's forearm, breaking the flesh, digging in.

As the pressure increased on Tom's neck, the lack of oxygen brought the stars out; motes of light that swam across Tom's vision. Tom changed tactics, going the streetfighter route and reaching between the man's legs.

But there was nothing to squeeze. Just scar tissue and a small nub that felt like a plastic tube.

Tom almost threw up, which would have killed him since he was presently being strangled. He managed to fight both revulsion and unconsciousness, and drew back the tactical flashlight and then struck, hard, at the man's temple. It was enough for him to release his jaw, but not his hands. He screamed, blood and spit spraying from his lips.

"ALL SHALL BE JUDGED!"

Tom hit him again. Blood flowed freely down the side of the man's face.

"ALL SHALL BE PUNISHED!"

Tom hit him once more, and there was a loud *CRACK!* like a walnut shell being crushed. The man's terrible grip relaxed, and Tom sucked in a breath as his attacker slumped onto the floor.

"Erinyes will get us all..." the man whispered, his eyelids fluttering as urine arced out of his catheter and all over Tom's legs.

That's when Roy and the rest of the team came running down the stairs, and Tom finally deemed it safe enough to throw up.

CHAPTER 23

Though she had too many people in her cell phone address book to ever possibly remember—so many that her assistant needed an entire day to send out holiday cards—Joan didn't really have any close friends. Joan's criteria for being close was crying on their shoulder, and the only person she ever did that with was Tom, and it was only after something truly horrible happened.

So Trish crying on her shoulder made Joan uncomfortable. The fact that she was uncomfortable made Joan dislike that part of herself, which made her even more uncomfortable, which is the reason she didn't have any close friends.

Trish was Joan's go-to when she came to Chicago to visit Tom. They enjoyed eating out, shopping, seeing an occasional show. They talked about their boyfriends, and sex, and stupid things in general that men did (which covered a lot of ground). But this was the first time Trish was asking Joan for emotional support. Joan could do it; she'd talked more than one A-list actor out of quitting, but it reminded her of work.

"I don't think I could find another man to love me," Trish said. She'd been saying variations of that since Joan had arrived. The poor waitress hadn't even taken their order yet, and Joan was on what felt like her second pot of mediocre coffee.

"He loves you."

"I can't have babies."

"You can adopt."

"Men want to pass on their genes. It's a macho thing."

"Did Roy tell you this?"

"No. But I know men. Technically, I'm a man."

Joan stopped short of rolling her eyes. "Fine. Slap your balls on the table and show me."

Trish laughed. "I don't have balls. But I do have testes, Joan."

"You have them *in your vagina*," Joan said, loud enough to make the surrounding tables peek their way. "Look, Trish, you were upfront with Roy about this when you started dating, right?"

"Yeah."

"And he was fine with it?"

"Yeah."

"So even if he is cheating on you—and that's still an *if*—why do you have to play the gender card here?"

Trish leaned over the table. "Do you know what it's like to not feel like you belong?"

"You know the Academy of Motion Picture Arts and Sciences? It's eighteen percent women."

"And how much of it is intersex?"

"Point made. But you asked what it feels like to not belong. I'm not African American. I'm not transgender. I don't know what these things are like. But I do know how it feels to be dismissed because I don't have a Y chromosome. And I know what it's like to be objectified rather than taken seriously. I walk past the old boy's locker room, and know they're making deals in there, and that I'm not allowed in. There's a long way to go before we see anything close to real equality. But you can't use gender as your default excuse. Once you define yourself by what you're not rather than what you are, you're playing their game."

Trish was nodding at her, but Joan wondered if she truly believed her own words. Because she could play the boy's game, better than most of the boys. Joan was pretty, and she used that. She knew that she was underestimated because of her looks, and she used that too.

"Has Tom ever cheated on you?"

"Not that I know of."

"What if he did?"

Tom? Joan couldn't really entertain the idea. He just wasn't that type.

"He's a good-looking guy. A cop. Cops have groupies, you know. Girls in their twenties, looking for daddy figures. There are hookers who work cops the same way they work johns. There are also other cops. How about Eva? Tom took her to that fundraiser formal."

"I was on a shoot and couldn't make it. Tom asked me first if it was okay. Eva is just a friend." Joan added. "And she's a lesbian."

"She's bi."

"Really?"

"Have you seen her picture?"

"No." For whatever reason, Joan pictured Eva as short and pudgy.

Trish flipped through her cell pics, and found one of Tom in a tux. The woman on his arm, in a gold dress, was stunning. Like six feet tall stunning, with boobs so big they had to be fake.

"That's Eva?"

"Yeah. Not a very good pic, though."

Joan signaled the waitress for more coffee. "Trish... what's your point here?"

"When I showed you her picture, did you, for just a split second, wonder if Tom slept with her?"

"No."

"No? She looks like Sofia Vergara, but with bigger tits."

"Well, I mean, she's tall. But Tom has told me he likes shorter women."

Joan wasn't tall. And the amount of money she spent on heels was proof she'd never really been comfortable with her stature.

"What are you? Four eleven?"

"I'm five three."

"And all guys prefer a B cup to a double D, right?"

"Okay, I get it," Joan said. "It's normal to doubt yourself, and then focus on your insecurities. But you need to stop dwelling on it and just ask Roy."

"And what if he's sleeping with someone else?"

"What if he is?"

"If Tom slept with Eva, and you learned about it, what would you do?"

Joan didn't have to think about it. "I'd leave him."

"Really?"

"Yes."

"But you love him, right?"

"Yes."

"Doesn't someone you love deserve a second chance?"

"When did this become about me and Tom, Trish? This is about you and Roy. Just man up and call him."

Trish raised a carefully made-up eyebrow. "Man up?"

"You're the one bragging about your testes."

Trish seemed confused, and then smiled her dazzling smile. She dialed Roy. Joan managed to get a coffee refill, and asked for a bagel while Trish talked. Joan purposely avoided listening, but Trish's face morphed from confident to devastated.

"What?" Joan asked, not bothering to wait until the call was over.

"Roy's at the hospital," Trish said.

"Is he okay?"

"It's Tom. He got attacked."

CHAPTER 29

Erinyes is irritated.

The house is compromised, but he can bear the loss. The place is clean. Nothing there can lead back to him.

He doesn't like losing his computer. His things.

The sinner in the basement.

But he has money. Erinyes can get a new place. A new computer. New things.

A new sinner to punish.

A new canvas to unleash Penance.

The timing is bad. There are still many things to do. He'll have to step-up his schedule. That's dangerous. These things needed to be savored, not rushed. And moving too quickly might lead to mistakes.

Erinyes checks the time. Checks his laptop. Checks the gas gauge. Does some quick calculations in his head. Takes his morning dose of Spironolactone. Then he goes in the back of the van to put on his scrubs.

Erinyes knows a lot about playing doctor.

Nurse, too.

He checks the chain on the metal barrel, making sure it's secure, and then drives to his destination, obeying the speed limit and minding traffic signals.

Being stopped by the police would be bad. Erinyes has a medical appointment to keep.

And being late is a sin.

CHAPTER 30

Joan was pretty pissed.

"You said you were taking the day off," she repeated for the third time.

Tom nodded. "I know."

"You swore to me."

Tom nodded. "I know."

"And now you're in the hospital."

"Just for observation."

Tom had gotten six stitches in the arm from the bite. Not too serious. But who knew what diseases that poor guy had? Tom's doctor decided to screen Tom for pretty much everything, from tetanus to rabies to herpes to AIDS to Rocky Mountain spotted fever.

Joan sat next to his bed, gave one of her Hollywood dramatic sighs. "Dammit, Tom."

"I'm sorry, Joan. I didn't want to wind up like this. Trust me. I had different plans."

"*We* had plans, Tom. Me and you. And *we* have rules about working when we're visiting each other. And *you* threw those rules out the window."

Tom thought about the engagement ring in his jacket.

Probably wasn't the right time.

Joan rubbed her temples—always a bad sign—and then turned to stare out the fourth floor window.

"I really don't want to be a bitch—"

"You're not. This is my fault."

"—but that's what I'm feeling like right now. Like the high-maintenance, always unhappy girlfriend. I don't like feeling this way, Tom."

"Joan, you're not high-maintenance. We have ground rules. I'm the one who broke them. You're a saint to put up with me."

"What if I did what you did?"

"What? Went to work when I was visiting?"

When Joan looked at him again, her eyes were glassy. "What if I went into some psychopath's house and got chewed on?"

Oh, man. This was worse than Tom had thought.

"Joan..."

"I'm serious. You love me, right?"

"Of course."

"What if I kept putting myself in dangerous situations? What if I chased killers? What if, every time the phone rang, you knew there was a chance it would be my boss, calling to tell you I was dead?"

What do you say to that? "I'm sorry, Joan."

Joan stood up. "Bullshit, Tom. I make movies for a living. The stuff I produce is as fake as the people I produce it with. The worst thing that can happen in my career is being attached to a flop. You? *You're in the hospital because a crazy man tried to bite your arm off.*"

Tom knew exactly what this was. It was the well-worn *what if you don't come home* argument. Every spouse of every cop came to that same conclusion, sooner or later. Tom had co-workers who'd gone through it. In many cases, it preceded a break-up, a separation, or a divorce. Tom had never dealt with it before, because he'd never been as close with anyone as he was with Joan.

The problem was, she was right. There was no way to win this argument. If a significant other couldn't accept it, the only recourse was splitting up.

They'd had a less extreme version of this fight before, and Tom had promised to quit the force. But he hadn't. And Joan hadn't pushed him. Now it was years later, and he was still on the street, chasing scumbags. Tom had thought his girlfriend's lack of complaints meant she was okay with his chosen profession.

He couldn't have been more wrong.

"I'll quit," he said.

"You've said that before."

"I mean it this time."

Joan dug out her cell phone and tossed it on the bed. "Okay. Do it. Call your Captain right now. Tell him today was your last day."

Tom stared at the phone.

"What are you waiting for?" Joan demanded.

"I can't just stop working, Joan. I'm a civil servant. I have to give proper notice. I could lose my pension."

"To hell with your pension. I make enough money."

"I can't just quit, Joan."

"Bullshit, Tom. It's not that you *can't*. It's that you *won't*. And it isn't because you're worried about your pension. It's this nutjob you're chasing. The Snipper. You can't quit until you catch him. Admit it."

Tom didn't answer. She'd nailed the truth, and any defense would be a lie.

Joan put her hands on her hips. "You aren't answering because you know I'm right."

"Okay. I'll quit as soon as I catch him."

Joan turned to the window again. Neither of them said anything for almost a minute.

"Chasing bad people... Joan, that's part of who I am. It's one of the reasons you fell in love with me. If you want me to change, I'll try. For you, I'll try. But it isn't going to happen overnight."

She continued to stare into the street below. "It's never going to happen, Tom. You said it yourself. It's who you are. But I don't think I can handle it."

"What are you saying?"

"I don't want to feel this way, Tom."

"Joan?"

She shook her head.

"Joan, please look at me."

Her shoulders shook. She was crying.

Tom reached over to the dresser next to the bed, and opened the drawer. He fished out his jacket, digging into the pocket for the ring. Then he swung his legs out of bed and walked to her. His IV stopped him before he could reach her, the needle pulling at the vein in his arm.

"Joan, I need to ask you something."

Joan turned.

Looked at his hand.

Saw the ring.

And then made the saddest face Tom had ever seen.

"No. You're not doing this right now."

"Joan..."

"This isn't fair, Tom."

Tom got down on one knee, the IV ripping free, causing a machine next to his bed to start pinging.

"Joan DeVilliers, will you—"

"Stop! Just stop!"

"Joan, I've never wanted anything more than this."

"Really?"

"Really."

Joan put her hands on her hips. "Then walk away from your job. Right now. Walk away, let someone else catch this maniac. You do that, I'll marry you."

Tom didn't say anything.

The silence was horrible.

"Well, then," said Joan. "Apparently there is something you want more than me."

She walked past him, past his outstretched hand, and toward the door.

"Marry me," he said. "Please."

She stopped in the doorway. "You know my terms. When you've made your decision, you can call me."

"Where are you going?"

"Home," she said.

Then she left.

Tom got up off his one knee. Got back into bed. Stared at the blood dribbling down his arm. Stared at the engagement ring. Tried to think of a worse moment in his life, and couldn't.

A nurse eventually came in, chiding him while replacing his IV. "This has antibiotics in it, Mr. Mankowski. You need to leave it in. We've diagnosed the man who bit you and..." His voice trailed off.

"And what?"

"There's a specialist coming in. He'll explain it."

That was a cryptic thing to say, and under normal circumstances Tom wouldn't have let the man leave until the nurse explained himself.

But at that very moment, Tom just didn't give a shit.

CHAPTER 31

It was twelve-hundred eighty-six steps to the Carpenter Clinic, and Kendal was four minutes late for her appointment. She waited outside until it became five minutes, because 5 was a better number, and then pulled at the front door.

The door was locked.

Kendal tried to push. That didn't work, either. She checked the hinges on the door, and pulling was correct, so she tried it again and the door opened.

Standing there was a tall woman wearing an expression somewhere between irritated and bored. She wore pink scrubs, white Keds, and her nametag read *Nurse Demeter*.

"Good morning, dear," the nurse said in the fake-sounding way people talked when they didn't care about you in the slightest.

She turned on her heels and Kendal followed her down a linoleum-tiled hallway, with many of the tiles torn up, as if the place were being remodeled. It took eighteen steps to get to the waiting room. The nurse took a seat behind the counter and focused all her attention on her cell phone screen. Kendal looked around the room. Empty chairs, an end table littered with magazines, a potted silk floor plant in need of dusting, an old coffee machine, the carafe empty.

Kendal counted chairs, picked the third one from the door, and went to sit down.

"Take a clipboard and completely fill out the information," the nurse said without looking at her.

Her nerves already shattered from last night, Kendal flinched at the order. She eyed the chair, and was compelled to continue toward it, touching the armrest three times before turning and taking five steps to the counter, taking the clipboard, returning five steps to the chair, and then tapping the armrest three more times before sitting.

She glanced nervously at the nurse, but the woman didn't notice Kendal's compulsive behavior. Or she simply didn't care.

Kendal pulled the provided pencil out of the clipboard spring and began to go through the health history questionnaire.

No anemia, arthritis, cataracts, diabetes, emphysema, gout, heart attack, high blood pressure, kidney stones, migraines, stroke, thyroid condition, or ulcer.

So far, so good.

No surgeries, no blood transfusions, not pregnant, no tobacco use, moderate alcohol use, drugs...

Kendal didn't see how smoking grass every once and a while was anyone's business, so she checked no.

Medication? Nothing in years. So not worth mentioning.

Family history. She had an involuntary image of her father flash into her mind, and checked off alcohol abuse.

Sexual history...

It didn't have any qualifiers for *consensual*, and Kendal didn't want to get into any of that, so she just checked *no* for everything.

Mental history...

Kendal looked over the checklist.

Bipolar disorder. Depression. Post-traumatic stress. Anxiety. Anger. Suicide. Violence.

This wasn't so much a questionnaire as a greatest hits of Kendal's psychiatric history. Yes to everything. Thank you, Father. You've given me so much.

Obsessive Compulsive Disorder.

She checked it off. Three times.

Schizophrenia.

Schizophrenia. That's the question, isn't it? Is this internal monologue I'm having with myself normal, or abnormal?

And what does any of this have to do with a goddamn mammogram?

Kendal left it blank, filled in her insurance information, and took the five steps back to Nurse Demeter, setting down the clipboard.

The nurse didn't so much as glance at her, or at the information Kendal had just filled out. She scowled at her smart phone, put it in her pocket, and said, "Follow me."

Kendal hurried to keep up as the larger woman took giant strides back down the hallway.

"You can change in here," she said, pointing to a doorway. "Take your sweater and bra off, there are gowns hanging up, behind you."

Kendal went inside the changing room and stood there, waiting for the nurse to leave.

The nurse didn't leave.

"The gowns are hanging up behind you," Nurse Demeter repeated, sterner this time.

Kendal turned and saw two drab, pale blue hospital gowns. She reached for one, took it off the hanger, and then glanced back at Nurse Demeter.

The nurse folded her arms across her ample chest. Apparently she wasn't going anywhere.

Kendal hesitantly removed her jacket, laying it on the bench, hating herself for having to touch it three times.

"Come on, now. Chop chop."

Kendal wasn't sure that *chop chop* was an appropriate thing to say to a woman when she'd come in for a breast exam, but she figured Nurse Demeter was one of those naturally rude people who was oblivious to her effect on others. And a pervert, too. Did she want to watch Kendal get undressed? She sort of looked a bit mannish. Something about her posture. Or her big hands.

If Linda were there, she would have made a joke about it. Linda was tough. A lot tougher than Kendal. She'd almost asked Linda to come with, but her roommate was still sleeping in her bed, and looked so peaceful Kendal hadn't woken her up.

Linda wouldn't be embarrassed. Or nervous. She'd take off her top, and stare the creepy nurse right in the eyes.

So that's what Kendal did.

And the creepy nurse smiled.

"Boobies that big, and you've never had a mammogram before?" Nurse Demeter asked.

Kendal felt her ears turn red, but she held the stare. "I'm only nineteen."

"Genetics don't care about age. Have you heard of Kallmann Syndrome? Some people never hit puberty, naturally. They have to take hormone supplements their entire lives. Obviously, that's not something you have to worry about. Now, the bra."

This had to be one of the most unprofessional nurses in the history of campus health care. Kendal considered walking out.

Nurse Demeter smiled that fake smile. "You seem nervous. No need to be. I've been getting regular mammograms since I was sixteen."

The nurse straightened her shoulders, jutting out her chest. "Believe it or not, I can thank my father's side of the family for these. Strange to think you got your boobies from your daddy, isn't it? Little girls worry they'll inherit traits like alcoholism." The nurse's smile faltered. "Or mental illness. Nature versus nurture. Genetic markers versus environmental factors. The parents are to blame, either way, aren't they? But it's the child who gets teased from fourth grade on, all because their pituitary gland is on a different clock than other children their age."

And then Nurse Demeter's face broke, and a tear rolled down her cheek.

Kendal's distaste for the woman was superseded by pity.

"I'll wait in the hall," the nurse said. "Put the gown on backwards, so it opens in front. I'll let the doctor know you're here."

Nurse Demeter left.

Kendal felt extremely alone.

She closed her eyes. An assortment of thoughts fought with one another for space in her head.

Strange nurse.

I'm too young to need a mammogram.

Why did she mention mental illness?

Has anything that has happened to me lately been real?

Is this even real?

How can you tell, for sure, when you're losing your mind?

Kendal's father was an alcoholic. And definitely mentally ill. But Kendal didn't know enough about his mental history. Could she have inherited his crazy? Or had she become crazy because of the things he'd done to her?

She took off her bra and reached for the closest gown.

Ultimately, it didn't matter what was real, and what wasn't. Kendal was an expert at acting like everything was okay. That was her special skill. No matter how horrible things became, she could soldier on. Dish it out, she'd take it. A pink dragon could have burst into the dressing room, and it would still be just another day in the life.

Survival, at its core, was all about rolling with the punches. Because life punches hard. Learn to accept that, or jump off a building.

Kendal left the dressing room, and found Nurse Demeter in the hallway, touching up her thick foundation in the round mirror of a compact. Any bit of frailty she'd shown before was gone.

"This way," she said, her long strides leading Kendal down the hallway. Again Kendal struggled to keep up, her right arm over her breasts, keeping the gown closed. The nurse opened a door, holding it for Kendal. She walked inside.

The room was cold, and smelled stale. At the far wall was a big machine that Kendal assumed was the mammogram.

The door slammed behind Kendal, making her jump.

"Do you give yourself regular self-exams?"

"What?" Kendal asked.

"Do you check for lumps?"

"I don't have lumps," Kendal said. "I don't even know why I'm—"

"Your blood test showed traces of cancer antigen 15-3," Nurse Demeter said.

"I haven't had a blood test in—"

"Raise both hands over your head," the nurse said.

Kendal followed orders, her hospital gown opening in front. Nurse Demeter put one hand on Kendal's right shoulder, and began to palpate her left breast.

The nurse was surprisingly gentle, given her rough demeanor. Her touch was decidedly non-sexual, but it didn't feel entirely clinical, either.

It was almost as if the nurse was trying to figure out what to do. Like she'd never examined a breast before.

This whole situation had gone from weird and uncomfortable, to warning bells ringing in Kendal's head. Maybe she was a paranoid schizophrenic with severe hallucinations, but she wanted to get the hell out of that clinic, immediately.

"Oh my God, I just realized I'm missing a major exam," Kendal began to pull away. "I really have to—"

"There's a mass."

"What?"

Nurse Demeter took Kendal's hand and placed it against the top of her breast. "There. Press. Can you feel it?"

Kendal pushed down.

And felt something. A bump of some kind.

"Isn't that my rib?"

"We need to get the doctor," the nurse said. She turned to leave and then stopped. "Wait, we should get you in the X-ray machine."

She maneuvered Kendal over to an ugly, beige piece of medical equipment at the back of the room. It looked like an oversized microscope, complete with a rectangular stage at shoulder-level. The nurse cupped Kendal's breast and slapped it up onto the platform.

"Hold still. We need to lower the camera."

Nurse Demeter kept one hand on Kendal's back, pushing her against the machine, and with the other she pressed a button at the end of a cord. The camera lowered, until it was smooshing the top of Kendal's breast.

Then it kept going.

"Ow!"

"We need to compress the tissue as thinly as possible."

Kendal watched, horrified, and the camera squeezed down until her boob was sandwiched tight.

"It hurts!"

"Hold still. I'll be right back with the doctor."

Nurse Demeter left.

Kendal began to cry. She tried to pull away, but that hurt even worse. This wasn't right. That crazy nurse had compressed her too tightly.

"Hey! Anybody!" Kendal yelled, her voice cracking. "I'm in here! Help!"

This had gone beyond mere discomfort, and Kendal didn't care about the embarrassment of some stranger coming in. She wanted out. Now.

She cast a frantic look around for the button the nurse had used to lower the top part that was squishing her, and saw it was a meter away, hanging from its cord.

Kendal reached for it.

Too far.

She tried to push against the machine, feeling like her breast was going to tear off her body, trying to get it to budge. The heavy piece of equipment didn't move a centimeter.

"SOMEBODY! HELP!"

No help came.

A minute passed. Maybe more than a minute. She'd left her phone in her jacket, back in the dressing room. An irrational fear descended upon her. Being stuck there for hours. What if the crazy nurse left? What if the doctor never came? What would happen if Kendal passed out? Would it rip her breast right off of her body?

Kendal fought against the fear. Refused to let it win.

She knew worst case scenarios. And the worst that could happen here was her being stuck for a bit. The nurse would get fired. Maybe Kendal could even sue. The concept was actually funny. She'd finally be able to leave HotSororityGirlsLive.com, even pay for college with the settlement. Sure, one tit would just hang there like a pancake, but that was a small price to pay for financial freedom.

"It's going to be okay," she told herself. "It's all going to be okay."

"No," said a male voice behind her. "It's not."

Kendal tried to turn and look, but she couldn't see whomever had come into the room.

"Doctor?"

"I'm not a doctor, Kendal."

She heard footsteps come closer.

"Help me," she begged.

No one replied.

"Who's there?"

The seconds ticked by, and Kendal began to wonder if she'd imagined the voice. Maybe this whole episode was a delusion. What made more sense? Some psycho nurse who clamped her boob in a mammogram machine and left? Or having another psychotic break?

Or maybe it was some combination of the two. Maybe Kendal was here, at the campus clinic, and she'd somehow done this to herself. Some kind of *Beautiful Mind/Fight Club* insanity where Kendal had put herself in this situation. Why wasn't anyone else here? Why was that silk plant in the waiting room so dusty?

Kendal remembered an app she and Linda had joked about, months before. It got you out of bad dates by autodialing your number, so you could say you were having an emergency. Had Kendal autodialed the sorority house yesterday, and set up this fake doctor's appointment with herself?

Maybe no one had been in her room last night. Or on her computer. Or her Kindle. Maybe her stalker was really her own broken mind, still crazy after all these years thanks to what her father did…

"It's strange," the male voice said, making her jump. "But this is the first time I've seen you naked."

Kendal again tried to turn around. She couldn't see anything.

"Who are you?"

"Don't be coy, Kendal. You know who I am."

"I don't."

"Do you always forget the boys you've had in your room? I actually came out of the closet for you."

Kendal began to sob. Hallucination or not, this was scaring the shit out of her.

"What... what do you want?"

"We both want the same thing. You're a sinner. You need Penance. Erinyes is here to give it to you."

"I don't know what you're talking about."

There was no reply.

"Hello?"

No answer.

"Hello!"

"We're still here," the man said, his mouth right next to Kendal's ear. "And we're just getting started."

Kendal felt something cold and wet press against her mouth. Something that burned her nostrils. Instinct took over, training from a self-defense class taken years ago.

Lift your foot.

Bring your heel down on the attacker's instep.

The man howled, pulling the chemical rag away from Kendal's mouth, and she began to scream for all she was worth.

CHAPTER 32

"We won't know for certain until we get your blood culture results back, but we're treating you for necrotizing fasciitis," said the specialist doctor standing next to Tom's bed. He looked like a casting company's stereotype; white, forties, balding, glasses, lab coat. His nametag read *Dr. Jones.*

"So give me a shot and let me leave."

Joan hadn't picked up her cell. Tom even tried calling Trish, thinking she might have gone there, but Trish didn't pick up either. And Roy, still at the perp's house collecting evidence, was no help in tracking down his girlfriend.

"Mr. Mankowski, I'm not sure you appreciate the seriousness of this condition. I've only seen one case of this in my career, and it was from the individual who bit you. The hospital has just alerted the CDC."

"You called the Center for Disease Control because some guy chewed on my arm?"

"We called the CDC because an outbreak of necrotizing fasciitis would be very serious indeed. It's also known as the flesh-eating bacteria."

"That does sound serious," Tom said.

"It is serious. We need to keep you under observation and on intravenous antibiotics. I also strongly recommend surgery to remove the tissue around your wound. The bacteria spreads very quickly."

"How quickly?"

"Immediately."

"The man who attacked me—"

"I'm frankly surprised that he even had the strength to attack you. Streptococcus is no doubt only one of the diseases he's carrying. The extent of his injuries is... extraordinary. Malnourished. Repeatedly beaten. He had spiders living in his hair. And some of his scars look to be years old. His captor had apparently been giving him antibiotics to keep him alive."

"Is he awake?"

"I got out of surgery half an hour ago. The amount of infected tissue I had to remove... it was extensive."

"Can I talk to him?"

"No, you cannot. What you can do is sign the consent form. Unless you'd like to risk losing your arm."

Tom knew a pain-in-the-ass ex-cop who'd lost his hand. He had no idea if the man's personality had deteriorated with the loss of the limb, or if he'd always been that way, but Tom didn't want to risk becoming that irritating. "I'd prefer to keep the arm. Will I just get a local? I don't want to be put under."

In case Joan called back.

"We can begin with a local. But I can't predict what kind of damage I'm going to find until I start digging in there with a scalpel."

The doctor seemed excited by the idea, which was more than a little disturbing. He left, a nurse came in with papers, and Tom tried Joan and Trish again. No luck. But he did manage to get Roy.

"Tommy, you ain't gonna believe what we found in the garage. We got barrels of bodies. *Barrels.* Son of a bitch pickled them like... like pickles. Got a hazmat team counting heads. Eight so far. You watching the news?"

"Roy, do you know where Trish is? I'm trying to find Joan."

"I haven't talked to her since this morning. You should see some of the freaky shit we've found here, Tommy. You remember that crazy whip from *The Passion of the Christ*? The one with all the spikes on the ends? This son of a bitch has got one. Also got a whole pharmacy here. Drugs up the ass. We could put him away for life just for illegal steroids. And I found this giant key ring of master keys. They'll open almost any lock. So now we know how he's getting into the vic's homes."

"Roy, listen to me. I need you to call Trish to try to find Joan. Trish thinks you're cheating on her, so they may be together."

"Trish thinks what? Say that again, Tom."

"Your woman found a credit card bill from the Sheraton. Eight hundred bucks."

"Man, I can't afford the Sheraton. Eight hundred bucks! Wait, Tom. That computer guy, Firoz, wants to talk to you. Just a sec."

"Roy..."

"Hello? Detective Mankowski? It's Detective Firoz Nafisi. The suspect's computer, as expected, is password protected. Before I try a blunt force attack, I was wondering if you had any ideas. Detective Lewis mentioned there was something about Greek demons that may be relevant to the case."

Greek demons? "I don't know what Roy is... wait. Roy was talking about the Furies. Greek deities of vengeance. Wikipedia it."

"I'll try. Thank you."

"Can you put Roy back on?"

Firoz didn't reply.

"Hello? You there?"

Apparently he wasn't. Firoz had hung up.

Tom was tempted to call Joan again, resisted, and located the remote control attached to the bed rail. He switched on the local news and saw the stack of barrels Roy had mentioned.

Jesus. They'd found a real bad one this time.

Found. Not caught. He was still on the loose.

Tom turned off the TV and considered Joan's words.

You can't quit until you catch him. Admit it.

Was she right? Tom thought he was willing to walk away from The Job for her. But watching the news, he couldn't deny his overwhelming feeling of...

Of what?

Responsibility? Civic duty? Joan teased Tom about being genetically wired for life, liberty, and the pursuit of happiness. Could that joke be true? Did Tom's need for justice and drive to make the world a better place outweigh his love for Joan?

Fighting monsters was a worthy cause. But it took a toll. Tom's former boss, a retired Lieutenant named Jacqueline Daniels, had suffered greatly by dedicating her life to chasing bad guys. Tom didn't believe in good and evil; those were absolutes meant to be debated in philosophy class, not applied to imperfect human beings. But Jack had done a lot of good in the world, and stopped a lot of bad, and she ranked up there with the unhappiest people Tom knew.

Was that Tom's future? Serve the greater good, but be miserable?

He glanced at the doorway to his room, and his navel-gazing was quickly replaced by curiosity.

The man who had bitten Tom in the basement. What did he know?

Tom swung his legs out of bed, gripped his portable IV stand, and wheeled it over to the tiny closet. He found his pants, fished out his badge, and then padded out into the hallway. The tile was cool under his bare feet, and he only wore boxer-briefs under his hospital gown, but he was strangely warm. Excitement from questioning a witness and possibly getting some answers? Or necrotizing fasciitis coursing through his bloodstream?

"You shouldn't be out of bed, Mr. Mankowski."

Tom turned, saw the male nurse who'd been in his room earlier. "Detective Mankowski," Tom said, flipping open his badge case. "Dr. Jones gave me permission to question the man brought in with me."

"Dr. Jones didn't tell me about—"

"Have you seen the news?" Tom interrupted. "They pulled a dozen bodies out of that house. We need to find the killer."

The nurse seemed to wrestle with it, then said, "He's in room 703, to the right."

Tom nodded. Thirty seconds later, he was staring at a mummy. The man who'd bitten him was swathed in so many bandages, he looked like he'd come straight from a Hammer film. Tom couldn't tell if his eyes were closed or not, so he moved closer.

"Are you awake?"

The man's eyelids fluttered. His voice was weak. "Where... am I?"

"The hospital. You're safe now. What's your name?"

"Wal... ter."

So this was Walter Cissick. And being locked up in his basement for years explained why he'd never renewed his driver's license.

"Who did this to you, Walter?"

Walter said something under his breath. Tom leaned closer.

"Can you repeat that?"

"Era... knees..."

"Erinyes," Tom repeated, recognizing the Greek term. "But what's his name?"

Walter didn't answer.

"Where is your son, Walter? Where's Dennis?"

"Erinyes..."

"Did Erinyes take Dennis?"

"Penance. Sinners... must be... punished..."

Tom recalled the bedroom he'd crawled into. "Do you have a daughter, Walter? Or some other girl living with you?"

"Crown..."

"Crown?"

"Crown... of spiders..."

Tom didn't seem to be getting anywhere. Either Walter was still drugged from surgery, or just flat out insane from years of captivity and abuse.

"Walter, I need you to tell me who did this to you. Do you know where he is?"

"Ken... dal."

"What about Kendal, Walter? Has the killer targeted another woman named Kendal? Another webcam model?"

"Detective Mankowski."

Tom turned and saw Dr. Jones in the doorway. Standing behind him, arms folded across his chest and looking smug, was the nurse.

"I'm trying to save lives here, Doc."

"So am I. Yours. Get back into bed. And while you're in bed, do a Google search for *Fournier gangrene* and decide if you're going to start listening to me or not."

Tom allowed himself to be led back to his room. After getting back into bed, he accessed the Internet on his smart phone.

Some things you just can't unsee.

He decided to follow the doctor's orders. Then he wiped some sweat off his brow, leaving the back of his hand on his forehead to check for a fever.

As usual, it was impossible to tell if you had a high temperature when your hand was the same temperature as the rest of your body.

Tom's phone rang, and he was in such a hurry to answer it he dropped it on the bed and got it lost in the flimsy blanket. Once he found it, Tom saw it was Roy, not Joan.

"Hey, Roy. That Iraqi computer geek hung up on me."

"Hello, Detective Mankowski. It's the computer geek. And I'm Iranian-American, not Iraqi. I'm calling because I was able to access the computer at the crime scene. You were right about Wikipedia. The password was *Demeter*, another name for one of the Greek goddesses associated with the furies."

"Sorry about the—"

"Not being able to tell the difference between someone with Iraqi heritage, and someone with Iranian heritage? I've lived in this country for all of my adult life, Detective. Your ignorance is commonplace. The amount of prejudice I've encountered, especially since 9/11, is—"

"I was sorry about the geek comment," Tom interrupted.

"Oh. Well, I don't mind being called a computer geek. I am a computer geek. It's not as if you called me a computer nerd."

"I don't remember the difference."

"Well, there's a big difference. Like the difference between someone from Iraq, and someone from—"

"Did you find something on the computer, Firoz?"

"Ah, yes. I found something. And nothing. The nothing was because he was using a Tor browser."

"I don't know what that is." Tom wiped more sweat from his brow.

"Tor is short for *The Onion Router*. It's a way to surf the Internet anonymously. It conceals a user's location by using a peer network of several thousand relays. So the NSA, or anyone else, can't track you. It also keeps no record of your browsing history, so if you're on the dark web—"

"The dark web?"

"The darknet, Detective. It uses the public Internet, but isn't searchable with normal engines. Instead of dot com or dot net, they are dot onion. You've heard of Silk Road?"

That Tom knew. "It was an Internet black market. You could buy illegal goods and services. The Feds shut it down."

"The black market never goes away. Where there is a demand, someone will find a way to supply it. So, because of Tor, I don't have our suspect's browsing history, and I can't think of any way to track him down. He has administration rights for the Fight the Feeling domain, but that is also password protected. I haven't been able to figure it out yet."

"Well, at least you tried. Can you put Roy on?"

"Roy is in the garage. I didn't call you to talk about what I didn't find, Detective. I called to tell you what I did find."

"Okay," Tom said, wondering why Firoz didn't start with that info.

"His computer is hooked up to twelve security cameras throughout the house. It's a very sophisticated, high-tech set-up. The cameras are miniature, and wireless."

"Do they record?" Tom asked, one eye on the doorway as the nurse came in.

"Yes. The files are on an encrypted hard drive, but I'm going to try a cold boot attack and—"

"I'm being operated on in a minute, Firoz. Can you get to the point?"

"The point, Detective Mankowski, is that the suspect no doubt has access to these cameras on his phone or laptop. Which means he knows we're here. He could even be watching us, right now."

CHAPTER 33

Erinyes is furious.

He tries to ignore the cops trampling through his house like a herd of elephants, because watching them paw through his things, his house, his life, is maddening. He doesn't want to look, but can't help himself, and with every glance his blood pressure escalates. One of the smarter ones even accessed his computer. It's the ultimate invasion of privacy, being stripped bare and exposed and helpless before a bunch of godless strangers.

They think I'm evil.

I'm no more evil than the police are. Or judges. Or priests.

I punish bad people. And by doing so, I save them.

I'm not a criminal.

I'm a god of vengeance.

Why don't they see?

Out of everyone in the world, I am the only true innocent.

Erinyes rubs his foot, wondering if any bones are broken from Kendal's stomping. He'd forced himself to limp away from her, because his rage hit a fever pitch and became so overpowering he likely would have killed her right there.

That would be sloppy. And wasteful.

She is a Kendal. Kendals deserve special attention.

Erinyes closes his eyes, centers himself.

It's just hormones. Making me act emotional.

Focus.

Do what you were put here to do.

The house being compromised doesn't affect plans very much. Erinyes has everything he needs in the van. He'd assumed the tricky part would be getting Kendal from the clinic to the vehicle, but was able to work out the logistics rather easily. Instead, the tricky part turned out to be properly subduing the sinner. He hadn't been fast enough with the ether mask.

Lesson learned. Erinyes switches on the stun gun, then pats his lab coat pocket to make sure the ball gag is there; Kendal's screams are becoming annoying.

"Doctor?"

Erinyes turns. Sees a man in a tan security uniform standing at the end of the hallway. Campus police.

"This building is closed for remodeling," he says.

Erinyes twists slightly, hiding the stun gun with his body. "I'm in the middle of a mammogram with a patient."

"Why is she screaming like that?"

Erinyes considers his options. The man is large, but fat. Probably not in shape. Probably armed. His left hand is empty, his right hand obscured by his belly.

Erinyes begins to walk toward the security guard, letting the irritation he feels show on his face. "Look, I don't have time for this. My patient is obviously in pain, and I need to see to her."

The cop has something in his hand, and raises it.

A gun?

No. A walkie-talkie.

"Got a guy in here, says he's a doctor, and a woman screaming. Request back-up."

Erinyes quickens his pace. He's only a few steps away. "I have my ID right here," he says, getting ready to lash out with the stun gun.

"We're right around the corner," squawks the radio.

Then Kendal screams, "Is someone there?! Help me!"

And the rent-a-cop draws his gun. Erinyes shouts, "She's in danger! Help her!"

The cop looks to Erinyes, then down the hallway, then back to Erinyes. "Stay here!" he orders, then jogs toward Kendal.

Erinyes doesn't stay there. He heads the other direction, into the waiting room, grabbing his bag and tugging on a trench coat. He's two steps outside the clinic before more security arrives.

"What's going on?" he says as they pass him by.

Close call.

When he visits Kendal again, he's going to have to be more careful.

More careful, and better armed.

CHAPTER 34

"Here's to not needing men," Joan said, raising her shot glass.

Trish clinked, then the women downed the whiskey. Joan savored the alcohol bite. It wasn't on par with the 23 year old Pappy Van Winkle she kept at her home in LA, but for a restaurant pub chain that had pictures of its food on its menu, it was surprisingly smooth.

The fact that it was her third in sixty minutes may have also contributed to her appreciation of the taste.

"So… was it nice?" Trish asked, picking at her cocktail napkin.

"What?"

"The ring."

"Really? We're supposed to be all *girls-night-out-and-to hell-with-the-boys*, and you're asking me about the ring?"

Trish shrugged. "I've never had a guy propose before."

"Proposals are bullshit. Marriage is bullshit. Pair bonding is bullshit. Do you know how many species are actually monogamous?"

"How many?"

"None," Joan said. "All animals cheat."

"Swans are monogamous," Trish said.

"They aren't. Ethologists just haven't caught them cheating yet."

Trish frowned. "I heard they were monogamous."

Joan had been hoping for some female commiseration and some good-natured mutual man-bashing. Instead. Trish seemed really sad.

"Aren't you angry?" Joan asked.

"Not really. I think I was expecting it."

"Why? You're gorgeous."

"For a woman with testes?"

"For a person," Joan said.

"What if Tom cheated on you?"

"He is. With his job. He'd rather spend time at work than with me."

"Isn't his job important?"

"Every job is an important job," Joan said. "I make movies that make millions of people happy. You help people get tax refunds."

"Most of my clients are too wealthy to get refunds," Trish said. "And I hate dealing with them. A bunch of rich, entitled, greedy little bastards."

"Even if you loved your job, would you put it first in your life, over your relationship?"

"What if we were surgeons?" Trish asked. "And we were on call 24/7 in case some terrible accident occurred?"

"That's different," Joan said. "Doctors save lives."

"So do Roy and Tom."

Joan raised her hand for the bartender—who was cute but too young—for two more shots of Blanton's.

"Trish… what I'm saying is that if our guys choose something, or someone, else over us, it's not worth stressing over."

"So you're not stressing?"

"I've dealt with A-listers threatening to walk off a two hundred million dollar picture five weeks into shooting because their hairdresser got their bangs wrong. I am not stressing this."

"He just proposed, Joan."

"I'm not looking for a husband. I'm looking for a guy who cares about me. And if Tom would rather chase after scumbags than spend time with me… well, maybe I would be better off with someone else."

Joan didn't like how it felt saying that out loud. And Trish, apparently, wasn't listening, because she was checking her cell phone.

"Roy still hasn't called," Trish said.

"Why are you even keeping your phone on? I turned mine off."

"What if it's an emergency?"

"Like this morning? I go running to the hospital, scared out of my mind, because some asshole gave Tom a little bite on the arm?"

"You are Tom's ICE, right?"

"Ice?"

"His *In Case of Emergency* contact. The person that someone else would call if anything happened to him."

"I think so." Joan wasn't sure.

"Then you should keep your phone on."

"So I can check it every five minutes to see if he called? No thanks." Joan waved for the bartender again.

"I bet he called."

"So what if he did?"

"I'm just saying it would be nice to have a man who called repeatedly to apologize when he screwed up."

"Roy doesn't call you when he screws up?"

"He used to. Until now."

"Did you even tell him you're upset?"

"No."

Joan had to willfully stop her own eye roll. "Trish, how can you expect him to apologize if he doesn't even know you're mad?"

"I'm not expecting an apology. I'm just expecting… I dunno… a text saying he loves me? A message saying he wants a booty call? But why would he, when he's getting his ass at the Hilton."

The bartender brought two more whiskeys, and winked at Trish.

He didn't even glance at Joan.

"Did you see that?" Joan just said. "Flirting with you. Didn't even look at me."

"That peach-fuzz bartender?" Trish snorted. "I'd break that kid in half."

They raised their glasses and shot again.

"So how was it?" Trish asked.

"The bourbon?"

"The ring."

Joan could picture it. White gold. Yellow diamond.

"It was perfect," she said. "Completely my style."

"Check your phone. See if he called."

Joan shook her head. "No way. I played the *wait-by-the-phone game* when I was in high school, hoping my crush would ask me to prom."

"Did you go to prom?"

"No. Asshole never called. But I'm friends with him on Facebook now. Works at a submarine sandwich shop, has an ugly wife, posts four times a day about his Yorkie. I dodged a bullet there."

"Is he happy?"

Joan frowned. "Yes."

"Is that the bullet you're trying to dodge? Happiness?"

Wow. That was sure on the nose.

"Way to kill my buzz, Trish."

Trish reached out, put her hands on Joan's. "I want my man to call me so I can be sure he loves me. You seem like you don't want yours to call you so you can prove... what are you trying to prove? That you don't need anyone?"

"I don't need anyone."

"Then why do you need Tom to give up his job for you?"

Joan didn't have an immediate response to that. And the liquor wasn't helping.

"Turn on your phone," Trish said. "See if he called."

"Because that will show he loves me?"

"Yes."

Joan shook her head.

"I bet he called you at least ten times."

"No way."

"Let's bet. If Tom called you ten times or more, you call him back."

"And if he didn't?"

"Then we'll both turn off our phones for the rest of the night."

"Deal."

They shook, and Joan whipped out her cell. As she powered it on, her stomach began to churn.

What am I nervous about? That Tom called more than ten times, and she'd have to talk to him? Or that he didn't?

"Ten missed calls," Joan said, staring at her screen.

Trish grinned. "See?"

"Nine are from Tom. One is my assistant."

Both of them were quiet for a beat.

"Nine is still a lot," Trish said.

It was a lot. But for whatever arbitrary reason, it didn't seem like it was enough.

"Bet's a bet. Phones off."

Joan and Trish powered off their cells, and then Joan tried to get the bartender's attention again. She had a strong feeling they were going to be there for a while.

CHAPTER 35

"Air aneeds?" Officer Ledesma said. He couldn't have been much older than Kendal, and he didn't have that world-weary dullness to his eyes that most cops had. Kendal sat across from him at his desk.

"That's what it sounded like he said. *Air aneeds* or *air aneece*."

He typed something into his computer.

"And you never saw his face?"

Kendal sniffled. Her boob still hurt, and she was still extremely upset. Over an hour had passed since the campus cop had saved her, but Kendal's heart rate was still double.

"I only saw the woman. Nurse Demeter."

Kendal didn't want to cry again. She'd cried in the squad car on the way to the police station. She'd cried in the Evanston PD lobby, waiting for a detective to speak to her. And she was about to cry in front of the detective, who was being really nice to her.

He offered her the tissue box, again, and Kendal took one and dabbed her eyes.

"Would you like to talk with a sexual assault counsellor?" he asked.

"I wasn't raped."

"You were sexually assaulted, Miss Smith."

"I just want to finish this up and go..."

Go where? She felt as if she were stalked everywhere she went. And how many people were actually after her?

Or was this all just in her head?

Kendal sobbed. The nice policeman waited patiently until she resumed self-control.

"Do you have any enemies?" he asked, gently. "Or has anyone been harassing you?"

Kendal wasn't sure what to say. That it might be her own brain, playing tricks? That maybe she clamped her own breast down in that horrible machine? That her cyberstalker, and the man in her closet, and the nurse and doctor could all be hallucinations?

"I think someone's after me," she said, breaking down once more.

Then she told the cop almost everything.

. . .

"Where would you like me to drop you off?" Detective Ledesma asked.

Kendal yawned. It wasn't nighttime yet, but she was exhausted. She'd been at the police station for five hours. Detective Ledesma had bought her pizza while she worked with an artist to create a picture of Nurse Demeter. She'd gone through everything that had happened to her in the last few days, and even mentioned some of the traumas of her past; stopping short of revealing her childhood schizophrenia diagnosis, and the fact that her sorority was filled with cameras that broadcast subscription webcam on the Internet.

But she told him the rest. She even told him about her OCD.

It felt good to talk about everything, and Kendal had never felt safer in her life. Something about Detective Ledesma—whose first name, she found out, was Jacob—had a calming effect on her. She didn't want to leave his squad car.

"I don't know," she said. The thought of going back to the house scared her. The thought of going anywhere scared her. "I just want to stay here."

"Fine by me." Jacob took his hands off the steering wheel and laced them behind his head. "We can park here forever."

"I like that idea. But what if we need to go to the bathroom?"

"No problem. We can always make a trucker bomb."

"What's a trucker bomb?"

"We pee in a plastic bottle, then throw it onto the street."

Kendal giggled. "That's gross. Cops shouldn't talk like that."

"Cops do it all the time. On a long stakeout. No toilet anywhere. Just drank that half gallon bottle of Gatorade. Just fill it back up, chuck it out the window."

"You don't really."

"Of course not. The men and women of the Evanston Police Department would never litter. We're responsible and law-abiding. So every trucker bomb gets put in the recycle bin."

They shared a laugh.

"So have you ever caught a murderer?"

"No. Population eighty thousand, only one murder in the last two years."

"How about a rapist?"

"Dozens."

"Stalkers?"

"I just delivered a restraining order last week. A man threatened to slap his wife, and she went to a judge. I had to physically remove him from his residence."

Kendal's eyes widened. "Was it dangerous?"

"Very. The man was eighty-eight years old. I was worried he was going to die on the way to the new retirement home."

They laughed again. "I think I figured out where I want to go," Kendal said. "College library."

Kendal had a research paper due in Biology and needed Internet access, but was still skittish about turning on her computer back at home.

"Done."

He started the car, and they enjoyed a pleasant, albeit silent, five minute trip back to campus. Kendal opened the door but didn't get out.

"It's okay," Jacob said. "I'll be right out here."

That wasn't the reason Kendal hesitated. She was actually trying to figure out how many steps there were, from this curb, to the library front door.

"You have my number in your phone, right?"

"Yeah."

"I'm not going anywhere, Kendal. Did you want me to come inside with you?"

Kendal did some quick math in her head and decided she could start her count at 1167. "No. I'm good. Thanks, Detective Ledesma."

Kendal left the car and didn't look back. Sixty-seven steps later, Kendal logged into Computer #17 using her Student ID as User 11892.

Twenty minutes into taking notes, her screen froze. After several seconds of ineffective tapping on the mouse and keyboard, she pushed her chair back and began to feel under the desk for an off switch to reboot.

Then a pop-up appeared onscreen.

Library Help Desk: What seems to be the issue?

Kendal tried the keyboard.

User 11892: Screen froze. Seems fine now.

Library Help Desk: Were you trying to turn off the computer?

User 11892: No. I didn't touch anything.

Library Help Desk: It is against Library Policy to manually turn off the computers.

Whatever, Kendal thought. She hit the esc button, but the chat box remained.

How do I get back to surfing the net?

It is against Library Policy to browse for online pornography.

Seriously? WTF?

I wasn't looking at porn.

I know. I'm watching you.

Kendal immediately looked around her. Her eyes found the Help Desk. Several librarians were at their computers, but no one was looking Kendal's way.

You were thinking about porn, weren't you, you bad girl?

This was getting freaky. Kendal removed her student ID from the card slot.

The screen remained.

You think squeezing your tit was the only punishment you'd get? You're going to suffer, Kendal. Suffer for your sins.

Kendal turned away from the computer.

Froze.

How many steps to the exit? Was it sixteen or seventeen?

Behind her, the computer began to broadcast a voice.

Kendal's voice.

"I just got a really weird phone call."

"Like obscene weird?" It was Linda's voice. *"Some guy yanking his crank and moaning? You lucky slut! I never get calls like that."*

"I mean like someone being beaten."

"That's even kinkier."

Kendal glanced over her shoulder, and saw the monitor screen showing the webcam video of her and Linda in the kitchen, from yesterday.

"Really beaten. Screaming for their lives beaten."

"Was it some kind of joke?"

"If it was, it wasn't funny."

"Who was it from?"

"It said caller unknown."

Then the image switched to the most violent thing Kendal had ever seen. Some guy with a chain around his ankle, getting beaten bloody with a whip as he screamed.

Kendal made it to the staircase in fourteen steps, then had to take two extra, plus touch the railing three times, before she could take the twenty-five steps back to the lobby.

Detective Ledesma was still parked in the loading zone, ten steps away. Kendal hurried to his car, then knocked on the window three times.

He rolled it halfway down.

"Done so soon?"

"Yes."

What else could she say? Kendal knew that if she dragged him upstairs to show him the computer screen, it would be gone by the time she got there.

If it was ever there at all.

"So where to?"

She considered the question. "Back to my sorority."

If her stalker was real, and could follow her anywhere, Kendal wanted to be in a place with eighteen cameras that broadcast live 24/7.

Being at that house was like living in a fishbowl, eyes on all sides. And that seemed like the safest place to be.

They drove in silence, and arrived at the house far too soon. When they pulled up, Kendal made no move to get out of the car.

"I used to work patrol in this area," Detective Ledesma said. "I know the Epsilon Epsilon Delta house."

"You do?"

Was he hinting that he knew about the webcams?

"Solid doors, front and back. Deadbolts. You've even got security windows. University rules. They want to keep their students safe."

"Locks can be picked," Kendal said.

"Sure. But I'll be out here all night, making sure everything is okay."

"How about when you leave?"

He smiled kindly. "When I leave, someone will replace me."

She didn't answer.

"Where is your bedroom?"

"Right there," Kendal pointed to one of the windows facing the street.

"Do you have a lock?"

"One of those flimsy, privacy locks with the slit you can turn with your fingernail."

"I've got something better than that. Step into my office."

Officer Ledesma got out of the car. Curious, Kendal followed him to his trunk. He popped it open, and there was a small cardboard box. He pulled out a small, blue bag, about the size of a cell phone. He opened it up and took out an odd-looking device made of metal and orange plastic.

"This is called an Addalock. Travelers use them in hotel rooms. You place the metal strip inside the door over the latch, close it, then put this orange piece in the slot. Now the door won't open, even if the knob is turned or the lock is picked."

He handed it to Kendal.

"It's so small."

"It works. Trust me. Once it's on, the door won't open unless you remove the whole frame."

She gripped the Addalock, tight. "Thanks."

"You've got my cell number. If anything happens, call me. Or just open your blinds and wave at me through the window. I'll be out here all night, drinking coffee and making trucker bombs."

Kendal nodded, gave the detective a quick hug, and then ran into the house, clutching the Addalock like a talisman.

CHAPTER 36

For the first time in as long as he can remember, Walter Cissick feels no pain.

He wonders if he has finally suffered enough for his sins. If his Penance is over.

And then he begins to laugh. He laughs so hard and so loud that a nurse comes in to sedate him.

Walter closes his eyes, blissful in the utter majesty of atonement.

CHAPTER 37

Tom opened his eyes, his brain still foggy from his drug-assisted nap. He checked the clock. A little past eight pm.

They hadn't put him under for surgery, but whatever they'd given him was enough for him to lose all memory of the last few hours. Not a bad thing, either. The last thing he remembered was Dr. Jones digging a scalpel into his stitches, which was an ugly, and gross, thing to see no matter who it was happening to.

He was thirsty, and reached for the water cup next to his bed. His cell was also there. He'd left it on, and the battery was dead. Tom plugged in his charger, then pressed the call button on his bed. His male nurse had been replaced by an older, Asian woman.

"Do we know how my surgery went?"

"The doctor is really the best person to discuss that with you."

"Is the doctor here?"

"He left."

"So can you tell me anything?"

"I'll see if I can find anything out. Is there anything else?"

"I think I missed dinner. Anything to eat?"

"Do you have any dietary considerations?"

"I'd prefer not to eat something lousy."

She smiled. "I'll see what I can do."

"Thanks."

Tom checked his phone. It had a 2% charge.

Joan hadn't called. Neither had Roy.

He thought about calling Joan one more time. If he did it from the land line, maybe she wouldn't know it was him and she'd finally pick up. And then...

And then, what?

If you had to fool your girlfriend into talking to you, the relationship was probably in trouble.

Instead of calling Joan, he went on Google and looked up the Tor thing Firoz had told him about, the browser that let you surf the deep web. He found out there was an onion browser for iPhones, downloaded it, and soon was poking around the darknet anonymously.

After quickly figuring out how to navigate, he went to a site called Ahmia.fi, a hidden-service search engine listing thousands of websites with names like *fzqnrlcvhkbgwdx5.onion*. Tom began to click on URLs.

Apparently, with Bitcoin, you could purchase practically anything, including all kinds of drugs (illegal and prescription), escorts, firearms, suppressors, cigarettes, electronics, passports, stolen credit card numbers, gift cards, counterfeit currency, and more drugs. You could hire assassins, hackers, and cyber bullies to target your enemies with online harassment or homemade computer viruses. There were a plethora of sites about mining bitcoins, most of them labelled *scam* by whoever did the labels on Ahmia.

Some sites were amateurish, looking like they were created with Dreamweaver back in '99. Tom couldn't imagine anyone, even the stupidest person on the planet, thinking they could get a real rocket launcher for the equivalent of four hundred dollars. But other sites looked like modern online retailers. Put some banana kush cannabis in your virtual shopping cart for only 0.0052 Bitcoin a gram. Add-on a hit of blotter acid for 0.0025.

Tom found it fascinating. Until it got weird.

While a firm believer in privacy and freedom, Tom grew increasingly uncomfortable surfing the hidden web. It was doubtful that the website selling leg-amputated Thai children—guaranteed to never run away—was legitimate. But the very idea of it was awful. And Tom knew that hate speech occurred on the Internet, but on darknet it went to a whole new level, with actual calls to violence. There were live webcams for things that were definitely illegal and non-consensual. There were pictures that made Fournier gangrene appear downright appealing.

On hunch, he searched for "*Fight the Feeling*". As he suspected, the web owner had an onion site that mirrored the public one.

Though *mirror* probably wasn't the right word. Rather than sex offenders trying to help one another avoid temptation, this forum had them trading tips on how not to get caught, tricks on how to seduce minors, advice on how much Rohypnol was needed to knock out a forty pound child.

According to the bot, the moderator was online.

There was a chat box. Tom turned his phone sideways so the onscreen keyboard was larger, then pecked out:

I'm looking for Erinyes.
Who's looking? came a quick reply.

Tom from Chicago.

There was no answer. Then, in a flurry of typing:

You pigs have sure done a number on my house.

He was chatting with The Snipper. Tom glanced at the phone, wondering if he could call Firoz to trace the...

Oh. Right. That was the point of darknet. No one could trace anyone.

Not me. Tom typed. **I'm nursing my wounds. Your friend in the basement bit me.**

You should see a doctor about that, Tom. That might get infected.

Thank you for your concern. He must have been a real bad boy for you to keep him locked up for years.

He was a very, very bad boy.

Did you enjoy keeping him chained up like a dog?

I have my job. You have yours. Do you enjoy your job, Tom?

I don't like the violence.

Neither do I. But it has to be done.

Why does it have to be done?

I punish sinners. I give them Penance.

Aren't you a sinner, too? We're chatting on a site dedicated to helping child rapists.

I only help them by making them pure.

Castrating them is making them pure?

Of course it is. I'm saving their souls. And saving future victims.

How about the webcam models? How did you save Kendal Hefferton?

Women are different than men. You know this. Men can't help themselves. They're led around by their cocks. Remove the cock, remove the sin.

And women?

I can't cut off something they don't have. Their sins run deep inside. There is no way to remove it.

So you torture them to death?

I cleanse them, Tom. I make them pure. Some need more cleansing than others.

Webcam models named Kendal?

Kendals are the worst sinners of all.

Why is that? Was your mother named Kendal?

No.

Tom took a shot. **Was your mother named Lilyana?**

I'll tell you about my mother sometime.

What's wrong with now?

I'm busy now. I've got to cleanse my next sinner.

That was exactly what Tom didn't want to happen. **This chatting thing is so impersonal. How about we meet?**

We will.

Now?

We'll meet. But it won't be how you imagine it.

So you've picked out the next Kendal?

Yes.

And you're killing her tonight?

Cleansing isn't killing, Tom. Your body has an expiration date. Your soul is eternal. If Kendal suffers for her sins while she's alive, she'll be saved in the afterlife.

Tom wracked his brain for the ancient Greek version of heaven. **Where? The Illusion Fields?**

It's the Elysian Fields. And don't be stupid. That isn't real.

But you believe you're a Furie, don't you? Is that real?

I am a product of my reality.

Tom recalled a conversation with a psychopath named Torble that went a lot like this one. The man seemed perfectly sane one minute, and then a raging loon the next.

Don't kill anyone else. Please.

Are you willing to make a deal, Tom?

Sure. What do you want?

The response was immediate. **Castrate yourself.**

Cut off my balls, and you won't kill anyone else?

Yes. You have my word.

I need to think about it.

No time for that. This deal expires in thirty seconds. And that's more than enough time to do the deed. I know, from experience.

Okay. I'll do it.

So do it, Tom.

I need to find a knife.

Tom waited. Then he typed, **OK, got one.**

Liar, Tom. The next whore I kill, I'm carving your name all over her body.

Erinyes left the chatroom, and the forum. Off to kill again. And Tom had no idea what he could do to stop him.

CHAPTER 38

Erinyes goes through her mental checklist. What's in the van, and what's on her person?

Duct tape.
Butcher knife.
Cardboard box.
Hand truck.
Moving blankets.
Master keys.
WD-40.
Stun gun.
Gamma-Hydroxybutyric acid.
Ball gag.
Taurus 9mm with suppressor.
Adult diapers.
Ethyl ether.
Ammonia ampules.
Doorstop.
Antique ether mask.

Thank you, Internet. What Amazon and eBay can't supply, the dark net does.

It's 2 A.M., and Erinyes is both tired and riled up. The chat with the cop was strangely exhilarating. The voyeuristic aspect of it added to the excitement.

You got a knife, Tom?

No... you don't. I know because I'm watching you on your cell phone camera.

Things have gotten more difficult. More complicated. Changing agendas at the last minute can lead to mistakes. But Erinyes is patient.

Erinyes is *patience.*

Slow and steady.

Silent and careful.

Erinyes is outside the sinner's door.

She takes out his cell.

Uses the app.

Turns on the sinner's phone.

Accesses her camera and speakers.

The room is dark. Only the sound of breathing.

The sinner is asleep.

Erinyes sprays inside the deadbolt lock with lubricating oil. She also sticks the thin, red tube into the door cracks and hinges, making sure everything gets a squirt.

The door used to squeak; Erinyes knows this from her online surveillance. Now, courtesy of the correct master key, it pushes open with a faint sigh.

Erinyes enters the dark, slipping inside quickly, securing the door behind her.

You shouldn't have lied, Tom.

You should have made the deal, and cut your naughty man parts off.

Because now I'm inside your house.

And I'm going to record some video. Of me carving your name into Joan's face.

CHAPTER 39

Joan awoke to a buzzing sound. It took her a moment to get her bearings.

I'm in bed. Tom's bed. Had a night out with Trish. Drank too much.

Another buzz.

My phone. On the nightstand next to the bed.

Joan reached for it, squinting at the text message. It was from Trish, in all caps.

INDENTITY THEFT!!!!

As Joan puzzled over what that could mean, and why it warranted four exclamation points, a follow-up text appeared.

Roy didn't go to Hilton! Someone cloned his credit card! He's not cheating!!!

Joan texted back an emoji smiley face. Then she checked her messages.

Nothing new from Tom.

She frowned in the darkness. Joan still hadn't listened to any of his previous messages. She had been waiting for him to come home, to deal with it in person.

Was he still at the hospital? Had that bite been more serious than Joan had guessed?

Or was he someplace else?

A bar?

A hotel?

With his incredibly hot, bisexual co-worker, Eva?

At work, chasing The Snipper?

Joan tried to tune into her feelings. Earlier, she'd been self-righteous in her anger. The man couldn't even take a few days off work to spend time with her. Yet he thought proposing marriage—something Joan didn't even want—was perfectly logical.

Marriage was a lifelong commitment, and Tom couldn't even commit to a week.

She had a right to be mad.

But now, all Joan felt was concern.

Was Tom okay?

They'd had fights in the past. On more than one occasion, Joan had turned her phone off to let things calm down. And things always worked out.

Wait... wasn't my phone off? How did it get back on?

Joan switched on the bedside light and sat up. The house looked empty.

But it didn't feel empty. It felt like someone was in there. Watching her.

"Tom?"

As her heart rate kicked up, fear and common sense fought for control over Joan's brain.

What was the likelihood someone had broken in, turned on Joan's phone, and now was hiding somewhere?

Unlikely.

But Tom was a cop. He had enemies. He chased killers. Joan had looked evil in the eye before, and an ounce of prevention far outweighed a pound of cure. Fear is your body telling you something. You should listen.

Joan eyed the front door. It was only three meters away. She could run for it, get into the hallway, and then—

Then what?

Call the police? Tell them she thinks someone is in the house?

If she was wrong, she'd look foolish. She and Tom would be the butt of jokes forever within the Chicago Police Department.

Call Tom?

That was a better option. In fact, it was the perfect excuse to talk to him.

But what if he didn't pick up? If he ignored her, like Joan had ignored him? Or if he was on a little bender at the neighborhood pub, like Joan had done earlier with Trish?

Try Tom first. If he doesn't answer, go to a neighbor.

And then? After banging on a neighbor's door at two-thirty in the morning, wearing nothing but a bra and tee shirt, the police would have to be called. Which led right back to the laughing stock scenario.

Then Joan remembered the nightstand.

Tom's back-up gun. A .380 Kimber that she'd practiced with at the range.

She slid open the drawer, found the weapon next to the TV remote control, and then quickly and efficiently checked the magazine and racked a round.

"I have a gun!" Joan announced. Just like Tom taught her to do.

Safety off, both hands steadying the weapon, Joan swung her feet out of bed and went to search the house.

CHAPTER 40

The moment after Joan's phone buzzed, Erinyes slipped into the bathroom. She knows the layout of the house well; people take their cell phones with them everywhere. As Joan texts, Erinyes reaches overhead and feels around for the ceiling lamp. She softly removes the glass cover, then loosens the light bulb by a quarter-twist.

Then Erinyes slips off her shoes and begins to carefully undress.

It pays to plan ahead. She has no zippers, buckles, or snaps on her clothing. Nothing that would make noise while being removed. Erinyes places her bag, shoes, baggy jeans, jacket, and dark flannel shirt in the bathtub. Beneath those clothes, she's wearing a full body vantablack unitard, with matching socks. She takes the tube of vantablack makeup from her jacket pocket, closes her eyes, and applies it over her lids. Then she pulls on the vantablack ski mask and gloves.

"Tom?"

No, it's not Tom.

Erinyes carefully takes the ether mask from her bag and sets it in the sink, then pulls up the stopper. Working in the dark, she pours half the bottle of ether onto the mask, judging the amount by weight. Then she places the stun gun and suppressed Taurus on the toilet seat behind her.

"I have a gun!" Joan said.

So do I. Erinyes closes her eyes and stands perfectly still, becoming one with the darkness. *Come find me, bitch.*

CHAPTER 41

Joan walked past the bed, checking every corner of the room and finding nothing. The bedroom closet door was slightly ajar, and with her finger lightly on the trigger she swung it open in one quick motion.

Empty.

She continued on past the edge of the bedroom, then turned the slight corner and hit the lights for the kitchen.

No one there.

That left a few more closets, the living room, and the bathroom.

Her fear level had begun to drop, and foolishness was taking over. She began to wonder if her initial panic had been rooted in guilt, rather than any actual threat. Joan imagined Tom walking in at that very moment, and her accidentally putting three shots in his center mass. She took her finger off the trigger and placed it alongside the trigger guard.

I'm being silly. And overly paranoid.

I should crawl back into bed.

And then, I should call Tom.

Joan promised herself she'd do just that.

But first, she needed to check the rest of the house.

Blowing out a stiff breath, Joan padded over to the linen closet.

Put one hand on the doorknob.

Swiftly tugged the door open.

Empty.

Joan considered how funny this story would be to tell at some far-off, future date. When she and Tom were elderly.

"Remember that fight we had when you proposed? When I was alone at your house, I missed you so much I thought there was an intruder."

"So what did you do?"

"I did what you told me to. Announced I had a gun, then walked around, looking for somebody to shoot."

They'd laugh about this someday, and just thinking about it made things so clear to Joan that she was, at that very moment, fearless.

Because I missed you so much.

She was making Tom choose between her and his job. Something Tom would never ask her to do.

Why did I do that? Jealousy? Insecurity?

Was I really worried he'd be hurt? Or did I just hate that he chose something over me?

Joan could picture him, on his knee, holding out that gorgeous ring, the love in his eyes.

Wow. I really fucked up.

She walked over to the bathroom, reaching for the light switch.

The light didn't work.

Joan flipped it a few times, squinting into the darkness.

It's empty. I'm being ridiculous. I have to call Tom.

She turned, thumbing the safety back on the weapon, and then noticed an odd, sharp odor. Then came fast movement and something jabbed her in the back.

Joan fell forward, onto her knees, trying to comprehend what just happened. Jolting pain had knocked her down, but she'd managed to keep hold of the .380, and she twisted and saw—

It looked like something floating in the middle of open air.

Joan aimed and pulled the trigger, but the safety was on. Then the stun gun punched her in the shoulder, and then she was on her back and something invisible was pressing down upon her.

No. Not invisible.

Something pure black. So black it was impossible to see.

Except for eyes. Floating in the blackness was a pair of staring eyes.

Her gun arm pinned, Joan lashed out with her free hand, clawing at the man's face, catching the edge of fabric and exposing a chin and some bared, snarling teeth.

Joan reached up, pressing a thumb into his eye. He leaned away, and Joan pushed, then brought up a knee and kicked at his groin—

—her bare foot not finding anything there.

Was this a woman?

The stun gun hit Joan in the thigh, a pain so piercing and absolute it was like a whole body charley horse. Joan's entire length went rigid, and the abrupt movement somehow knocked her attacker off.

It also made Joan drop the gun.

Joan managed to twist onto her side, get her shaky knees up under her, and sprint, full speed, to the front door.

She grabbed the knob, turned it, and yanked.

The door didn't move. Joan pulled hard, then looked down and saw the doorstop wedged at the bottom. As she reached down for it, the stun gun zapped her in the small of the back. And this time the agony didn't let up until Joan had blacked out.

CHAPTER 42

This one is a real fighter.

Erinyes continues to stun Joan until the woman passes out, then she quickly goes into the bathroom and grabs the ether mask in the sink, squeezing out the excess.

Too much ether, and the sinner never wakes up.

Erinyes holds the damp mask to Joan's face until she is sure the woman is under.

Then, a quick check of Tom's phone, to make sure he's still at the hospital.

He is. And he's sleeping.

He likely wouldn't be back for several hours.

Erinyes gets her things from the bathtub, dresses in the thrift shop clothing she isn't worried about bloodying up.

As she scrubs off the black make-up, Erinyes considers her next move.

There was a promise made to Tom. His name carved all over the whore's body.

But something like that takes time. And energy. Erinyes is tired. It has been a very long day. Her eye hurts, from where Joan had poked her.

Still, a promise is a promise.

Erinyes sets her bag down next to Joan, then takes out the duct tape, and the smelling salts.

CHAPTER 43

"So… success?" Tom asked. It was a little after seven am, and the doctor was standing at his bedside.

Dr. Jones nodded. "I didn't see any necrotic tissue. I cut around the wound just to make sure—necrotizing fasciitis is nothing to play around with—and sent the samples to the lab. The prognosis is good."

"Can I go?"

"I recommend another day of intravenous antibiotics."

"Isn't there an oral version?"

"Oral medication isn't as effective against this form of streptococcus."

"I have to take my chances, Doc. There's a serial killer who might have added to his list last night, and I need to make things right with my girlfriend."

He prescribed Tom some azithromycin pills and topical clindamycin cream, which took an eternity to get at the hospital pharmacy on the first floor. While waiting, he grabbed a Hostess Apple Pie and a Little Debbie Honeybun at the gift shop. Tom had skipped breakfast; cold, rubbery scrambled eggs and stale toast delivered by the male nurse he'd lied to. As he feasted on crap, he decided whom to call first, Roy or Joan.

Tom thought it spoke well of him that he chose Joan.

No answer.

He tried his house, and his machine picked up.

Was she still ignoring him?

Tom remembered their last words to one another.

"Where are you going?"

"Home."

Maybe home wasn't Tom's place. Maybe Joan meant she went back to Los Angeles.

That was a five hour flight, longer with connections. Depending on what flight Joan took, and when, she might not be back in LA until later today.

Tom called Joan's assistant, and got an answering service. Of course he did; it was two hours earlier in California. He left a message, saying it was urgent, and then called up his partner.

"I'm gonna find that son of a bitch, Tommy. I'm gonna find him, and I'm gonna wrap my hands around his neck and squeeze until his eyes go dead."

"I think he killed again last night, Roy."

"Who?"

"The Snipper. Who are you talking about?"

"That asshole who took my credit card number and bought himself a suite at the Hilton. Poor Trish was a wreck all day. Thought I was messin' around. Didn't Joan tell you about it? Why didn't you let me know, man? We're like brothers."

"I tried to tell you. Has Trish heard from Joan?"

"Ladies tied one on last night. Trish is still a little green. Heard you got shut down. Sorry about that. Joanie will come around."

"Did Joan tell Trish she was going back to LA?"

"Last I heard, they took cabs home around ten. Hold on." Tom heard Trish talking in the background. "Joan texted Trish last night, at 2 A.M."

That was good to know. Odds were high Joan was at Tom's house, probably sleeping it off.

"What about the case? Are there any leads?" Tom asked.

"Man, credit thieves are like ghosts."

"The Snipper, Roy."

"It's gonna take a month to sift through all the shit we got. Meet you at the office?"

"No. I'm on vacation."

"Okay. I'll keep you in the loop. Good luck with Joan."

"Thanks."

"Oh, Tom! Almost forgot to tell you. Top of the police blotter this morning. Terrance Wycleaf Johnson did a jackrabbit parole last night. Street name was T-Nail. War Chief of the Eternal Black C-Notes. Bad dude. Got his nickname nailing people to walls."

Tom wasn't sure why Roy was telling him this.

"He kill some people while escaping?" Tom asked.

"Dunno. Two guards, three paramedics missing. He was being taken to a hospital, and the ambulance disappeared."

That was one of the worst parts of being a cop. You put away bad guys, and then they got out again to do more bad things. "Sounds shitty, but we're not the gang unit, Roy."

"I know. Not our problem. But Captain Bains told me to tell you."

"Why?"

"The undercover officer who arrested T-Nail was our old Loot."

"Jack?"

"Lieutenant Daniels put the banger away for life. Dude might be holding a grudge. Bains called her house, no answer. No answer from her old partner, neither."

Tom knew Sergeant Herb Benedict as well as he knew Jack. Good man, good cop.

"Bains asked if I had her cell number," Roy continued. "You got it? You guys still tight?"

"Yeah. I'll call her right now, let her know."

"Have a fun vacation, my man."

Roy hung up. Tom flipped through his address book and found Jack, who'd devoted herself to The Job, and was still paying for it in retirement.

"This is Jack."

"Loot, sorry to call you so early. It's Tom Mankowski."

"I'm not a lieutenant anymore, Tom. What's up?"

"I just found out about it, and haven't been able to get in touch with Sergeant Benedict. Did he call you already?"

"Herb's on a staycation. He turned his phone off. Found out about what?"

"Last night, Terrence Wycleaf Johnson escaped from prison."

There was a pause. Then Jack said, "T-Nail."

"Two guards and three paramedics are missing."

"What happened?"

Tom repeated what Roy had told him.

"Sounds like he had help. Has the ambulance been found?"

"No."

"Have you talked to anyone in the gang unit? Are they making a move?"

"I just heard about it on the blotter, immediately called. Want me to send a car over?"

"No need. We're up north. Harry's got a place near a lake. I'm pretty sure we're okay. T-Nail never even learned my name. I testified undercover."

"Where are you?" Tom caught himself. "Wait, don't tell me. I'm working a case, and electronic security is a lot less secure than I had thought."

"The Snipper?"

"Yeah. Got me and my partner running in circles. Don't know if you've heard, but there's been a second murder."

"Describe the scene."

Tom gave Jack the ugly details of Kendal Hefferton's demise.

"It sounds like a sex crime," Jack said.

"No semen. No evidence of rape."

"Were her breasts mutilated like her mouth and vagina?"

"No. Untouched. Like the last one."

"Was the bra left on?"

"Yeah."

"Men sexualize the female breast. Unusual that the killer left hers alone."

"Are you thinking the perp might be a woman?" Tom had been thinking the same thing.

"I'm thinking that even though it looks like a sex crime, the killer may have an agenda that isn't sexual. Have you run a ViCAT report on the vic's name? You can also run an alert to inform you automatically if anyone inputs new data. It's likely the killer is looking for a new victim. If the pattern is followed, there will be harassment first. Maybe you'll catch a break."

"Good idea." Tom hadn't used ViCAT in a while, because the website was so poorly done, and cops weren't good about updating information, Tom himself included. "You have a second to spitball?"

"Sure."

Tom did a quick recap of what went down at Hector Valentine's, and Walter Cissick's. "I just chatted with the perp, online. I think it could be Walter's son, Dennis. But the dual bedrooms is bothering me. And so are the vics. The men, castrated. The women, tortured to death. There was a transgender, or maybe intersex, woman who came to us, pretending to be a witness. At the least, she's an accomplice, but she might be more than that."

"How did you know she was transgender?" Jack asked.

"Roy mentioned it, after she left. If he didn't say anything, I wouldn't have known. What I keeping coming back to is—"

"—that it sounds like two perps."

"Yeah. We don't know how many kids Walter Cissick had. You ever work a case with two siblings, killing together?"

Jack made a sound that sounded like it could have been a snort. "Yes. I have. Crazy tends to run in families."

"So it could be brother and sister. Each with a similar, but distinct, agenda."

"Or two brothers," Jack said. "One who identifies as female. Identity is more than how we view ourselves. It also colors how we view others. We're pack animals. We tend to want to be around people like us."

Good insight. "And what if we can't find anyone like us?"

Tom noticed the pharmacist had finally gotten around to filling his script. He walked over to the register.

"Jack? You there?"

Jack didn't respond. Tom tried redialing, and got her voicemail.

He paid for his prescriptions, shoved them into his pocket, and headed for the hospital parking lot. Once inside his car, he called Jack again.

And again it went to voicemail.

Odd. They were in the middle of a conversation, and had obviously been disconnected. But phone etiquette dictated that one or both parties keep trying until connection was re-established. Jack hadn't left him any messages, so Tom wondered if she was just having bad reception wherever she was.

But there was a very small percentage it was something else. Something bad.

Much as he didn't want to, Tom dialed Harry McGlade, the ex-cop who'd lost his hand and was a pain in the ass. He still worked with Jack, in the private sector, and Jack mentioned she was staying at his place. As much as it would be a pain in the ass to talk to him, he should be informed about the T-Nail situation.

"What?"

Nice way to answer the phone. "It's Detective Tom Mankowski, McGlade."

"So?"

"I'm calling about Jack Daniels."

"Jack's not here."

"I know. I just talked with her."

Tom gave McGlade the highlights, ending with, "Is there a landline at your place?"

"No landline. I bet it's just bad reception. I'll bug her on my autodial until I get through."

McGlade hung up.

Tom tried Joan again, both on her cell, and at his house.

No answer.

Tom's stomach sank. As a cop, he often relied on intuition.

And he had a hunch that things were about to go very, very wrong.

CHAPTER 44

Erinyes awakes.

Sleeping in the van is awkward. She's parked at a gas station oasis off of I-90, amid all the semi-trucks sporting snoring drivers.

She stretches, notes it's seven in the morning, then checks on Tom. His doctor is talking to him.

"I didn't see any necrotic tissue. I cut around the wound just to make sure—necrotizing fasciitis is nothing to play around with—and sent the samples to the lab. The prognosis is good."

Erinyes has to look up what necrotizing fasciitis is.

Gross. So that's what happened to Walter's lips.

The Tom Mankowski Show continues on through several phone calls.

Erinyes learns a lot.

The cops have no leads from her house. And they won't find any. Even if that computer geek decrypts her files, there is nothing that can lead them to her.

Someone escaped from jail, and the story is intriguing enough that Erinyes looks up Terrance Wycleaf "T-Nail" Johnson.

His body count puts hers to shame. And his mugshot is downright terrifying. Erinyes actually shivers looking at it. They manage to put an animal like that away, and he still escapes. Yet the ridiculous War on Drugs—which persecutes people for using chemicals deemed illegal by a bunch of tight-assed, paid for politicians—arrests users once every 1.9 seconds for a drug-related offense. In what universe does it make sense to lock people up for doing what they want with their own bodies, and let out psychopaths who nail people to floors and walls? There's something seriously wrong with the penal system in this country.

The conversation with Tom's mentor, a former cop humorously named Jack Daniels, is also fascinating. Listening to them discuss her is like listening to juicy gossip. Most things they're off base on, but a few of their guesses are surprisingly close.

Erinyes searches for Jacqueline Daniels, and finds a lot of information. Jack used to be a star. She's dealt with some very high-profile serial killer cases, including some big names Erinyes has heard of.

Maybe, when I'm finished with Tom, I'll pay his mentor a little visit. Jack Daniels no doubt has many sins she needs to atone for.

The Tom Mankowski Show continues with an abrupt call to a boor named Harry McGlade—someone even more famous than Jack—and Erinyes switches off after Tom makes yet another desperate and pathetic attempt to contact his would-be fiancée.

Aren't you going to be surprised when you find out what happened to her?

Erinyes exits the vehicle, and walks across the lot over to the 7-11. After using the ladies' room, she buys a breakfast croissant sandwich and a large coffee, choosing to use extra cream and sugar.

The extra calories will be put to good use. Lots to do today.

She's down to her last ten dollars, and makes a mental note to get some cash.

Back inside the van, she checks on Joan, her wrists securely taped to the eight inch steel U bolt attached to the floor of the van, next to the aquarium.

She's still knocked out.

After laboring over the decision hours before, Erinyes chose to abduct Joan rather than kill her outright. A shrewd move, in case she needed to use Joan as a bargaining tool with the police. But Erinyes also had a bigger, deeper reason; she's never given Penance to two sinners at the same time.

The concept is provocative. As they watch one another suffer, it will make their own suffering more exquisite.

In theory, anyway.

So, rather than tie Joan to Tom's bed, wake her up, and do her business with the butcher knife, Erinyes went back to the van and brought up the hand truck and cardboard appliance box. After securing Joan in moving blankets and tape, she wheeled her outside and loaded her into the vehicle without anyone giving her a second glance.

Not that there were many people paying attention at four am. But if any were, they would have seen a person moving a large box.

Then Erinyes put a diaper on her—there was no telling how long it would take to grab Kendal—tied her to the rod, and put a GHB tablet under her tongue to keep her compliant. She didn't bother with the ball gag yet; if Joan started getting too noisy, the option was available. But it wasn't worth the risk of her possibly vomiting and choking to death.

Besides, listening to them confess their sins was one of the most enjoyable parts of the whole Penance process.

After starting up the van, Erinyes headed for the nearest BTM. They were becoming prevalent in Chicago, so she finds one only five minutes away. It's located inside of a liquor store.

She's halfway to it when she sees the flashing red and blue lights in her rearview mirror.

Police.

Not good. Not good at all.

Even worse; she left her Taurus in the back of the van.

Erinyes slowly pulls over to the side of the street. The cop is no doubt recording the stop, plus she sees his eyes are focused on her side mirror. If she gets up to gag Joan and grab the gun, he'll notice the movement and become suspicious.

So Erinyes remains seated. But when she stretches for the glove compartment to get her insurance information, she makes sure the security curtain separating the front and rear of the van is pulled closed.

The policeman does his swagger up to her door, and Erinyes cracks open the window.

He gives her a once-over, then cranes his neck to see inside the van.

Nothing to see here, officer.

"License, registration, and proof of insurance."

"Can I ask why you pulled me over?"

"You ran a red light back there."

Erinyes hadn't run a red light. It had barely turned yellow when she entered that last intersection. She's always extremely careful about such a thing, because cops are such pricks.

Arguing with him will be fruitless. Better to take the ticket and get the hell out of there.

"Sorry about that." She digs through her wallet, making sure she selects the correct driver's license. Then she hands it to him along with her insurance card and plate sticker registration, and then waits, drumming her fingers on the steering wheel, hoping her fake identification is worth the crazy amount she paid for it.

He goes back to his squad car.

A minute passes.

Two minutes.

From the back of the van, Joan whimpers.

Erinyes checks the rearview. He's still writing the ticket.

"Tom?" Joan says, her voice slurring.

"Shh. Quiet."

"Who are you?"

"I said, be quiet," Erinyes orders.

The cop exits his car and begins to walk toward her.

"I want Tom," Joan is louder this time.

"Sweetie, I'll bring Tom to you, but you have to be quiet for a full minute. Count to sixty and you can talk to Tom."

"Why am I tied up?"

The cop is only five steps away. He has one hand on his belt, next to his holster.

"You've been in an accident," Erinyes tells her. "Do you want Tom?"

"Yeah."

"First you have to count to sixty."

"One... two..."

"In your head, sweetie."

The cop raps a knuckle on the window. Erinyes opens it a few centimeters. He feeds in a small clipboard with a ticket attached.

"Sign the bottom."

Erinyes takes it, eagerly.

There's no pen.

"Tom? That you?"

The police officer squints at her, a question on his face. Erinyes shrugs. "Do you have a pen, officer?"

"Tom?" Joan is getting louder.

"Is someone in the van with you?"

"No. All alone. Just the radio." Erinyes quickly turns the radio knob, even though it's already off. "Oh, lookee, found one."

She hurriedly snatches a ballpoint from her purse pocket, scrawls across the bottom of the ticket, hands the clipboard back, and shuts the window.

The cop doesn't leave.

"Tom? Where's Tom?"

The cop knocks again. Erinyes opens the window once more.

"Here's your copy, and your identification. Information on paying your fine, or contesting the violation, is on the back of the ticket."

"Thank you, officer."

He stares, still not leaving. What the hell else does this sadistic fascist want?

"Are you sure you're okay, Miss?"

"I'm fine."

"Are you sure?" The cop touches his own eye.

Erinyes isn't sure what he's talking about. Then she checks her own eyes in the center mirror.

Sees traces of dark black make-up.

He thinks someone beat me up. She almost laughs at the absurdity of it.

"I can take you someplace safe. Get you help."

Seriously? He gives her a two hundred dollar ticket, now he wants to play hero?

"It happened at the gym, officer. Thank you for your concern."

"Okay. Drive safely."

Erinyes nods, shutting the window. Behind her, in the back, Joan begins to snore.

GHB, the date rape drug of choice since 1960.

Erinyes pulls back onto the street. Two minutes later, she parks in front of the liquor store, goes in the back of the van, gags Joan, and then wanders inside to find the Bitcoin Teller Machine.

Erinyes flashes the QR code from her phone, punches in her password, and checks the exchange rates. Bitcoins are currently worth four hundred and twenty US dollars. Erinyes withdraws two bitcoins in twenties. That leaves her with slightly over eight hundred and six bitcoins in her digital wallet.

Free money. She's been mining bitcoins for years, along with selling various hacking services on darknet. It's more than enough to start over in a new state, buy a house for cash, and set up several new identities.

But first, she has to finish up things in Illinois.

Erinyes pulls out of the parking lot and heads for the expressway, toward Evanston.

On the way, she stops at a pet store and picks up a bag of crickets.

Her Eratigena agrestis eggs have begun to hatch, and she doesn't want the little darlings to start eating each other.

CHAPTER 45

Tom opened the door to his house, hurrying inside, hoping to catch Joan still asleep.

But Joan was gone.

He placed his hand on the unmade bed, as if there could still be some residual heat from when Joan had slept there. But the sheets were cold.

Tom sat, and for the hundredth time he thought about how it all could have gone differently.

"Walk away, let someone else catch this maniac. You do that, I'll marry you."

That was Tom's moment. If he had agreed, Tom could have been on his honeymoon right now.

But instead of a happy, safer life, starting a family with the woman he adored, Tom chose instead to surf the moral black hole of darknet and chat with psychopaths online. Psychopaths that he would one day have to worry about escaping from prison and going after him and those he loved.

Tom didn't want to become Jacqueline Daniels. He could feel the despair in her voice over the phone. The only time she perked up was when they discussed The Snipper case.

It was sad. And it was also the road he was headed down.

Thinking about Jack, Tom considered her advice; checking the Violent Criminal Apprehension Team national database for similar cases. The chance was slim. Filling out ViCAT reports was a lengthy, and often fruitless process. State and local authorities weren't required to do so. Because of this, not every cop did it, so police departments didn't know what other police departments were doing. That allowed perps to hop from jurisdiction to jurisdiction, with every new investigator having to start from scratch with no prior evidence.

Tom stared at his computer, at his corner desk.

Search ViCAT? Or send a letter of resignation to Captain Bains?

Tom sat down and began to type.

Consider this letter the beginning of my two weeks' notice.

Tom stared at the sentence. Then erased it and started again.

Please accept this letter as formal notification of my resignation from the Chicago Police Department.

Delete.

I fucking quit.

But why, exactly, was he quitting? For Joan? Or for himself?

Maybe some combination.

He considered what Erinyes asked him in the chatroom.

Do you enjoy your job, Tom?

Tom dealt with the worst that humanity had to offer. He felt like he made a difference, but seeing man's unrelenting inhumanity to man really took a toll on his psyche. It was depressing. And frustrating. And never-ending.

The only good part of his job...

The only good part of my job is when I leave for the day, and talk to Joan.

I like helping others. I like making a difference. I like justice.

But I don't like being a cop.

The realization hit with such force, it was like a blind man seeing for the first time. Tom stood up.

To hell with a letter of resignation. I'm going to march into the Captain's office and give him my badge and gun, right now.

He sat down again.

But first, might as well do a quick ViCAT search. What does another few minutes matter, anyway?

CHAPTER 46

Erinyes parks a block away from the Epsilon Epsilon Delta house, and then logs onto www.HotSororityGirlsLive.com as administrator. She flips through all the live webcams. Seven girls are asleep, even though it was already past eight am. Made sense. The little whores stayed up late, chatting with their johns.

Erinyes can't see Kendal. She must still have her cams off. Her computer, cell, and Kindle are off as well. Erinyes remotely powers up Kendal's cell—she'd manually put the app on it when Kendal was stuck in the mammogram machine.

She's asleep.

Erinyes goes into the back of the van. Joan looks up at her, groggily.

"You're about to get a roommate," Erinyes tells her as she gathers her things. She finished her old tube of make-up at Tom's townhouse and takes the new one she'd just ordered out of a cabinet.

"This is vantablack," she says to Joan. "It's made of carbon nanotubes. It's the blackest substance known, absorbing 99.965% of the visible spectrum. That's why you couldn't see me in the bathroom. It absorbs light rather than reflects it."

Erinyes tucked the tube into her duffle. Then she takes the bag of crickets she bought at the pet shop and shakes a few into the aquarium. Joan's eyes go wide when she sees what is in the tank, and she whimpers.

"Yes, Joan. These are for you. They will help bring you atonement for your sins. Want to hear something really ironic? You could have prevented this easily. If you had said yes to Tom's proposal, you wouldn't be here right now. That was a really, really mean thing to do."

Erinyes squatted at Joan's level, looking her in the eyes. "I know. Because I watched the whole thing."

Another whimper. Erinyes pats her on the head, then looks for and finds the folding map. She makes sure no one is on the street before she gets out of the van. After locking it, she heads for the sorority house.

A squad car is parked in front. Erinyes unfolds the map to full size, then walks slowly past the cop. She stops. Waits. Then turns back and walks briskly toward the car, her duffle bag hiding the Taurus in her hand.

"I'm looking for this street," she says, handing him the map as he opens the window. It's not the cute cop Kendal was with earlier. This guy is old, pasty-looking. When his face is obscured by the map, Erinyes quickly checks for witnesses, then brings the 9mm up and shoots him six times in the head and chest.

There's no such thing as a true silencer. But the suppressor Erinyes bought online is a good one, and the shots are no louder than a strong cough.

She opens his door by sticking her hand inside through the window, shoves his dead body over, and shuts the window. The map is all bloody, so she can't keep it. A shame. Big paper folding maps were getting harder to find in the digital age.

Erinyes locks the door, then briskly crosses the street to the sorority.

The master key works as intended. Once inside, she strips down to the unitard, spreads on eye make-up, and puts on the gloves and ski mask.

Then she puts a fresh magazine in the 9mm, and almost sheds a tear at the tragedy that is about to unfold.

These sinners need to atone. A bullet in the head isn't nearly enough Penance. They should suffer more than that. But this environment is too risky. Too daring. She needs to kill the girls, grab Kendal, and get out quick.

Hopefully God will have mercy on them anyway.

Erinyes heads for the first whore's bedroom.

Stops.

Turns.

Goes back to her duffle bag, and takes out the duct tape and butcher knife.

Because there is always time for a little suffering.

CHAPTER 47

The ViCAT homepage, like a lot of the scam sites on the dark web, looked like it was designed by a high school kid running Windows 98. And it was just about as user-friendly.

Tom did searches on the word *Kendal.*

Three hits. None were recent, or fit the current MO.

Next he tried *Erinyes, Furies, Tilphousia, Megaera*, and *Alecto*.

Nada.

Tom searched for *castration*, and got too many hits to wade through.

Okay. I tried. Time to go resign.

ViCAT had apparently outlived its usefulness. Just like everything else when user-interface ceased keeping up with technology. He wondered if some computer geek, like Firoz, could somehow update the system, make it more—

Thinking about Firoz, Tom has a tiny blip of inspiration. What was that password he'd used to unlock Cissick's computer? Demented? Demeanor?

Demeter.

Tom typed the word into the search box.

He got a hit. A recent hit, for only an hour ago. A cop in Evanston named Ledesma had posted an entry about a girl on campus who had been sexually assaulted by someone who identified herself as Nurse Demeter.

Tom read on, feeling the hair on the back of his neck tingle.

Nurse Demeter had attacked a girl named Kendel.

Kendal was spelled wrong, but that was close enough to get Tom on the phone with Evanston PD as fast as he could dial. After a few words with their operator, Detective Ledesma picked up.

"Detective Tom Mankowski, Chicago Homicide. I just read your ViCAT report."

"So that old system really works? I just put that in this morning. Have you got something?"

"You know The Snipper case? He's cyberstalking webcam models named Kendal."

"Kendal Smith is a student at the university. She didn't say she was a webcam model."

"Where is she?"

"The Epsilon Epsilon Delta sorority house."

Evanston was maybe a twenty minute drive. "I can meet you there in fifteen."

"No need. She was really scared, so we've got a car outside."

"Radio him. Tell him to wait inside with Kendal."

"He just checked in fifteen minutes ago. But let me get him on. Give me a second."

Tom waited.

"He's not answering," Ledesma said.

"Send every cop you've got over there, right now."

Tom ran out the door.

CHAPTER 43

Kendal yawned, knocked on the shower door to make sure it was empty, and then went inside. The floor was damp, indicating recent use. Hopefully there would still be warm water. Kendal shut off the shower camera using the wall switch. The green light on the camera's base blinked, then became red.

She hung a hand towel over the lens, just to be sure, and then turned on the water in the shower. Even though it was likely already hot from whoever just used it, she still counted to thirty-five before checking the spout.

The perfect temp.

Then she checked it again.

And again.

Someone in the house must have had a bad cold, because Kendal could hear the coughing even with the water and vent on.

While under the spray she didn't even try to avoid counting the tiles. She counted the soap dish in the wall as two, since it took up two spaces.

Three shampoos and three minutes later, Kendal stepped out of the shower, toweled off, and walked down the hallway back to her room, closing the door behind her. She began to lay out some clothing on the bed, heard more coughing from the hallway, and remembered the Addalock Detective Ledesma had given her. Kendal wouldn't be in her room long, but she attached it to the door anyway.

When you had OCD, new habits died just as hard as old habits.

Kendal dressed in black jeans, a red crew neck sweatshirt with her school logo on it, and was pulling on socks when someone tried to open her door.

"Hello?"

Kendal watched the knob jiggle.

"Linda? Hildy?"

No one answered.

But there was a faint knock. And then—

Scratching.

Someone is scratching on my door.

"This isn't funny, Hildy."

The scratching stopped.

Then the privacy lock in the center of the doorknob twisted, someone unlocking it from the other side.

The doorknob turned.

The door began to push inward.

But it didn't open. The Addalock stopped it.

Kendal grabbed her new cell phone and hurried to the window, splitting the blinds with her fingers and peeking through. The police car was parked on the street, but with the sun's glare Kendal couldn't see who was inside.

BAM!

Someone hit her door, hard.

Kendal was so scared she dropped the cellphone.

BAM!

She quickly scooped the phone up, accessed the onscreen keyboard, and dialed 911.

"Kendal?"

Kendal knew that voice.

"911, what's your emergency?"

"Kendal?"

It was Linda.

Kendal switched off her phone. "Linda?"

Another faint knock. Kendal took the three steps to the door, reached for the Addalock, then paused.

"Linda? What do you want?"

"I'm hurt… hurt bad…"

Concern for her own safety was instantly replaced by concern for her friend, and Kendal disengaged the Addalock and opened the door.

Linda's face was pale, her eyes wide, her mouth open. She was wearing her red University tee shirt.

No… it was her Spongebob shirt. Her favorite.

Except that her Spongebob shirt was white. So why was it—

Kendal's breath caught. Linda's shirt was completely soaked with blood. And then she fell to the side, revealing something black crouching behind her.

Kendal didn't think. She reacted. As the scream left her lips, Kendal dropped a shoulder and shoved past the man in the doorway, pushing him to the side as she sprinted down the hall.

Twelve steps to the front door!

Eleven-ten-nine-eight-sev—

Kendal slipped on something, breaking the fall with her hands, phone flying, skin rubbing off the heels of her hands as they skidded across the hardwood floor. Her legs were caught in something. Kendal twisted onto her side, her eyes trailing the blood all over the floor, and coming to rest on Hildy, lying next to the wall, her eyes wide and a slash of gray duct tape covering her mouth.

Hildy was quivering, making a keening, high pitched whine through her flared nostrils. Kendal tried to scoot away, and Hildy's whine became a sealed-lip scream.

Kendal looked at her own feet, and in that incongruous instant wondered how they'd become tied up in rope.

Half a second later she saw the rope wasn't rope—it was coming out of the big gash in Hildy's belly, where both of her hands were pressed, like an expectant mother caressing her nine month old baby.

But Hildy wasn't caressing her unborn child.

She was trying to stuff her insides back in. And Kendal had made the process much more difficult, because her feet were tangled up in loops of Hildy's intestines.

Kendal's reaction was visceral, and she kicked and kicked until she was free of the innards and then she got a slippery foot under her, ready to dash to the front door only two meters away.

And then she froze.

I forgot my count.

Twelve steps to the front door from the bedroom.

Where did I leave off?

Kendal stood there, rigid and immobile as a statue, as tears exploded from her eyes.

Then something grabbed her from behind and clamped a wet cloth over her mouth, and Kendal's lungs burned as the whole world became one, giant blur.

CHAPTER 49

While Detective Ledesma vomited into a garbage can, Tom winced at the corpse on the bed. Her bare thighs had been carved open, from the hip to the knee, and Tom inadvertently thought of the hot dogs his mother used to make when he was a kid, splitting them almost in half along their lengths to stuff them with cheese.

"That's seven," Tom said. "And this isn't Kendal?"

"She had the bedroom facing the street," Ledesma said into the can.

"Can you check her face to make sure?"

"Is it… all there?"

The Snipper had cut the cheeks and nose off the girl one bedroom over.

"Mostly," Tom said. "What color are Kendal's eyes?"

"Brown," Ledesma said, turning to look. "Oh—fuck—he cut out her eyes—"

More retching. Tom knew this couldn't be Kendal. He turned to leave.

"I can't tell if it's her," Ledesma said, catching his breath.

"It's not. This girl's eyes are blue."

"Her eyes are gone, man!"

"They're not gone," Tom said. "They're on the dresser."

Tom left the bedroom, walking through the throng of cops and techies, walking to the front door, tugging off the blood-soaked paper crime scene booties he'd put on over his shoes, dropping them into the garbage can with five other pairs, and stepping outside where he stared up at the sun until his head began to throb.

"What now?" Detective Ledesma, from behind him.

"I'm done."

"Look, if this is a jurisdictional thing, we work with Chicago PD all the time. What's our next move?"

Tom closed his eyes, still seeing the afterglow of retina burn. "I'm done. I quit. My next move is going to my captain's office and turning in my gun and badge."

Tom turned and stared at the guy, wondering if he was ever that young. "Is this your first murder scene?"

"Yeah."

"It's my two hundred and nineteenth. And each one of them," Tom jammed his index finger against his temple, "is still up here. I'm done. I'm going to fly to LA, beg my girlfriend to take me back, and get a normal job. This—" Tom spread out his hands, indicating the two of them, the house, the whole world. "This is not normal. And it's not healthy."

"He took her, Detective Mankowski. This animal took Kendal. I've been following the case. He's never kidnapped before."

"So he's branching out."

"Kendal could still be alive."

"I hope she is. I really do. And I hope you find her."

"The only thing necessary for the triumph of evil is for good men to do nothing." Ledesma blinked. "That's Edmund Burke."

"I fucking quit. That's Tom Mankowski. Good luck with your investigation, Detective. It's a kidnapping, federal crime, so the Feebies will probably take over. I'll make sure my partner, Roy Lewis, gets in touch."

Tom didn't bother with a handshake. He headed for his car, parked a block away.

He didn't feel guilt. He didn't feel regret. His finely honed sense of civic responsibility wasn't berating him to turn around and assist.

Instead, Tom felt an overwhelming sense of relief.

He checked his phone, and was pleased to see there was a voicemail. But he wasn't pleased to see who it was from.

"It's McGlade. I've been trying Jack, and her husband, Phin, for the last few hours. They didn't get through. Then I checked a few sources and found out the Folk Nation—T-Nail's gang—had been mobilizing for something big. So I picked up Herb and we're driving up north to Spoonward, Wisconsin. If you ever owed Jack a favor, you can repay it by coming with us. Call me back, pronto."

Ah, shit. Tom owed Jack a lot of favors.

He Googled Spoonward, saw it was a seven hour drive north.

Then he tried Joan again. She didn't pick up, so he left another message.

Tom unlocked his car, climbed into the driver's seat, and rubbed his face. Then he texted McGlade, since that was preferable to talking to the man.

That Edmund Burke line that Ledesma had quoted; Tom knew it well. He'd used it himself, when arguing with Joan.

The only thing necessary for the triumph of evil is for good men to do nothing.

It was true. But Burke had another equally famous, equally true quote:

Those who don't know history are destined to repeat it.

Tom stared into the sun again.

He knew doing so hurt his eyes.

But he did it just the same.

CHAPTER 50

Joan was dreaming about Tom, about how she hurt him, and she woke up hearing his voice.

"…can't live without. Call me back."

Then reality slapped her, full force.

She was sitting up, her hands bound in duct tape behind her. Her ankles were also encircled, the tape wrapped around a curved, metal bar bolted to the floor of some sort of small room.

No, not a room. A truck or van. Joan could hear an engine, feel the movement of the vehicle.

Patchy, dreamlike memories of being carried, being gagged, were superseded by much sharper recollections of being attacked in Tom's house.

Someone has abducted me.

Pain came next. A scorching headache. Bruised from the stun gun. A sore jaw. Pins and needles in her fingers.

Then, nausea. Joan turned away to throw up, and saw a young woman was bound next to her, wrists and ankles also secured with duct tape, a red ball gag in her mouth. Joan made a gagging sound, and managed to choke back the puke and she felt the vehicle stop.

Movement, to her right, and some curtains parted.

It was a young man. Longish blonde hair. Wiry frame. He wore khakis, a polo, and gym shoes.

"Are you awake? All cylinders firing? Mental faculties intact?"

"Who are you?" Joan managed to say.

"Erinyes." His eyes narrowed. "Say it."

Joan repeated the strange word. "Erinyes."

"You might have heard of our work. They call us The Snipper. My better half took you from Tom's house last night."

Joan felt a scream building, and Erinyes put a finger over his lips. "Shh. There is a time and a place for screaming. This isn't it. I only have one ball gag, and I took it out so you wouldn't choke on your vomit from all the drugs you've taken. But I can pick another one up."

Joan swallowed the scream, and tried to keep the fear out of her voice. She failed.

"What do you want?"

"Are you familiar with the Furies? Ancient Greek deities of vengeance from the underworld, sent to earth to punish sinners?"

He pointed both fingers at himself and made a *that's me* expression.

"I heard..." Joan stopped her sentence short.

"You heard Tom. You are correct. I was being a bit nosy listening to your voicemail."

Erinyes held up Joan's cell phone, and began to play Joan's messages.

"I'm sorry. Can we talk? Please? I love you."

"Isn't he so sweet?" Erinyes said. His words were like pouring salt on a third degree burn.

"Me again. You're right about everything. I'm really sorry. Please call me back."

Hearing Tom's voice, and him sounding so sad, made it hard for Joan to breathe. Her eyes glassed over.

"Joan, you're my everything. I know I messed up. The ring... I wasn't thinking. You told me marriage was stupid. I guess I thought... I dunno what I thought. Just please call me back. I... I love you so much."

The tears were flowing freely now. Erinyes paused the messages. "He sold all of his comic books to buy the ring," he said. "It cost him over seven thousand dollars. White gold, a yellow diamond. Tom was particularly excited that it was an antique Cartier, and came from France."

The sob came out of her like it had been ripped out.

"I bet you feel like such a bitch right now," Erinyes said. "I'm a Greek deity. I see all. I know all. And let me tell you, Joan; you should have said yes."

He played another.

"Joan, I gotta stay here overnight, for observation."

Erinyes paused. "He's sugar-coating it. He had surgery on his arm. Some horrible infection, flesh eating bacteria, pretty serious stuff."

"I've been thinking a lot about you. About us. You... you're the only thing I want. The only thing I can't live without. Call me back."

"Please..." Joan said. "Please let me go."

"Shh. Last message."

"I'm at a crime scene in Evanston. The Snipper just slaughtered seven sorority girls, and kidnapped an eighth. I'm done, Joan. I'm quitting. I'm going in right now to turn in my badge. I assume you're on your way back to LA. Please call me when you get in. Please. I love you so, so much."

Erinyes put Joan's phone into his pocket and said, "So you got your way. How do you feel?"

Joan felt...

Helpless. Terrified. Ashamed. Devastated.

No matter what Erinyes did to her, Joan couldn't imagine it hurting more than she already hurt. If only she'd stayed with Tom. If only she'd said yes to his proposal. If only—

The slap was abrupt, rocking her head back.

"Penance works best when you confess your sins, Joan. Tell me what you're feeling."

Another emotion took over.

Anger.

Joan stared hard at the man. "I'm not telling you shit."

He smiled, stroking her stinging cheek with his thumb. "Oh, you'll tell me everything. By the time we're through, you'll tell me every detail, every sin, every secret you've ever had. Then you'll beg to tell me more."

He slapped her again.

And again.

And again, until she could no longer hold the sick feeling back and the vomit came. Erinyes quickly reached on top of the sheet-covered box on the floor next to her, and held a plastic bag under her head until she stopped throwing up.

"The drugs I gave you made you sick," he said, tying the handles of the bag into a knot. "But if you do it again, I swear, I'll cut off all your fingers, drop them in your puke, and make you lick up the whole mess."

CHAPTER 51

Captain Bains wasn't in his office. Tom asked around, and found Bains had taken a personal day. Station gossip said it was health-related.

Tom would have left his gun and badge on the man's desk, along with a note, but his office was locked. So, instead, he went back to his house.

He lasted five minutes, staring at his empty bed, then texted Harry McGlade.

`I'm in.`

`OK. I'll pick you up.`

Tom packed a backpack with overnight essentials; shirt, underwear, socks, toiletries, phone charger, extra ammo. Then he made the bed, flipped on the television, caught a brief glimpse of Snipper coverage, turned off the television, and then got on his phone and downloaded a casual game he'd gotten addicted to. When Joan came into town, he'd removed it so he wouldn't be tempted to play while she was there.

If only he'd had that same self-control with his job.

McGlade eventually texted that he'd arrived, and when Tom went to meet him he saw the private eye standing in front of a full-sized, candy-apple red RV.

Harry was a dozen or more years older than Tom, salt and pepper scruff on his face, eyes manic. His clothes were expensive, but in need of an ironing.

"Glad you could make it."

"I owe Jack."

"Hop in the side door."

Tom opened it, and saw the familiar rotund and mustachioed face of Sergeant Herb Benedict, sitting on one of the couches. Herb was in his fifties, his suit cheap and wrinkled, and there was a stain on his tie that was probably as old as the tie itself. Next to Herb was a sleeping baby, and across from him, in a cage, was a parrot.

Tom nodded at the sergeant, climbed in, and closed the door behind him.

"Welcome to the Crimebago, Tom," Harry said from the driver's seat. He pronounced it *Crim-ee-baygo*, like *Winnebago*. "That's Harry Junior, and Homeboy. Harry Junior is the one wearing the diaper and napping next to Herb. Homeboy is the one in the cage. Herb is the land whale. Help yourself to whatever is in the fridge, and if the ride gets boring you and Herb can play some chess, assuming Herb knows how. Board is in the cabinet with Junior's toys, next to the dishwasher."

"Why is the parrot named Homeboy?" Tom asked Herb as he sat down.

"Former owners. I don't know whether to blame their parents, or society in general. Something went wrong somewhere."

"Why is it naked?"

"He's addicted to methamphetamine, so he plucked out all his feathers."

Tom nodded. A parrot with trichotillomania made about as much sense as a giant, red recreational vehicle. Such was Harry's world. Tom looked around, taking in the expensive furnishings. The ride was certainly pimped. McGlade travelled in style. But it was a loud, abrasive style.

"So, how have you been, Sarge? Haven't ran into you in a while."

"I spent all morning with McGlade, that's how I've been. You?"

"Not that bad. But close."

Partly from nervous energy, partly because he didn't want to discuss Joan, Tom began to talk about The Snipper case. He stopped short of mentioning his impending resignation.

"I've been following that one," Harry interrupted. "Seems like a real nutjob. Herb and I have run into a few of those."

Tom absently touched his arm, the bandages hidden by his jacket.

"Herb had his eyes sewn shut by a psycho," Harry said. "I had it even worse. I was electroshocked by the same guy."

"One guy kidnapped me, broke my arm, and kept twisting it to lure Jack to him," Herb said. "That one was bad."

"Dude, electroshock is worse than a tiny little fracture," Harry said.

"He was grinding bone on bone."

"Bone on bone is like foreplay. I still don't have full control over my bladder."

"Did you ever?" Herb asked.

So that's what they were doing? The scene in *Jaws* where everyone compared scars? The two of them went back and forth like that for a minute, bickering like brothers. Tom stared out the side window. He wondered if Joan was also staring out a window, in Business Class at thirty thousand feet.

"I was tied up and branded by a guy," Tom said.

"How much branding are we talking here?" Harry asked.

"Enough that I passed out. And then the killer licked the burn."

"Sounds like a fairy princess tickle party compared to my hand." Harry waved his prosthetic limb. "Fingers cut off, one at a time, stumps cauterized with a blowtorch. Doctors couldn't save anything, had to amputate. Remember that one, Herb?"

"Yes. I got a chest full of roofing nails."

"Yeah! Right! I remember making a joke about you getting nailed. You missed it because you were in the ER, under sedation. Also, I didn't go visit you. What else you got, Tom?"

"I was just bitten by a guy."

"Bitten, huh? Well, it's not a contest. Because if it was, you'd lose. But you're young yet. Plenty of time for more maniacs to torture you before your career is over."

"Fingers crossed," Tom said.

Then he sat back and tried to settle in for the long, boring drive ahead.

CHAPTER 52

Joan's phone buzzes.

Tom again.

Erinyes waits for him to leave a message, and then listens.

Interesting. He's heading to northern Wisconsin.

Erinyes drums her fingers on the steering wheel, thinking.

He's following the news on his laptop. Things are getting hot in Illinois. Between the house being raided, and the sorority adventure, the police and the media are all whipped up in a convulsive frenzy. There are rumblings about bringing in the FBI, and even mention of road blocks.

Exciting. But risky.

This might be a good time to leave the state for a while. Let things cool down.

Erinyes reaches out to his better half, who agrees.

He tracks Tom's location by his phone, and then points the van north.

CHAPTER 53

Fear threatened to devour her.

One-two-three… one-two-three…

She was bound, gagged, and waiting to be killed by the maniac who had butchered all of her sorority sisters.

One-two-three…

This wasn't in her head. It wasn't a dream. It wasn't a paranoid delusion. It wasn't a hallucination or a fantasy.

It was real. And there was no escape.

One-two-three… one-two-three… one-two-three.

Kendal managed to retain her sanity by tapping the back of her head against the interior wall of the vehicle.

One-two-three… one-two-three… one-two-three.

The woman next to Kendal had her eyes closed and was jerking and twisting her arms. It wouldn't do any good. You can't break duct tape. Kendal owned a purse made entirely out of duct tape, bought on a whim at a craft fair. That stuff was stronger than leather.

One-two-three…

"We're stopping, ladies." It was the man driving. "I need you to behave. The walls of this van are soundproof, so if your scream all it will do is make me angry."

He parked the vehicle, and shut it off. After more than a minute, the curtain moved back, and her abductor appeared.

Kendal wet herself with fear. It was only then that she realized she was wearing a diaper.

The man squatted next to her, grinning. "Hello, Kendal. I'm going to take your gag off. Do you want that?"

He nodded, and Kendal nodded along with him.

"And will there be any screaming?" he asked, shaking his head.

She repeated the gesture. He unbuckled the ball gag and pulled it from her mouth. Kendal closed her sore jaw, swallowing several times.

"I'm Erinyes. Say my name."

"Erinyes," she whispered.

He gave her a rough pat on the cheek, then turned to the other woman. "Guess where we are, Joan?"

The woman doesn't answer.

"Don't want to talk to me? I'm hurt. Is it because your heart belongs to him?" Erinyes raised up a cell phone and showed her the screen. "I just took this picture of Tom a minute ago. He's right outside, walking into that restaurant. Less than twenty meters away."

"TOM!" Joan screamed.

Erinyes grabbed Joan by her bangs and began to slam her head into the side of the van, until she was either dead or unconscious. Then he smoothed out her hair, pulled back his hand to stare at his fingers, and wiped the blood off on Joan's jeans.

"I told her not to scream," he said, turning to Kendal. "Are you going to scream?"

"No."

Kendal felt herself shrink, like she was about to disappear. The psychological term was *disassociation*. She was detaching from her surroundings, going to a safe place in her mind where she couldn't be hurt.

It was an effective way to cope with horrifying situations. But it was a last resort. If Kendal detached, she'd have no chance to get away.

So she focused on the head tapping, this time harder.

One-two-three-one-two-three-one-two-three...

"What are you doing?" Erinyes asked.

"I have obsessive compulsive disorder."

Erinyes nodded. "I thought there was something odd about you. Like Jack Nicholson. In that movie. Do you wash your hands all the time?"

"No. I count."

"Count what?"

"Everything. Steps. Ceiling tiles. Cars that pass."

Erinyes tilted his head, seeming to appraise her. "So you're crazy."

"We're all a little crazy."

He took her throat in his hand. "Are you saying that I'm crazy, Kendal?"

One-two-three-one-two-three...

"My father had antisocial personality disorder," Kendal said, speaking as quickly as she could.

"Is that what you think I have?"

Kendal began to spit out what she memorized for Abnormal Psych class. "Several behaviors must be present before a diagnosis of ASPD can be made. The subject must fail to conform to social norms or laws; lie or use aliases; be impulsive, aggressive, and irritable; have a reckless disregard for the safety of themselves or others; show consistent irresponsibility; and lack remorse."

"And what did Daddy do to make you think he was a sociopath?"

One-two-three-one-two-three-one-two-three.

"There are seven subtypes of ASPD, according to Theodore Millon. My father was the unprincipled type. He did whatever he wanted to," Kendal swallowed the lump in her throat. "Regardless of who he hurt."

The man's eye twitched. "Sometimes fathers do things we don't understand."

"My father raped me."

Erinyes had no reaction. "Were you tempting him? Acting like a whore?"

"I was eleven."

"AGE DOESN'T MATTER!" Erinyes screamed in her face, flecking it with spittle. "We're all sinners, Kendal. All of us. Even little babies."

ONE-TWO-THREE...

"Stop that head tapping thing. It's irritating me."

"I can't," Kendal whimpered.

"Men naturally lack discipline," Erinyes said. "My father taught me that. Impulse control is directly linked to the penis. But women... they have control, Kendal. They don't do things impulsively. They calculate. They plot. That makes them worse sinners than men. With women, everything they do has intent. So stop that damn head tapping."

"I wish I could," she cried, "oh god I wish I could."

Erinyes narrowed his eyes, and Kendal cringed. She was sure he was going to hit her, or slam her head into the side of the van, or worse.

But instead he said, "The Erinyes are Greek deities of vengeance. They give Penance to sinners. When a sinner suffers, their soul is cleansed. The more sins they have, the more they must suffer. Do you think it's easy to be Erinyes, Kendal? It's a great burden, punishing the wicked."

He moved next to the small box, on the floor of the van next to Joan. It had a sheet over the top.

"All of the furies wear a special crown," he said, pulling off the sheet.

It revealed a small, glass aquarium, no more than ten gallons. The interior appeared to have been speckled with mud.

Then Kendal realized the specks of mud were moving.

"It's a crown of spiders," Erinyes said.

Kendal began to thrash her head back and forth.

Oh no. No-no-no-no-no...

"I think Joan should be awake for this, don't you?"

He reached into his pocket and pulled out something small and white. There was a snapping sound, and Kendal smelled ammonia. Joan's head popped up.

"Welcome to the party, Joan. I was telling Kendal about my pets, here. Eratigena agrestis. Also known as the hobo spider. It is one of the very few spiders known to attack humans. That's why it has picked up another name. The *aggressive house spider*."

Erinyes took the screen cover off the tank, setting it aside. Spiders began to crawl onto the van's floor, spreading out in all directions like a creeping stain. Some of them were at least two inches long.

"I was telling Kendal that all of the furies must wear a crown of spiders. I did, when I was sixteen years old." Erinyes lowered his voice to a whisper. "A word of warning. If you move too much, they bite. And it really, really, *really* hurts."

He reached into the bottom of the aquarium and pulled out—

A plastic bag. The grocery store kind.

Erinyes held the bag by one of its handles, bouncing it on his fingers. "A few ounces of spiders. That's a lot."

He moved to Joan, who began to violently flail, stretching to move away, but with nowhere to go.

Erinyes went to her—

—and pulled the plastic bag over her head, tying the handles in a loose knot under Joan's chin.

Erinyes reached into the tank once again, removing a second bag.

"Remember our game, Kendal? Would you like to sing along?"

ONE-TWO-THREE-ONE-TWO-THREE…

"The eetsy…beetsy… spiiiiiiiider… went… up… the… waaaaaaater spout."

He opened the bag, holding it up to her face. Kendal couldn't stop herself; she peered in horror at the bottom, which was teaming with hairy, scurrying, eight-legged monsters.

And then the bag was on her head, and thousands of hobo spiders began to explore their new environment.

CHAPTER 54

Contrary to expectations, the trip wasn't too boring. They stopped once to eat, stopped once to drop Harry's child off with some babysitters, and stopped several times for gas. Between stops, Tom played his cell phone game, and time passed pretty quickly.

Up until they got way up north and lost cell coverage.

"My phone reception is gone." Herb held his cell up in the air and began to wave it around.

Tom did the same thing, searching for bars. But no matter where he held it, his screen said NO SIGNAL.

"Try adjusting the rabbit ears," Herb eventually suggested.

"Huh?"

"They were on old TVs."

"Rabbits were on old TVs?"

"That's what the antennas were called. You're probably too young to remember."

Tom frowned. "Can we switch to WiFi or Bluetooth?"

Herb shook his head. "I just had a case where a killer hacked a neighbor's WiFi connection to spy on her. It's easier than you think. With normal equipment, WiFi only has a range of about thirty meters. Bluetooth, less than ten. And both need some sort of WAP."

That made no sense. "They need a derogatory term for Italians?"

"W-A-P. Wireless access point. Like a router. We don't have one. No hotspot either. And no ad hoc network. With a hotspot or ad hoc, we could maybe text each other, but we still couldn't connect to the Internet or reach anyone beyond our short range."

"Fascinating," Tom lied.

"I'm full of useless bits of information."

To make polite conversation, Tom asked, "Such as?"

Tom paid half-attention as Herb talked about Argentina, and Nikola Tesla, and sharks, and all Tom cared about was that his cell service had vanished, and Joan still hadn't called him back.

He wondered what she was doing, at that very moment.

CHAPTER 55

Joan pursed her lips together, her whole body quaking with effort not to scream.

Because if she screamed, the spiders crawling all over her face would creep into her mouth.

CHAPTER 56

Erinyes checks his cell phone.

No signal.

He tries Joan's phone, and his 4G laptop, and has similar results.

Maybe there's just no signal out here in the boonies.

He speeds up. Tom and his buddies are two miles ahead. Prior to the service disruption, Erinyes had been listening in to their conversation. He knows where they're going—to the local police station—and he considers beating the trio there and surprising them.

But that poses a problem. If they change plans, it will be impossible to find Tom out here.

The other option is to stay behind them, keep them in sight. It shouldn't be that hard; even though the sun has gone down, that private investigator's RV stands out like a giant, bright red thumb.

The danger there, however, is that McGlade person noticing he's being tailed.

Decisions, decisions…

The choice is made for him when Erinyes comes upon road construction, and fifty meters ahead sees that Tom and the others have pulled over to the side of the road.

If he slows down, or stops, he risks being spotted.

Erinyes opts for the original plan, turning off his headlights before cruising past them, heading toward the tiny, one horse town of Spoonward, Wisconsin.

When he arrives, he isn't sure where to go. He doesn't have the police station address, and the whole town seems to have locked up and retired for the night. Worried about the time, and how far behind Tom and company are, Erinyes begins to drive up and down the streets, looking for someone, anyone, to ask directions. He finds a billboard that announces a Walmart nearby—open 24 hours—and begins to head for it, but luckily notices a simple street sign that says POLICE.

He turns on Main, cruises past dark shops and buildings, and sees a sole light at the end of the street.

Sure enough, it's the stationhouse.

Erinyes rolls past, parks a block away, next to a bait shop. He kills the engine and goes into the back of the van. When he removes the bag from Kendal's head, spiders scurry everywhere.

Kendal's eyes are open, but she's staring into space. She has a few bites on her cheeks, her nose, and the hobo spiders have begun to spin webs in her hair.

"Are you here with us, Kendal?"

Kendal doesn't answer. She's somewhere else. Which is fine, for now. He wants her docile.

Erinyes turns to Joan. When he pulls off the bag, her eyes are open as well. But she stares directly at him, defiant. She also has several spider bites. And her hair is so mottled with webs, she looks like a gray-haired old lady.

"I see you're with us, Joan. I'm stepping out for a few minutes. You know by now I make good on my threats. If you scream, if you try to escape, if you so much as move an inch out of place, you're getting twice as many spiders. But this time, I'm going to slice off your eyelids and your lips, first. Do you understand?"

Joan doesn't respond.

"Answer me. If you don't want to use your tongue, I'll cut that out, too."

"I understand," she mumbled.

Erinyes strips down to the vantablack leotard, and then puts the make-up on his eyelids. After he slips on the gloves and ski mask, he strikes a model pose for Joan.

"Does this outfit make me look fat?" he says, then giggles.

Joan doesn't seem amused. "It doesn't matter what you do to me. Tom is going to find you."

"Not if I find him first."

Erinyes takes his bag and steps out into the night, blending in like he's part of it.

When he gets to the sheriff's office, he peeks in the streetside window. Rather than seeing the expected country bumpkin cop smoking a corncob pipe and eating cracklins, he spots three African American youths with submachine guns loitering inside.

Interesting. Erinyes knows very little about street gangs, but he knows some of them have hundreds of members. He wouldn't want to be that Jacqueline Daniels person they'd come here for.

The youths are preoccupied, gathered around a desk and throwing dice. They're also smoking pot.

Erinyes is outgunned and outnumbered, but has vantablack, surprise, and sobriety on his side. Flicking off the safety on the Taurus, he quickly enters the room and shoots all three, hitting two of them in the head and one four times in the neck and chest.

They died without even reaching for their weapons.

Erinyes loads a fresh magazine as he searches the rest of the station, which is really nothing more than two offices, a hallway, a storage room, a back door, and a single, barred cell. On the floor of the cell is a dead old man with a star pinned to his chest. Eight of his fingers are gone.

My my my. Those gang guys had been very naughty.

Such a shame they died without Penance.

Erinyes sticks his head out the front door, checking to make sure the street is still empty. Then he turns off all the lights except for the single bulb lamp on the desk, and stands in the window, silhouetting himself, waiting for Tom and his friends to arrive.

CHAPTER 57

"Welcome to beautiful downtown Spoonward, Wisconsin," McGlade said. "Don't blink or you'll miss it."

Tom looked out the window. He knew the town was small—a population of five hundred—

but this was nothing but a main street in the middle of a forest. And everything was dark. None of the shops or buildings had their lights on, except for one.

Luckily, it was the one they'd come for. The police station. Though, judging from the size, it was less of a station and more of a small office.

The plan, which they'd discussed earlier, was to go in, inform whatever authority was present what the situation was with Jacqueline Daniels, and then round up some cops to take along to McGlade's hideaway in case T-Nail and his gang had already shown up.

"The locals can provide more manpower, more guns, and the necessary stamp of approval," Tom had argued. "If things go bad, we'll be up to our necks in bad media and local politics. We're a long way from our jurisdiction, and Harry isn't even a cop. We do this wrong, it isn't just a slap on the wrist. It's jail time."

"I vote against jail time," Harry agreed. "I'm too pretty for prison. The lifers would pass me around like a pack of cigarettes."

McGlade pulled up to the station house and parked.

"Let's be quick about this," Herb said. "We run in, tell whoever's there what's happening, and go get Jack. How far away is your place, Harry?"

"About ten more miles."

"Just let me out here," Tom said. "I'll talk to them."

"We can all go in."

"We don't know how long it will take. You and Harry need to go find Jack."

Plus, Tom thought, *if they have a land line, I want to try calling Joan again.*

"You sure?" Herb frowned. "What if there isn't anyone there?"

"I see people through their window. Someone is home. You got a paper map, McGlade?"

Their GPS had died at the same time their cell service had.

"Yeah. In the good old glove box."

Harry opened the glove compartment and found a map amid all the snack food, then wasted thirty seconds finding his hideaway and circling it in pen before handing it to Tom. It was one of those free tourist maps, listing all the shops, gas stations, and motels. There weren't many.

Tom chose to leave his overnight bag in the car, figuring he'd be back. He offered Herb his hand and they shook. "Be careful. I'll be right behind you guys. If the Chief doesn't give me a ride, I'll steal his squad car."

"Good luck," Herb said.

"Who needs luck when I have natural charm?" Tom asked.

"Ned Beatty had natural charm, too," Harry said. "Things didn't work out well for him in *Deliverance*."

Tom opened the side door, and then smiled. "They're cops like us. What's the worst that can happen?"

CHAPTER 53

Joan shook her head, trying to get the spiders out of her hair. The first hour had been one of the worst experiences in her entire life, and she'd had some doozies.

But when she ran out of adrenaline, her panic eased. And the bites, though painful, weren't nearly as bad as a bee sting.

"Kendal," she said. "You okay?"

Kendal didn't answer. She was obviously in shock.

Joan had been waiting for Erinyes to leave. During the past few hours, while trying to snort spiders out of her nostrils, she'd come up with a plan to escape. It was a long shot, but it beat the hell out of waiting to be tortured to death.

Strangely enough, the plan involved the spiders that had scared her so badly.

Or rather, their aquarium.

Joan leaned over, stretching for the edge with her chin, sticking her face in the tank and pulling it closer. The spiders didn't like their habitat moved, and several dozen scurried up the side of the glass, swarming over her.

Joan managed to tip the tank onto its side. She fit her whole head in, until her nose was buried in spiders, and the back of her skull touched the opposite end. Then, in one sudden move, Joan snapped her neck up and jerked into a sitting position, sending the whole aquarium flying through the air.

But rather than land next to her, the tank arced in Kendal's direction.

The aquarium broke, as expected. Into shards large enough to cut their duct tape bonds.

But all the glass had broken too far away for Joan to reach.

She flopped onto her side, stretching for it with her chin and cheeks, straining against the duct tape until her ankles were about to snap in half against the steel U bolt.

The nearest piece was still half a meter away. There was no way she could grab it.

But Kendal could.

"Kendal. Listen to me. There's broken glass next to you. You can use it to cut the tape and get free."

Kendal continued to stare blankly into space.

"Dammit, Kendal! Listen to me! We can get out of here!"

Kendal didn't respond.

"KENDAL!" Joan cried, as loud as she ever had in her life. She cried for herself, and for all the life she had lived and the life she hadn't lived yet. She cried for the world, and all the people who would suffer and die because Erinyes continued to be free. But most of all, she cried for Tom, whom she hurt so badly and needed to see again because her answer was yes, yes, GODDAMIT YES, she would sure as hell marry him.

Kendal didn't even blink. She was too far gone.

CHAPTER 59

Tom gets out of the Winnebago.

He's by himself.

Then the RV leaves.

Erinyes smiles, his hands tightening on the 9mm.

This is absolutely perfect.

He can already imagine the look on Joan's face when he hands her Tom's severed head.

. . .

Tom opened the door to the police station—

—smelled blood—

—immediately dropped to his knees and yanked out his Glock as bullets blasted into the air where he'd been standing a moment ago.

Tom let gravity take him onto his side, and he brought his weapon up as his shoulder slammed into the floor, aiming where he'd seen the muzzle flash, squeezing the trigger and firing six rounds.

One of his rounds hit the desk lamp, and the office plunged into darkness.

Tom quickly got a foot under him and tore ass out of the office, back onto Main Street. The gunfire had deafened him, but he could still feel his own pulse in his ears, thrumming like a Tommy Lee drum solo.

Crouching, he put his back against the side of the doorway, and waited for the shooter to come out.

. . .

The pain is exquisite.

Erinyes doesn't know how bad the wound is, but he can feel the hot blood trickling down his arm.

He shot me. The bastard shot me.

It all happened so fast, and then Erinyes was on the floor in the dark, bleeding, not sure what to do next.

Get out of there.

He winds the strap of his bag around his neck and crawls through the blackness on three limbs, over to the hallway, running on pure memory, heading for the back door. It lets out into an alley, and Erinyes waits, trying to hear above the ringing in his head, hoping against hope that Tom has followed.

• • •

A minute passed.

Tom stayed put, determined to wait this SOB out.

• • •

Tom doesn't show himself.

Erinyes dares to probe the wound in his upper arm. It cut a trail across his triceps, so deep he can feel the impression.

As the pain builds, so does the anger.

Erinyes digs into his duffle, finds his first aid kit, and opens a packet of Celox with his teeth. He dumps the powder on the wound, stopping the bleeding.

This is no longer about simply killing Tom.

Erinyes wants to hurt him.

He wants to punish him.

He wants to make him suffer like no one has ever suffered before.

He wants Tom to watch as he violates Joan with the butcher knife, unable to look away because his eyelids are gone.

He wants to chisel out Tom's teeth, and break his fingers and toes and arms and legs, and burn every bit of his body with a blowtorch.

But how can he get him?

Tom is a cop. He's had more training then Erinyes. And he's already shown that he's better in a gunfight.

Erinyes stares into his bag, looking for inspiration, and notices Joan's cell. He snatches it up.

No 4G service.

But her phone has its own WiFi hotspot.

. . .

Another minute passed.

The shooter didn't emerge.

Tom decided not to press his luck, and he ran, keeping low, up Main Street. If the gang had already taken out the local cops, they'll be moving on Jack soon.

If they hadn't already.

Tom needed to find a vehicle, to get to Harry and Herb and warn them before—

His phone vibrated, tingling in his pocket. Had cell service returned?

Tom stopped, crouching down, squinting at the screen.

No service, but his WiFi was activated, and Tom found himself staring at a text. From Joan.

`snipper has me`

At first, Tom's mind couldn't process what he was reading.

`in spoonward dark van main st`

She was here? The Snipper had grabbed her? And they were in Spoonward?

Tom checked the WiFi signal, and saw his phone had automatically logged onto Joan's hotspot.

That meant, according to know-it-all Sergeant Herb Benedict, that she was within thirty meters.

`can u c anything` Tom typed, fast as his fingers could move.

He held his breath, waiting for a reply.

`bait shop`

Bait shop? Tom didn't remember seeing a bait shop.

Where the hell is the damn bait shop? Why didn't I pay more attention to—

Wait. Harry's map.

Tom tugged it out of his jacket pocket, using the light from his cell phone to see.

The Spoonward Bait Shop was a block away from the Police Station, in the other direction.

Tom didn't think. He ran.

When he saw the van, parked on the street in the distance, he ran even harder.

. . .

Kendal blinked.

It was never easy to come back from the safe place. But she returned, bit by bit.

Hearing came first. Someone yelling at her.

Then sight. It was a woman yelling. A woman wrapped up in duct tape.

Then realization.

I'm in a van.

A psycho has me.

The woman was named Joan, and she was shouting something.

"The glass! Pick up the glass!"

The glass? What does that even mean?

The back door of the van swung open and Kendal turned to gape at the strange man standing there.

"Tom!" Joan cried.

Then the man fell backward as two gunshots rang out.

. . .

Tom hadn't seen Erinyes hiding under the van. He hadn't even stopped to look.

Love is blind.

Erinyes waited for him to run right up, open the back door, and see the woman he loved.

Then he shot Tom once in each leg.

• • •

Tom dropped like a marionette with its strings cut, his legs no longer supporting him. He managed to hold onto his gun, but there wasn't anyone to shoot at. For a moment he locked eyes with Joan, sitting on the floor in the back of the van, her hands behind her and her legs wrapped in duct tape.

"He's wearing black!"

Tom cast frantic looks in all directions. To his left, his right, behind him, under the van.

He didn't see anyone, anywhere.

The pain came. Like he'd been hit in the shins with a sledgehammer. Tom grimaced, yelled.

Then a gun pressed against the back of his head.

"If you even breathe, I'll kill you. Put the weapon down."

Once again, Tom stared at Joan. He tried to tell her, with a look, that he wasn't going to give up. That he was going to make a move, even if it was his last.

Joan said, "I love you."

And then Tom was pistol-whipped so hard that his whole world went sideways, then winked out.

CHAPTER 60

As Tom flops over, Erinyes kicks away his gun, then hurries to retrieve his bag, which he left alongside the bait shop. He puts his Taurus inside, doses the mask with ether, and holds it to Tom's face until he's sure the cop is out.

Then he turns his attention to the van.

The aquarium is smashed.

Rather than beat the bitches to death, he uses a bit of ether on each of them. Joan tries to hold her breath, so he kicks her in the stomach to make her inhale.

Then he needs to regroup. Take a little breather.

His arm has stopped bleeding. He looks at the wound in the dashboard light.

Nasty. He probably needs stitches. He settles for an injection of local anesthetic, and some Tylenol 3.

As the drugs kick in, Erinyes considers his next move. He's tired. Very tired. It's easy to make mistakes when you're exhausted. The smart thing to do is to make sure Tom is secured, then drive someplace safe and sleep. The suffering can start in the morning, after Erinyes has rested.

He uses more of the blood clotting powder on Tom's legs. The wounds aren't too bad, but it would be a tragedy if Tom bled to death after Erinyes put in all this effort.

It isn't easy to get Tom into the van. He's a big guy, and dragging him is difficult. Lifting him inside, impossible.

Then the codeine takes effect, giving Erinyes use of both arms. Using a spoon he crushes and sniffs four methylphenidate tablets, and then drinks a whole liter of water. While he waits for the pills to work their magic, he wipes off the vantablack make-up, then cleans the van, using an old tee shirt to sweep all broken aquarium pieces out into the street. Many of his Eratigena agrestis have gone, escaping into the night. But he's pleased to see that some have stuck around.

The amphetamines kick start his metabolism, and Erinyes finds he can easily pull Tom inside the vehicle. He duct tapes his hands behind him, but tapes his legs to the floor of the van, spread-eagled.

They'll all stay put until tomorrow.

But Erinyes doesn't want to wait for tomorrow. He's wired and pain-free and ready to dish out Penance.

So he snaps on some latex gloves, everyone gets a big whiff of smelling salts, and then the show begins.

"You up, Tom?" he slaps the man, hard, as Tom blinks rapidly.

"Joan? How about you? You don't want to miss this."

Joan shoots arrows at him with her eyes.

"How about you, Kendal? You ready to atone for your sins?"

Kendal has that far away stare again. But Erinyes knows many interesting ways to get a person's attention.

"First things first. Tom, you made me a promise earlier. Remember? You told me you'd castrate yourself. And then you went back on your word." Erinyes waggles a finger at him. "A man is only as good as his word, Tom. So I'm going to help you keep it."

Erinyes unzips Tom's fly.

Then he freezes.

This isn't right. It's not right at all.

I shouldn't be doing this.

This isn't my job.

Erinyes backs away from Tom, then goes to his medicine bag and finds the vial of spironolactone.

This job belongs to my better half.

He gives himself a dose in the thigh.

"It isn't like Jekyll and Hyde," he tells his captive audience as he peels off the top of his unitard. "I don't transform. Women have testosterone. Men have estrogen. It's the proportions that give us traditionally masculine, or feminine, characteristics."

He stares down at his own chest, then tweaks his nipples. "With hormones, I once got up to a B cup. But I missed my beard. So now I go back and forth, as the mood strikes."

Erinyes goes into the duffle bag and puts her falsies on. They're already stuffed into a bra, and both look, and feel, extremely realistic.

"I wasn't born gender-fluid. I'm not trans by choice. My father made that choice for me, when I was five."

She kicks off her shoes, then pulls down the rest of the unitard, and then her boxer-briefs, exposing...

"Nothing," Erinyes says, touching the scar tissue between her legs. "Just a hole to piss through."

The sinners are silent. All that can be heard is the spiders crawling around, but Erinyes knows she might be imagining that because of the uppers she just snorted. Thank you, Ritalin. The amphetamine also makes her chatty, but there's nothing wrong with that.

She's not even bothered that the conversation is one-sided. Erinyes feels like she could gab all night.

"I'm sorry," Tom finally says.

"No need to be. You're going to see how it feels to be like me, soon enough. Well, not exactly. I never went through any sort of traditional puberty like you did. Or like the biological ladies here. I hit puberty thanks to illegal drugs ordered off the Internet. When my mother left... wait... I'm getting ahead of myself."

Erinyes digs through the duffle bag, finds some pink panties, and her butcher knife. She sets the knife aside and pulls on her underwear.

"So, when I was little," she continues, "I thought my mother left. My father told me stories, about what a bad person she was. He told me she took—and in retrospect, this is pretty funny, but I was really young and didn't know better—that she took my penis with her. Dad raised me as a girl. He called me his little Ken doll."

Erinyes shoots a look at Kendal. "Get it? Barbie's boyfriend doesn't have any junk. It's all smooth. So I became Kendal, Daddy's good little girl. He did me a favor, really. Men start wars. Men rape. Men destroy everything they touch. Thank you, testosterone." Erinyes gave a military salute. "Dad spared me all of that. He was my hero."

Erinyes kneels next to Tom, and pulls out his man parts.

"Or he was. Until I found out that Mom never left. He had her chained up in the basement. I used to hear her scream at night. He told me it was Erinyes down there, punishing sinners."

Erinyes laughs.

"He was lying, of course. It wasn't Erinyes. It was my mother. I caught him, late at night, burying her in the backyard after she died. I could barely recognize her. Dad had kept her down there for years. Cut all of her fingers and toes off. Her tongue. Her nose. Whipped her a lot."

Erinyes stretches out her hand, staring at it.

"You know, he even used to carry one of her fingers around with him? And then the stupid son of a bitch dropped it. Anyway, when I saw him with the shovel and my dead mother, he insisted that Erinyes wasn't a monster. Erinyes was a deity of vengeance, who punishes sinners. It's a good thing, really. Sinners are given Penance through suffering, so their souls are cleansed. But he was full of shit. He wasn't Erinyes."

Erinyes smiles. "I'm Erinyes."

Then she grips Tom firmly and brings the butcher knife up under his testicles.

CHAPTER 61

Kendal wasn't paying much attention to the psychopath's rant.

She was too busy sawing away at the duct tape with the piece of glass she'd grabbed before Erinyes brushed it all out of the van.

And then, suddenly, she was through. Her hands were free.

Now she needed to grab the gun. Erinyes had put it in the duffle bag, just a few feet away.

Kendal was terrified. But her fear wasn't as strong as her resolve.

She'd had enough.

Had enough of being victimized.

Had enough of being helpless.

Had enough of being just a thing, rather than a person.

When Erinyes was occupied with Tom, Kendal moved.

In one smooth motion, she bent forward, dug into the bag, and came up with a gun.

Erinyes went wide-eyed.

Kendal pointed the weapon at her head and squeezed the trigger.

Nothing happened.

Erinyes began to laugh.

"You stupid little girl. You've never used a gun before, have you?"

Her father had taught Kendal a lot. Some of what he taught her was terrible. Things little girls should never have to know.

But not everything he did was terrible.

That was the thing that fucked with Kendal's head the most; that her father wasn't a complete monster. He raped Kendal. But he also did all the things that other fathers did. He taught her how to tie her shoes. How to read. How to ride a bike.

How to shoot a semi-automatic pistol.

Erinyes lunged.

Kendal thumbed off the safety and shot the crazy fucker twice in the face.

Erinyes went down.

Bits of skull that had gone airborne came down a moment later.

Kendal didn't like the number two. She preferred things in threes.

But somehow, for some reason, she was able to resist shooting Erinyes again.

There was no need to.

No person, male or female or anywhere on the gender spectrum, could get any deader than that.

CHAPTER 62

As soon as Kendal cut her free, Joan rushed over to Tom, took his face in her hands, and kissed him.

"I do," she said, half into his mouth. "I do I do I do…"

EPILOGUE

The drugs wore off.

The pain came back.

But Walter Cissick is no stranger to pain. He has endured more than any other.

And it has cleansed his soul.

He looks around his hospital room, then stares through the open doorway, into the hall.

There have been no cops since that one who questioned him about Dennis.

It's funny. Really funny.

Those dumb pigs have no idea. None at all.

His son/daughter told him about the people he gave Penance to. The men and women. S/he described every detail. Including the whores from that sorority house that Walter saw on CNN, and those baby rapers he castrated, Dennis still had only punished forty sinners.

Such a small number. True, the boy/girl was young. But s/he lacked discipline. Always had. Even when s/he'd grown enough to drug Walter while he slept, and chained him up in the basement, s/he'd still shown weakness.

Forty is a small number.

Walter Cissick has given Penance to over ninety sinners.

And no cop ever came sniffing around. No suspicion was ever leveled at him. Even after he dropped that finger in the street and reported his wife missing. The police had been sympathetic, not inquisitive.

Cissick sits up. He's dizzy. With pain. With medication. With possibility.

He will be healthy again. Soon.

Healthy, and ready to punish more sinners.

For he is Erinyes. And he shall make them suffer.

THE END

JOE KONRATH'S COMPLETE BIBLIOGRAPHY

JACQUELINE "JACK" DANIELS THRILLERS

WHISKEY SOUR (Book 1)

BLOODY MARY (Book 2)

RUSTY NAIL (Book 3)

DIRTY MARTINI (Book 4)

FUZZY NAVEL (Book 5)

CHERRY BOMB (Book 6)

SHAKEN (Book 7)

STIRRED with Blake Crouch (Book 8)

RUM RUNNER (Book 9)

LAST CALL (Book 10)

WHITE RUSSIAN (Book 11)

SHOT GIRL (Book 12)

CHASER (Book 13)

OLD FASHIONED (Book 14)

BITE FORCE (Book 15)

JACK ROSE (Book 16)

LADY 52 with Jude Hardin (Book 2.5)

JACK DANIELS AND ASSOCIATES MYSTERIES

DEAD ON MY FEET (Book 1)

JACK DANIELS STORIES VOL. 1 (Book 2)

SHOT OF TEQUILA (Book 3)

JACK DANIELS STORIES VOL. 2 (Book 4)

DYING BREATH (Book 5)

SERIAL KILLERS UNCUT with Blake Crouch (Book 6)

JACK DANIELS STORIES VOL. 3 (Book 7)

EVERYBODY DIES (Book 8)

JACK DANIELS STORIES VOL. 4 (Book 9)

BANANA HAMMOCK (Book 10)

KONRATH DARK THRILLER COLLECTIVE

THE LIST (Book 1)

ORIGIN (Book 2)

AFRAID (Book 3)

TRAPPED (Book 4)

ENDURANCE (Book 5)

HAUNTED HOUSE (Book 6)

WEBCAM (Book 7)

DISTURB (Book 8)

WHAT HAPPENED TO LORI (Book 9)

THE NINE (Book 10)

SECOND COMING (Book 11)

CLOSE YOUR EYES (Book 12)

HOLES IN THE GROUND with Iain Rob Wright (Book 4.5)

DRACULAS with Blake Crouch, Jeff Strand, F. Paul Wilson (Book 5.5)

GRANDMA? with Talon Konrath (Book 6.5)

STOP A MURDER PUZZLE BOOKS

STOP A MURDER – HOW: PUZZLES 1 – 12 (Book 1)

STOP A MURDER – WHERE: PUZZLES 13 – 24 (Book 2)

STOP A MURDER – WHY: PUZZLES 25 – 36 (Book 3)

STOP A MURDER – WHO: PUZZLES 37 – 48 (Book 4)

STOP A MURDER – WHEN: PUZZLES 49 – 60 (Book 5)

STOP A MURDER – ANSWERS (Book 6)

STOP A MURDER COMPLETE CASES (Books 1-5)

CODENAME: CHANDLER
(PETERSON & KONRATH)

FLEE (Book 1)

SPREE (Book 2)

THREE (Book 3)

HIT (Book 4)

EXPOSED (Book 5)

NAUGHTY (Book 6)

FIX with F. Paul Wilson (Book 7)

RESCUE (Book 8)

TIMECASTER SERIES

TIMECASTER (Book 1)

TIMECASTER SUPERSYMMETRY (Book 2)

TIMECASTER STEAMPUNK (Book 3)

EROTICA
(WRITING AS MELINDA DUCHAMP)

Make Me Blush series

KINKY SECRETS OF MISTER KINK (Book 1)

KINKY SECRETS OF WITCHES (Book 2)

KINKY SECRETS OF SIX & CANDY (Book 3)

Alice series

KINKY SECRETS OF ALICE IN WONDERLAND (Book 1)

KINKY SECRETS OF ALICE THROUGH THE LOOKING GLASS (Book 2)

KINKY SECRETS OF ALICE AT THE HELLFIRE CLUB (Book 3)

KINKY SECRETS OF ALICE VS DRACULA (Book 4)

KINKY SECRETS OF ALICE VS DR. JEKYLL & MR. HYDE (Book 5)

KINKY SECRETS OF ALICE VS FRANKENSTEIN (Book 6)

KINKY SECRETS OF ALICE'S CHRISTMAS SPECIAL (Book 7)

Jezebel series

KINKY SECRETS OF JEZEBEL AND THE BEANSTALK (Book 1)

KINKY SECRETS OF PUSS IN BOOTS (Book 2)

KINKY SECRETS OF GOLDILOCKS (Book 3)

Sexperts series

THE SEXPERTS – KINKY GRADES OF SHAY (Book 1)

THE SEXPERTS – KINKY SECRETS OF THE PEARL NECKLACE (Book 2)

THE SEXPERTS – KINKY SECRETS OF THE ALIEN (Book 3)

MISCELLANEOUS

65 PROOF – COLLECTED SHORT STORIES

THE GLOBS OF USE-A-LOT 3 (with Dan Maderak)

A NEWBIES GUIDE TO PUBLISHING

OLD FASHIONED

Former Chicago Homicide Lieutenant Jacqueline "Jack" Daniels has finally left her violent past behind, and she's moved into a new house with her family.

But her elderly next door neighbor is a bit… off.

Is he really as he appears, a kind old gentlemen with a few eccentricities?

Or are Jack's instincts correct, and he's something much, much darker?

And what is it he'd got in his basement?

Jack Daniels is about to learn that evil doesn't mellow with age.

OLD FASHIONED by JA Konrath
How well do you know your neighbors?

LAST CALL

A retired cop past her prime…

A kidnapped bank robber fighting for his life…

A former mob enforcer with a blood debt…

A government assassin on the run…

A wisecracking private eye with only one hand…

A homicide sergeant with one week left on the job…

And three of the worst serial killers, ever.

This is where it all ends. An epic showdown in the desert, where good and evil will clash one last time.

His name is Luther Kite, and his specialty is murdering people in ways too horrible to imagine. He's gone south, where he's found a new, spectacular way to kill. And if you have enough money, you can bet on who dies first.

Legendary Chicago cop Jacqueline "Jack" Daniels has retired. She's no longer chasing bad guys, content to stay out of the public eye and raise her new daughter. But when her daughter's father, Phin Troutt, is kidnapped, she's forced to strap on her gun one last time.

Since being separated from his psychotic soulmate, the prolific serial killer known as Donaldson has been desperately searching for her. Now he thinks he's found out where his beloved, insane Lucy has been hiding. He's going to find her, no matter how many people are slaughtered in the process.

All three will converge in same place. La Juntita, Mexico. Where a bloodthirsty cartel is enslaving people and forcing them to fight to the death in insane, gladiator-style games.

Join Jack and Phin, Donaldson and Lucy, and Luther, for the very last act in their twisted, perverse saga.

Along for the ride are Jack's friends; Harry and Herb, as well as a mob enforcer named Tequila, and a covert operative named Chandler.

There will be blood. And death. So much death...

LAST CALL by J.A. Konrath

The conclusion to the Jack Daniels/Luther Kite epic

WATCHED TOO LONG

Small town Wisconsin cop Val Ryker is about to move in with her longtime firefighter boyfriend when her old boss asks for a favor. Former Chicago Homicide lieutenant Jacqueline "Jack" Daniels, needs Val to babysit for a few days.

Val isn't comfortable around toddlers, but she accepts.

Then one baby becomes two, and some criminals from Jack's past come calling with child abduction and arson on their agenda.

Val might not know babies. But she knows a whole lot about putting up fight...

WATCHED TOO LONG by Ann Voss Peterson and J.A. Konrath

Some would kill for a good babysitter...

Sign up for the J.A. Konrath newsletter. A few times a year I pick random people to give free stuff to. It could be you.

http://www.jakonrath.com/mailing-list.php

I won't spam you or give your information out without your permission!

Made in the USA
Middletown, DE
30 June 2023